JACK BE NIMBLE

By the same author

My Life Closed Twice

Nigel Williams

JACK BE NIMBLE

Secker & Warburg
London

First published in England 1980 by
Martin Secker & Warburg Limited
54 Poland Street, London WIV 3DF

Copyright ©Nigel Williams 1980

SBN: 436 57155 2

Filmset by Reproduction Drawings Limited

Printed in Great Britain by
Redwood Burn Limited
Trowbridge & Esher

For Suzan, Al and Donald

Jack be nimble
Jack be quick
Jack jump over
The candlestick

Old rhyme

PART ONE

"I 've got a . . ."

A what? thought Jack. A tumour? A jellybaby?

"A . . proposal."

Ah hah! It seemed doubtful, however, that Jack would ever learn what the proposal might be. Schooner was looking at his spoon as if it had just told him its mother was dying of cancer. Jack leant back in his chair, savouring the quality of Schooner's silence, taking in the hum of the restaurant and the bright day outside.

"I wondered how you'd feel," Schooner continued, laying down the spoon with a sigh, "I wondered how you'd *feel* if I *said* we were *interested* in you writing an episode of *The Wheebles?*"

He jerked up his head suddenly and stared deep into Jack's eyes. Perhaps he loves me, thought Jack. Perhaps he wants me to go away with him. *How would I feel if someone asked me to write an episode of* The Wheebles? *I would feel terrible. I would feel as if someone had just asked if they could urinate on my head.* The Wheebles *are –*

"*The Wheebles,*" said Schooner, picking up the spoon again, "at the moment are pretty bloody awful actually. At the moment."

"Yes," said Jack, startled out of his reverie, "yes, they are."

"But," said Schooner, "who knows?"

The Wheebles were a family, weren't they? They lived in a bungalow. Near Taunton? Doncaster? Aberystwyth? There were a lot of them, that was for sure. Dad Wheeble Gran Wheeble Ma Wheeble Jimmy Wheeble. . . And that was it. There wasn't a lot more to be said about *The Wheebles.* They were a lethal mixture of situation comedy and soap opera, combining the worst elements of both. Schooner was talking again now, with a madman's cunning.

"The thing about *The Wheebles is,*" he said, "they are capable of being subverted. They are capable of being something. They're just a huge question mark really, are *The Wheebles.*"

One way of describing them, thought Jack. They were so lacking in

3

any of the things usually considered necessary for characters in drama that it was almost impossible to say what, if anything, they were like. It would not surprise *Wheeble* fans if the whole family suddenly decided to emigrate to the Soviet Union or to take to waylaying young girls and jamming hot pokers up their behinds. A waiter blasted through the double-doors of the kitchen. He had the sallow complexion of one who avoids the sun, and he was carrying three silver dishes, piled high with veal.

"I'd like to *take The Wheebles*," said Schooner, "and make them go places. I'd like to put them through the mill. I'd like to *say* something about sex, about life, about *politics*. Using *The Wheebles*. You know?"

Jack knew. Saying something about politics was one of the major ambitions of his life. Saying something rather that doing something, because he wasn't as good at doing as at saying. Schooner, with all the low insight of a television producer, had spotted this way back when Jack and he first met. Jack had made an impassioned speech about Chile, while Schooner, as well as giving him the impression that he was marking him out of ten, awarding points for content, delivery and average length of sentences, wrinkled up his eyes, nodded and leered. You, Schooner seemed to be saying, cannot possibly *believe* any of this. In the world of showbiz, Jack, nothing, but *nothing* is for real.

"Think about it anyway," said Schooner, pushing himself back from the table, "El Bill, *per favore*."

This last remark was addressed to the sallow waiter, who genuflected in Schooner's direction as he thundered back towards the double-doors. To his horror, Jack realised that Schooner was in a wheelchair. Again. This was always happening with Schooner. He would ponce around, gesture unpleasantly and get you to dislike him, then, without warning, reveal the fact that he had lost the use of his legs. The sallow waiter was accepting a heap of crumpled notes.

Manager, assistant manager and traditional woman in traditional black peasant dress were lining up at the door to give Schooner the kind of send-off that was supposed to make him feel better about his disablement. Things were moving too quickly, thought Jack, for the twentieth time that day. Too quickly, too quickly.

"Goo'bye sah thangyou 'bye 'bye sir thangyou 'bye 'bye!" This from the line at the door, then out into the afternoon, where light rocketed harshly from the pavement, the walls and the windows opposite. Jack's face felt red and several sizes larger than usual.

4

Schooner, his proposal forgotten, wheeled himself keenly towards his waiting Volvo. He wrenched open the door and, dumping his legs on the front seat, fell forward towards the wheel. Jack bobbed and ducked on the pavement, wondering whether he ought to do something, but Schooner, ignoring him, began to dismantle his chair with a smooth and practised hand. Passers-by looked at Jack as they passed as if to say, "This man is crippled. And all you can do is stand there goggling at him." When Schooner was securely instated at the wheel, Jack got in beside him, and they pulled away from the kerb, through the busy midday traffic and out towards Elstree. There lay Schooner's office, Schooner's drinks cabinet, Schooner's deep-pile carpet and Schooner's beautiful secretary.

Why had Schooner suggested having lunch in Barnet? Jack watched his face as the Volvo accelerated up through posh Arkley, past the mansions of estate agents and pop-singers, the landed gentry of the suburbs. Schooner had a face like one of those puzzle pictures in Kiddies' Corners – if you were to turn it upside down, it would make a different but equally acceptable countenance. Jack could pick out a fairly clearly defined mouth on his forehead, and it was quite easy to think of his real-life mouth as no more than a disastrous wrinkle.

"I think," said Schooner's real-life mouth, "the thing about *The Wheebles* is, basically, I need to sort out the writer now-ish."

In other words, "Do you want to do it? Yes or no? If No – there are a million other hacks who would give their right bollock to write an episode of The Wheebles.*"*

Jack closed his eyes and scratched his ear, nervously.

"I don't think," he said, "that *I* could really do it."

"No?"

"No, really. But I think Luke Danby could."

"Ah hah. Ah hah!"

Schooner pursed his lips and looked both cunning and sad.

"I'm not sure," he said.

"No?"

"No."

To Jack's mild surprise and horror they seemed to be slowing to a halt at a deserted crossroads. Nothing much seemed to be happening at the crossroads. Tall trees and high fences fronted the road. There was a bench on the pavement to their left, and, to their right, a bus-stop. Was Schooner going to leave him here to die as a punishment for suggesting

Luke Danby?

"Is here OK for you?" said Schooner.

"Fine," said Jack, "absolutely fine." And then added, brightly – "I could get a bus!"

"You could," said Schooner thoughtfully, and opened Jack's door for him. Jack got out.

"Think about *The Wheebles,*" he said, as Jack blinked down at him from the pavement in the hot June sun, "Think about them. Because it's *you* I want. Not Luke Danby. Danby's dead. Finished. Kaput. Don't you think?"

And, slamming the door, he settled back to the more serious business of driving. Jack watched the car until it was out of sight, then, after offering up a prayer that the brakes of Schooner's wheelchair might fail at the top of the steepish gradient, he walked across to the bus-stop.

So Luke Danby was dead, was he? Not as far as Jack was concerned he wasn't. Not by a long way.

L uke Danby had, somehow or other, managed to occupy a central place in Jack's life. Unasked, he had pushed his way into Jack's meagre social round, preening, sneering sardonically and making friends wherever he went. Where Jack wore a green corduroy jacket and never combed his hair, Luke sported a tiny bum, wore tight leather jackets and was coiffured by someone called John of Chelsea. Where Jack smoked Number Six Tipped, Luke sucked greedily, stylishly at a special brand of cigarette called American Verithins; where Jack shambled, Luke strutted, from car to flat to TV studio.

Television was Luke Danby's natural home, and he had first come on the scene by writing a thirty minute play about rape, a subject with which he, like Jack, was totally unfamiliar. But Danby never let a little thing like ignorance get in his way. Once Danby had ingratiated himself with figures in the media establishment, he held on to them, pestered them with ideas for drama series about fishermen, astronauts, politicians, unmarried mothers, anything, in fact, that would earn the ten thousand a year he needed to "tick over" — to use his own appalling phrase. As usual, when thinking about Danby, Jack found he was sweating with wonder and resentment.

He wasn't going to think about Danby. That way lay madness. Concentrate on the issue in hand. Which was, essentially, how to get out of here, wherever here might turn out to be. Jack headed for the bus-stop (which was a two-tone affair, half red, half green) as, underneath his grubby collar, his skin pricked with moisture. Heat. Danby. *The Wheebles*. It was all getting out of hand.

The sheet of paper that should have told him when the local buses left places like The Old Bull, Whetstone, and the approximate times of their arrival at places like The Forge Garage, Arnos Grove, had been doctored by the local youth. Some bright spark had written Q.P.R. WANKERS in a neat, educated hand, twenty or thirty times; the script matched the London Transport style rather accurately. It occurred to Jack that such artistry was probably the result of terrifyingly long waits for the buses of the region. He looked up the empty road.

To his surprise, around the corner, travelling at a speed of about twenty miles an hour, came something that looked like a large, red taxi. It was obviously in severe mechanical difficulty, because its driver did not take the risk of stopping at the crossroads — he eased his vehicle out into no-man's land, shaking violently with the rhythms of the engine. It was, Jack realised with amazement, a bus. It was either the bus of the future or the bus of the past, for he had never seen anything quite like it — snub-nosed, single-deckered, fat-arsed, and bearing a number that looked like 140P. Jack started to wave his arms at it frantically, like Robinson Crusoe greeting people from the white man's world. But the bus driver wasn't taking any risks. He, and the bus, shook and jolted past Jack as if bus-stops had never been invented. They were bound somewhere or other and they weren't going to let a little thing like passengers get in their way.

Jack started round the corner after it, running in long, easy strides, his hair flaring out behind him. In spite of the fact that it had no cross-winds to contend with, the bus did not stand a chance against a determined human opponent. Jack was almost up to its boot, when, from the other side of the road, he heard a voice, calling out to him. It was a voice

7

he hadn't heard for years, but, as soon as he heard it, he realised that, for a long time, longer than he could say, a part of him had been expecting to hear those mocking, strangled tones, speaking of a shared childhood and a shared education, speaking, now, of something else too, a half-buried worry about . . . About what? Before he had a chance to consider that, Mike Snaps had stepped out from the shade of a plane tree, and caught his eye. He hadn't changed — he had a light tweed jacket slung over his left shoulder, his black hair stood up like a brush from his forehead and he looked as if he had just finished a rather painful shave. "Saturnine Good Looks," that was the conventional description of Michael Snaps, but to Jack there had always been something innocent about the clash between the Mephistophelean eyebrows and the milkmaid complexion, the wicked eyes and the carefully reserved manner.

"I would say," said Snaps, looking down his nose satirically, "I would say that this could be Jack Warliss."

"I would say it could be," said Jack, picking up the old rhythms of their speech, as if no time at all had passed between now and their last meeting. Which must have been at Leeds. Why, then, did he have the feeling that he had seen Snaps only yesterday or the day before that, that there was something inevitable about their meeting now? Snaps had always represented a variety of conscience to Jack; a man with even less sense of where he was going than Jack himself, he had the subversive humour of the drifter, coupled with a genuinely low opinion of himself. He would have made a good beachcomber, but, like many other aimless young people, he had wandered into the middle management of the Ford Motor Company. That was when Jack had stopped seeing him.

"What are we doing here, squire?" said Snaps, looking like a shark who wants to make friends.

"We seem to be lost!" said Jack.

"Aieeou!" said Snaps, and flung his head back, suddenly rather girlish.

"And what," said Jack, "are *we* doing here?"

Snaps looked him straight in the eye. He seemed to be weighing his answer with unusual care. Jack still had the feeling that he had seen Snaps in the recent past, that over the last weeks (or was it months? or longer than that?) there had been times when he'd glanced off a busy street to catch the edge of Snaps' back, his hands or some part of him anyway, half out of frame.

8

Mercifully, at that moment, hard on the heels of the 140P (if it was the 140P) came a huge, double-deckered bus with the words POT-TERS BAR written on its front. It looked in reasonable working order – its only concession to eccentricity being the fact that it was bright green. Jack turned and ran for the bus-stop.

"I would say – " began Snaps.

Jack sprang on to the platform as the bus pulled away from the stop, gathering speed.

"Ring me!" he shouted back, "435-9601!"

"I would say – " said Snaps again, but did not attempt to complete the sentence.

When they were round the corner, twenty or thirty yards down the road, they passed a blue Cortina. Its windows were open and the car radio was blaring out a tune about a girl who loved a boy who thought she loved his o-w-n be-est friend. For some stupid reason, Jack decided that this was Snaps' car, that Snaps had been following him from the restaurant, from further back than that, for some ghastly, twisted reason of his own. He looked back down the road and saw his one-time friend jog into vision. He still had the jacket slung across his shoulder, but his face was turned away, as if from some catastrophe.

H e was going to be an hour late for Lucy. Damn. Still, there were worse things to worry about. Jack had never had his name put forward instead of Luke Danby's before; it gave him an unpleasant, breathless feeling. It was clear that Schooner thought that Jack Warliss was the kind of person who would be interested in writing rubbish like *The Wheebles*; it was this, not the suggestion itself, that made the whole thing so frightening.

Jack bought a ticket for Potters Bar, which seemed to be the nearest centre of population; he sat back in his seat and looked out at the pretty fields of Hertfordshire, pocket-sized arable land and over-neat herds of cows, awaiting urban sprawl, innocently, in the summer afternoon. Perhaps he should ring Annie and explain things to *her*. She would know what to do about Schooner. By the time Annie had finished with Schooner he would never want to hear Danby's name again. But that still left Lucy, did it not? Was he going to abandon Lucy with no money, no means of support? That was precisely the sort of thing Danby did all the time ("Honey," Jack could almost hear him say, "I'm not a one-woman man"), but it was quite definitely *not* Jack's style. Grubby, inefficient, disorganised and weak he might be, but he wasn't actually unpleasant.

After the brief attempts at countryside, Hertfordshire had got back to its real talent – ribbon development. They were grinding through a High Street that rang the changes on butcher, greengrocer, supermarket and dry-cleaner for mile upon pointless mile. Past an old-fangled pub, with a cobbled yard and a sign reading NO COACHES, they came to a service-road; in the window of one of the shops was a sign that said CAR-HIRE SERVICE. Opposite the shop was a telephone box. Jack pushed his way through elderly ladies, and, Lucy once again at the forefront of his mind (by now he must be two hours late), he scuttled for the booth. Four panes of glass had been smashed, and there were several graffiti mentioning football teams, sheds, self-abuse, local whores etc, but those responsible had decided to let the telephone live. Jack felt in his pockets for change. He had none. After a wild glance over his shoulder he phoned the operator, told her he had just put in ten pence and been connected to the wrong number, and, as a reward for his ingenuity, was connected, free of charge, to Lucy's flat. He held the phone away from his face and prayed that she might be out, but, after two rings, she answered. Lucy was never out.

"Hullo?"

She said this in a reedy, fearful little voice, as if testing out her caller's response to the notion of greeting. Jack, fighting off the urge to shout rude words at her and slam the phone down, tried to inject a note of gaiety into the proceedings.

"Hi!" he said breezily. "Luke!"

"Oh," said Lucy, "hi!"

"Sorry I'm late," he went on, the Luke Danby voice coming more easily now, distant, mocking, "held up!"

"Oh," said Lucy, as if this was the first time anyone had ever been held up in the history of the world.

"I'll get a minicab down to you right now."

"Oh," said Lucy, "good. Yes."

Outside, a fat woman, who, in spite of the heat, was wearing a tweed coat and a pork-pie hat, started to bang on the glass, threateningly.

"How's Egbert?"

"Watching telly."

Egbert was Jack's four-month-old son by Lucy, a child with a big body, a huge head and even huger eyes, like those of a bat or a bush-baby. He spent most days slumped in his Babee-Bounce watching everything the television had to offer. He seemed especially fond of Westerns and Current Affairs. His name was not Egbert but Ben; nonetheless, for some reason Jack had been unable to understand, they never called him anything else but Egbert.

"Got to go, darling. People banging."

"Oh Luke – "

The woman was now kicking the base of the telephone booth, lustily, as if for her own amusement.

"*What?*"

One of the things about Luke Danby was that he had a very short temper – howling at traffic wardens, barking at untalented directors, he was a master at well directed spleen. Some said it was the secret of his success.

"There's something I want to tell you."

"It'll have to wait."

"Lukey, it's important."

But Luke did not have the time to discuss Lucy's emotional problems. Although not dressed for the gay world of television, Jack could feel his alter-ego calculating, plotting. He would get back to Lucy's, put in a brief appearance, manufacture a story and disappear back to Annie to cross-question her about Snaps. The pips went. The operator asked him for more money, but Jack, or rather Luke (or maybe Jack), shouted a farewell to Lucy, slammed down the phone and bumped out on to the pavement, past the one-woman queue. He needed a drink. Both he and Luke needed a drink. Several drinks.

Snaps *was* definitely up to something. Other incidents were coming back to him – half suppressed memories, doubts. Minicab down to Finchley soonest. Plan of action. And decide what to do about *The Wheebles*. Very soon. It would have to be soon. Oh God, *The Wheebles*.

11

The pointless, vulgar, boring, lucrative *Wheebles*. Perhaps if he could sort that out he could make a start on the rest of his life. Whose life? Luke's? No, of course not, Jack's. He was Jack, after all. Snaps, though. What a sod, eh? What a devious sod. Snaps, *Wheebles*, Lucy, Annie to be sorted out in that order. No. *Wheebles*, Snaps, Annie, Lucy. Or was it Annie, Lucy, *Wheebles*, Snaps? Or was it, perhaps, none of them? Was it, instead, a few pints followed by a tasteful suicide in a small hotel? Oh God oh God oh God.

Minicab anyway. Plus drink. That was a start.

A nnie Warliss felt very bad about persuading Snaps to spy on her husband. She hadn't, in the beginning, intended to spy on him, and, in her more sensible moments, did not suspect him of anything at all. It wasn't, after all, twenty-four-hour surveillance, but a casual, infrequent affair. The worst thing about it was that it had been going on for over two years.

Maybe it was unfair to blame it all on Snaps. Her suspicions had started, really, with Luke Danby's sudden and undeserved success. Annie had been against his using the name, against his writing the kind of rubbish that Luke seemed to write, against the whole fucked-up system that considered it necessary to feed the working classes of England with improbable tales of life in newspaper offices, degrading half-hour comedies and advertisements that patronised and sneered at the same time. She had also been saddened at the ease and speed with which Danby became successful.

Annie bit her nails, and tapped the big, shabby table with the edge of a paperback book about Guerilla Warfare.

She should never have talked to Snaps in the first place. For it was Snaps who had conjured up the person he, and she, always referred to as The Mistress. Annie saw her as a hard, bosomy woman of thirty-five, while Snaps was convinced she was a Television Woman. Annie had got to know some Television Women since Luke's arrival – heavy on chic and light on brains, they often rang up and left messages for Luke, their voices rich with sympathy and jealousy for her condition as wife and mother. The fact that for about six years it was Annie who had earned the money by slogging into NALGO every day, the fact that it was Annie who had given Jack his principles, his talent, his politics (even if she couldn't persuade him to join her in the Communist Party), the fact that it was Annie who had given Jack the confidence to dream up a creep like Danby, none of this seemed to matter.

She smoothed back her shoulder length blond hair and crossed to the window. Thinking about Schooner and Television Women always got her ratty. Come the Revolution all Television Women would be re-deployed into heavy industry. At the thought of Julie Wetherby Crouch (or whatever spurious name she went under) handling large quantities of molten pig-iron, Annie's day looked up. Julie Wetherby Crouch was Schooner's secretary, a woman who expected Annie to be familiar with Jack's, or rather Luke's, whereabouts at every single moment of every single day of the year. She wondered what would happen to Schooner after the Revolution. Her mind drifted between regret and malice, as, outside, the sun shifted behind the elm trees and there was a sense of evening beginning in the dusty London gardens that lay between their flat and Hampstead Heath. Jack was a long time, even if he *was* having lunch in Barnet. She'd got home early too. She was almost asleep now. Her last thought was of Schooner and Wetherby Crouch together at a work camp in the Ukraine. "I think," Schooner was saying as he raised his pick above the frozen earth, "I think the lunch worked in our terms." And Wetherby Crouch, strangely, was doing her nails, un-concerned, as the icy Russian wind whipped through her skirt . . .

BEEP! BEEP! BEEP! BEEP!

She jolted up in her chair and crossed to the other window, that looked out over Highgate West Hill. Snaps, it had to be Snaps. He was never a man to get out and walk. His car, his *Company* car, as he kept telling her with some self mockery and some pride, was his first line of defence. What puzzled her was why he had chosen this afternoon to fulfil his often-used threat of visiting her at the flat. Previously, they had met in pubs or at absurd secret rendezvous in parks or quiet streets. It was all part of some complex plan of his, and as Annie no longer cared about whether The Mistress was real, or whether Jack found out

13

that she was spying on him, she felt no anger, merely dull surprise as she looked down at Snaps, leaning out of the driver's window, blue shirt open at the neck, mouth open in a loose grin. He looked, from a distance, like an all-American kid, cruising through for an evening of hamburgers and the juke-joint.

"I finally made it!" he replied up.

"What's so special about today?" called Annie.

"Day of decision," Snaps replied.

He didn't look wicked. But to Annie, who had known for months that this would happen, that one afternoon Snaps would arrive to involve her more deeply in his scheme of things, ask her to make cruel and awkward decisions, there was something wicked about him as he nodded up at her, his elbow lying rather saucily across the open window. Just recently he had talked more and more about The Mistress, about how they would have to confront her, face it out. He fancied Annie of course, that was why he was so anxious to provoke a breach with Jack, that was why he had approached her at that party. She strode to the door, rather too decisively for her outfit, cramming a wide-brimmed hat on her head as she went.

His car radio, as usual, was on at full blast. A man was asking a woman in Leeds if she could identify a Sound of Yesteryear. The woman was having difficulty. The man offered her a T-shirt. This did not improve her memory. Snaps looked, bleakly, at the dash-board, suddenly nervous. Annie remembered long, half-joking conversations about The Mistress – an image of Snaps that put Jack and The Mistress, naked, in the back of a Mini.

"We go?" said Snaps.

"Yes," said Annie, "we go."

A cloud moved across the sun. There was shadow, then light again. Annie's face was frozen, as she remembered Jack, Jack's face and their life together.

T hey had met at a demonstration, one rainy afternoon in Leeds. A small, not very successful demonstration, at which the number of political groups represented was only slightly less than the total of the participants. Annie had been handing out leaflets demanding the immediate return of all bourgeois imperialist forces from Vietnam, Rhodesia and everywhere East of Dover. The star of the show being a small Maoist called Hovis who kept shouting, "YOU RIP OUT THE GUTS THE HAND LETS GO!" Standard stuff.

What had Jack's role in the demonstration been? she wondered, as Snaps drove them at breakneck speed through blocks of evening sunlight falling across the Finchley Road and mellowing the forefronts of red-brick shops, flats or offices. Jack had never been anything quite as silly as a Maoist. She and a girl called Julie had wandered over to him and Julie had offered him a *Morning Star*.

"*So-ocialist Worker!*" Jack had shouted in reply. "Girls! Girls! Girls! Girls! Read All About It!"

"*Morning Star!*" shouted Julie, who came from three generations of Communists,"*Racing News! Morning Star!*" and then sloped off.

"*Socialist Worker!*" Jack went on, "What are you Doing Tonight?"

"*Morning Star!*" said Annie, "Not a Lot!"

"The Only Paper That Tells the Truth About The Working Class!" carolled Jack, "See You In The Trafalgar Eight Sharp!"

Annie had wandered back to the demo, where some local toughs were baiting the enraged Hovis. "YOU RIP OUT THE GUTS THE HANDS LET GO!" Hovis was shouting. "What do you rip out, mate?" the toughs were asking. "THE GUTS!" Hovis replied, stamping his desert boot wildly on the pavement, "THE GUTS! THE GUTS! THE GUTS!" Annie remembered Jack, papers clutched to his chest, staring dreamily at all this as if unsure whether he had a right to be there.

Snaps was driving with his usual priest-like care, stamping the foot on

15

the clutch, greasing the gears forward; his mouth was set in a pout of what looked like disapproval as he whipped past unsuspecting commuters, in and out of vacant spaces.

Now she thought of it – Jack's self-mockery and uncertainty extended, in those days anyway, to his sexual behaviour as well as his politics. He'd looked down at his prick on their first night in bed together and said, "Well. It seems to be going up." But there was a doubt in his voice – as if at any moment it might do a U-turn and hurtle back between his legs. This was typical of the male members of the bourgeoisie. They all expected to be coaxed, wooed and cheered as they expanded a muscle from three to seven inches. What was so fucking clever, important and hence neurosis-making about expanding a muscle a few inches? And yet, from the way they went on, you would think that the fate of empires hung in the balance every time they decided to spur their organs into action.

They were now coming up to Tally Ho Corner. Annie looked sideways at Snaps, suddenly filled with a violent hatred for him. Did he imagine that she was going to bed with him as a kind of quid pro quo for leading her to the scene of Jack's Other Life? Did he think that women were as near to machines as that? Some of the bitterness must have shown in her face because Snaps said:

"I'm not just doing it for me, you know."

"Then who the fuck *are* you doing it for?"

"Never mind. It's not just *me* trying to get *you*. It's got a lot more complicated than that."

Oh sure, thought Annie. Sure. You're probably doing all this for the Pentecostal Church of Christ or the CIA. Still – there was something helpless and out-of-his-depth about Snaps that lent this last remark a curious kind of conviction. Annie didn't have time to think about Snaps.

"Where the fuck are we going?"

"I would say Finchley."

"Whereabouts in Finchley?"

"The heart of Finchley."

If this was the heart of Finchley, then the suburb was close to death. Somewhere away to their left a window opened and a grey head appeared; they passed an open-air, rather folksy-looking tube station and a labrador tottered into their line of vision, and looked up at the car expectantly, as if he thought it might feed him. Snaps slowed to a

16

tasteful forty miles an hour.

"I don't want to go – " began Annie.

"This is it!" said Snaps and jammed on the brakes outside a house that seemed to have been constructed so as to minimise the resistance it might offer to the wind – the façade looked like a piece of dated science fiction. Jerking his head over his shoulder, his face contorted horribly, Snaps reversed into the one available parking space. Reversing was one of the things Snaps did best. Why, then, was the rictus of concentration slowly changing to an acid-indigestion face?

Annie swung round to see the rear of an elderly Austin thrusting towards them, blindly. There was a loud crash of metal and Snaps winced, as if suddenly embarrassed.

"Oh God!" said Annie.

Out of the back of the Austin came a tall, shabby man, having some difficulty in getting his legs out neatly. Jack.

"Oh God," said Annie again, "Oh God oh God oh God oh God!"

"This is true," said Snaps.

F rom the door of the house a woman of about Annie's age emerged, carrying a small baby. She was wearing a blue nylon housecoat and her hair – of a dull, mousey colour – was set in curlers. If her dress was that of the hardened housewife, however, her face suggested something completely different: the delicate nose and the huge, straggling eyes were those of a junior Russian princess, and her manner, now tentative, now down-to-earth, did nothing to resolve the conflicting impressions of her appearance. It was as if her clothes had just sprung a nasty surprise on her, and, to intensify the effect, a psychotic hairdresser had jammed her hair full of rollers, against her will.

Snaps had gone very red in the face. He kept saying, "*Too* much. *Too* much," and slapping the steering wheel. Occasionally he gave a rather stagey laugh. Annie, feeling that something was required of her, got out and walked towards Jack, who was marching in the direction of the woman in curlers, as if he was a particularly crusty Colonel-in-Chief and she was a particularly badly drilled platoon.

"Oh *yeah*," Jack said as he passed her, "all this and *The Wheebles* too. Eh?"

Annie decided that he had gone barmy. The woman and the baby sidestepped shyly into the limelight of the road, the baby screwing up its eyes and making little punching motions with its fists, as if warding off insects. Jack stopped about three yards short of it and pointed disdainfully at its head, saying –

"*There* you are. A baby. See? It shits. It cries. That's all. A baby. Now you've seen one. OK?"

He said this in a way that implied that Annie, or indeed unspecified women of Finchley behind and beyond her, had been plotting to trap him into fatherhood, which, as Annie didn't want or *need* a baby (did she?), was as ludicrous a distortion of the facts as she had yet heard from Jack's lips. But he was, quite definitely, suffering some kind of brainstorm, and could not, fairly, be described as Jack at all, for he was now saying to the woman in curlers –

"Luke here. Luke bloody Danby. I've come for my things."

"Oh *Lukey!*" said the woman in a soft, London whine, "oh *Lukey*. I was so worried."

"Got to go," Jack said loudly, "Documentary. Zambia. Ten years." And he strode past her, to the house.

Annie and the woman now met at the gate.

"Hullo," said the woman, "are you a friend of Luke's?" There was a touch of deference in the way she said this.

"Not exactly," replied Annie, who was unable to feel anything as strongly as she thought she would have done, "and you must be . . . "

"Lucy," said the woman nasally, "that's it."

And she nodded, anxious to be placed. Jack had now disappeared inside the house. Out of the corner of her eye Annie could see that Snaps and a small dark man, who had the classless, dishevelled appearance of a minicab driver, were talking. The small dark man was holding on to Snaps' collar and saying "'Snart true I fooking jrunk. Not true!" Drunk. Was Jack drunk? "All zer time," the small, dark man was saying, "You make conspiracy for him. Is it you follow heem, eh? Make spy? Eh?" A window upstairs opened and Jack pushed his head out.

"Packed and ready to go!" he said.

"He often," said the woman called Lucy, "has to leave at short notice. For filming and so on. Are you in television?"

"Afraid not," said Annie.

"Quite glamorous really," said the woman, and giggled. Her giggle was another surprise, an unattractive, unexpected sound that altered Annie's idea of her yet again. When the giggle had stopped she drew in her chin to her neck, like a lizard trying to turn its head, and watched Annie narrowly, as if her new acquaintance might bite her for her indiscretion. Jack leaned further out of the upstairs window. He *was* drunk.

"*The Wheebles*," he said, "are a force for change. Potentially."

"Who in God's name are *The Wheebles*?" said Annie.

"Egbert would know," said the woman. "They're on in the afternoons. I think."

At this point, Egbert, aware that he was by no means the centre of attention, narrowed his mouth to a tiny, disapproving O, and, arching his back, started up a tiny, strained cough.

"He'll scream now," said Lucy, like a guide introducing a point of interest to tourists.

Egbert, confirming her prediction, began to scream. He set his back in a bow and flung his body back against Lucy's. Each time his head hit her shoulder he redoubled his vocal efforts, throwing himself forwards and then backwards, thus provoking another round of screaming, the volume of which seemed to be increasing in geometric progression. Lucy seemed unconcerned. She bashed him on his well upholstered behind and said, almost absently – "There there, Eggie. There there."

Jack seemed to have disappeared. Snaps and the minicab driver were now having one of those stylishly aggressive conversations that Annie had noticed other men enjoying – usually when neither party had the slightest intention of letting a verbal dispute become physical.

Lucy had now, to the consternation of an elderly lady opposite, fished out a breast and was pointing the nipple in Egbert's direction. Egbert, like a fighter pilot with the Hun in his sights, lined up on the nipple and altered his scream to a surprised whine. His hands, feet and mouth were all revving up like Donald Duck preparing for a quick getaway.

Then, suddenly, he struck. Mouth, eye, hand and brain worked in unison, and he swooped on to the tit, clawing, biting, wriggling and sucking. Lucy looked down at him admiringly. "Hungry!" she said.

"That's what it was."

It was now quite difficult to hear anything over the noise made by Egbert eating. Lucy said, over the chomping, slurping and sucking sounds, "What did you say you did in television?"

"I didn't," said Annie, "I don't work in television."

"No?"

"No," said Annie, "I'm his wife."

"Luke's wife."

"His name isn't Luke. It's Jack."

"Oh," said the woman sadly, "he told me it was Luke."

Lucy looked as if someone had just hit her in the groin with a baseball bat, although whether this was at the news of Jack's marital status or his *nom de plume* was impossible to tell. At this moment, Jack emerged from the front door carrying a lightweight leather suitcase, and, in his left hand, a pair of two-tone shoes – under his shoulder was what could well have been an atlas. He marched down towards them unsteadily. Egbert, for a brief second, unclamped himself from the nipple and looked at Jack through narrow, suspicious eyes. Lucy looked from Jack to Annie to Egbert and back again, respectfully, as if honoured to be taking part in something quite so complicated.

"You're off then?" she said to Jack, no note of reproach in her voice.

"Off," said Jack, "away. Off."

"I think," said Annie, "that before you go there are some explanations due."

"Perfectly simple," said Jack, swaying. "Me Jack Warliss also Luke Danby. Complicated. Schizophrenia. Two women. You. Lucy. Chewing up the balls. Staking a claim. Danby. Warliss. Complete waste of time. Priority Grade A is Warliss, eh? Who is Warliss? Who the fuck is Danby come to that? Who are he? Who am I? Right? I mean me and where my head is at and all that jazz, eh?"

"Listen – "

"Listen nothing. One lot going tremendously revolutionary socialism terrific join union work for universal brotherhood unions aren't brotherhood far as I can see simply another form of organised crime. Others say very good Danby terrific stuff commission you do four episodes terrific idea *Wheebles* worked well in our terms load of old rubbish. Me at centre of row. Cultural dilemma. Me. Work *myself* out OK? Start on my head, man. Ecology. Tremendous fun."

"What are you blithering about?"

20

The minicab driver was headed towards them in an attempt to gatecrash their row, Snaps having given up and prostrated himself on the bonnet of his car. Jack strode off down the pavement, followed by Annie, Lucy and Egbert, who, miraculously, managed to keep eating. The minicab driver waylaid Jack and shook him warmly by the hand – "You – " he said, "are a fookin' good feller me lad an' a fookin' Wheeble all the way, hein?" They then embraced and the minicab driver, his bolt shot, retired to the scrubby lawn in front of Lucy's house in order to be sick. Jack went on down the road, stopping when he came to Snaps' car.

"You," he said to Snaps, "are a cunt."

"Sorry about this, squire," said Snaps, "really sorry."

And then Jack, atlas, two-tone shoes and suitcase hanging round him, strode off down the pavement, followed by the two women, Annie now walking in what she tried to think of as a rational fashion, trying to make all of this a little less absurd, and Lucy seeming to be driven by terrified interest rather than the intention of contributing something to the discussion. About twenty yards down the road Jack stopped. Annie stopped. Jack turned round to face the two women.

"Are you following me?" he said.

"Yes," said Annie.

"You can follow me as long as you like, it will do you no good." Suddenly his voice became calm and rational.

"Just leave me alone. Both of you. OK. I need time. *Time*. To myself. OK?"

Lucy sank on to the pavement and bowed her head over Egbert. One roller had come adrift and a curl, half-completed, fell across her forehead. She started to sob quietly. Egbert seemed to be blissfully happy, and, as his mother wept, he squirmed, as if in the grip of a slow, delicious orgasm.

"Please, love," said Jack, addressing the two of them as one, "don't expect to see me. I'm off." And he turned and walked away down the street, moving very slowly and firmly, like a military man, who, though out of style, intends to preserve the honour and dignity of his profession.

Annie watched him go. Then she too sat on the ground. She did not cry, but did not speak either as she stared ahead at the dry gardens opposite. It occurred to her that she might never see Jack again, so she looked at him once more before he turned the corner and was lost to their sight. He looked less like a soldier this time, more like one of those refugees seen in films of the last war, trudging from city to city, hopeless, pursued by avenging planes.

After a while Egbert fell asleep and this seemed to calm Lucy. Her face dirty with recent tears, she turned to Annie and said –

"Cup of tea or something?"

"Might as well."

A little later they went into the house together. The minicab driver was asleep on the grass, but Snaps watched them go in, a malevolent smile on his face. He seemed to be waiting for something.

J ack hadn't gone to Zambia or anywhere else. He hadn't even got as far as the station. He was sitting up against a wall just around the first corner, staring at his feet in a manner reminiscent of Egbert.

What were the bitches up to now? It didn't really matter what he did. If he retired to a log cabin in the Appalachians to re-think his life, Lucy and Annie would still be there . . . yack yack change his nappy . . . yack yack the Revolution . . . yack bloody yack. Unstoppable. How could he even start on himself when he knew those two would already be discussing him in that slippery, gentle way women have?

He got up from the pavement and squared his shoulders. He had the beginnings of a headache. Never mind. He picked up the suitcase and turned back to Lucy's house.

Of all the faces Jack had at his command, perhaps the most successful, and certainly the most used, was one called Nice Guy A Bit Out Of His Depth, which could modulate into either Plain Man Not Afraid To Speak His Mind or Nice But Dim Guy Totally And Completely Out Of His Depth – depending on how actually out of his depth Jack was. The last face had been used brilliantly in the one Communist Party meeting he had attended with Annie. Where hardline Stalinists were failing to win over the meeting with lines that always began, "Lenin said . . . " etc etc, Jack stepped in with a formula never previously heard, i.e. "As far as I can make out, I get the *impression* that Lenin may have said something along the lines of . . . " etc etc. This allowed his listeners to feel (a) intellectually superior, and (b) that Lenin sounded such a nice bloke that even if he hadn't said anything on the lines Jack was suggesting, he would have done if asked nicely.

Jack retraced his steps, past the high hedges and open windows of suburbia.

Nice Guy A Bit Out Of His Depth was perhaps a little over the top. It was plain that Jack was wildly out of his depth. Any man whose wife has just met his mistress and hitherto concealed son is bound to feel wildly out of his depth. And Nice But Dim Guy Totally And Completely Out Of His Depth would, in these circumstances, draw nothing but a giant raspberry from the wife and mistress concerned.

It was Plain Man and Plain Speaking Time. Since, obviously, the last thing in the world that Jack was capable of doing was speaking the truth − it was time for him to look the Lucy/Annie squarely in the eye and tell it that he loved it. Both of it. He couldn't see a way of dividing it. He couldn't choose. This not only had the merit of being an emotional pitch, of leading with the feelings (a thing the Lucy/Annie would enjoy), but also of transferring the responsibility for any decision about Jack's future, sexual, political, literary and social, back on to the Lucy/Annie.

Plain Man and Plain Speaking had been used most successfully at Jack's school, a cheap-ish public school in North London. The headmaster, a man known for his firm moral sense (i.e. obsession with corporal punishment) and strong sense of the community (i.e. desire to divert motorways towards the homes of the proletariat), had taken a slow, leisurely dislike to Jack, culminating in an attempt to have him removed from the school on the basis of what was described as Jack's Attitude. Jack's Attitude, in his headmaster's mind, was a combination of Faust, Hitler and Robespierre with the bit between his teeth; he was accused of laziness, iconoclasm, subversion and, finally, the crime Jack had always been accused of for as long as he could remember − Cynicism. Jack had, in fact, always fancied being a cynic, but was far too lazy, iconoclastic and subversive to maintain such an effortful and demanding position.

He remembered that afternoon in the study now, as the tall flowers

23

glared back at his progress, and the pavement, white as chalk, hammered at his eyes. He had been a hair's breadth away from Leeds University, and, more importantly, a hair's breadth away from escaping from his mother, fighting for his reputation. "What do you feel?" Jack's headmaster had said in the high, fluting tone he adopted for such occasions, "What do you feel you *care* about, Warliss?" And Jack had sized up the situation at a glance. Hadn't he? Shaking his head slightly he had met the headmaster's gaze and replied, "My Poetry, Sir." Brilliant. The kind of thing an unhappy adolescent would feel most dear to his heart, and also connecting Jack to a whole company of acceptable aberrants − boffins, eccentric scholars, loners in the field of athletics and countless other perverts tolerated by the public school system. The fact that Jack had never written poetry, would never write poetry, hated poetry and was, in fact, a sort of low energy anti-hero, a person as devoid of clearly defined ambition as it is possible to be without being actually downright wet and depressing, did not matter. The Plain Man had spoken the Plain Truth.

Transfixed with embarrassment, the Head had said:

"What kind of poetry, Warliss?"

Jack, too, had reddened with embarrassment.

"Love poetry, sir. Mainly."

To other boys, he could see the headmaster thinking, his yellow eyes fixed on this troublemaker who now appeared to be a pansy as well.

"I see, Warliss," he said eventually, "and . . . do you want to go . . . on . . . with this . . . this . . . "

He couldn't bring himself to say the word "poetry".

"Yes, sir," said Jack, "I want to be a poet."

The Head did not ask Jack, at this point, why it was, if he wanted to be a poet, he was proposing to study engineering. He goggled at Jack as if he had just turned into a frog, indeed, as if the two of them had both turned into frogs, large, green frogs, approaching the end of long and pointless lives.

"Well, Warliss," the Head had said, nearly in tears by this time, "I'm glad to know you care about something."

"Thank you, sir," said Jack.

"Er . . . why don't you show me some of this . . . poetry some time?"

"Yes, sir," said Jack, hoping that it wouldn't be necessary to write any.

There was another long, agonised pause, while the Head looked dewy-eyed at his pupil, now re-classified as troublesome, hopeless, but ultimately capable of better things.

"Goodbye, Warliss."

"Goodbye, sir."

"And . . . good luck."

And good luck to you too, mate, thought Jack.

His face was now getting rather too twisted and cynical to manage Plain Man and Plain Speaking. He looked, he decided, catching sight of his reflection in one of the windows, rather more like Stunted Man and Pack of Lies. He stopped by a discreet, four-storey block of flats, just within reach of Lucy's, and tried to cobble together some sort of introductory dialogue.

"Hullo, you two."

No.

"I forgot my car keys."

Worse. He didn't drive anyway.

Maybe a letter. He had written a letter to Jill, his first girlfriend, telling her it was all over. A stylish letter, full of lines like . . . "I hope this isn't arrogant, or, even worse, humble, but . . . " you are an old slag, or words to that effect. The problem, of course, with letters, was that women didn't write graceful, agonised letters back. They rang you up and screamed at you and jumped off bridges, or something equally tasteless.

He took a deep breath and walked towards Lucy's front door.

L ucy answered the door. She didn't seem surprised to see him. Jack, who was by now looking positively furtive, said in a fresh, open voice –

"Hi!"

"Hullo," said Lucy.

And then they were inside the cramped hall, shutting out the sweetness of the evening. Just as the door closed, out of the corner of his eye, Jack noticed that Snaps' car was still parked outside. Had he been there a moment ago? It was curious how Snaps seemed to have acquired a talent for vanishing and re-appearing, like some Shakespearian sprite. Annie was coming towards him, holding Egbert in a suspiciously professional manner.

"Hi!"said Jack again.

"Hullo," said Annie.

Egbert swung his head round from Annie's shoulder and grinned at Jack. Jack, who had never felt less like grinning in his life, felt it would be rude not to manage some response. He gave a sick, Dracula-like smile. Egbert seemed satisfied.

"Look," said Jack, very plainly and squarely indeed, "let's talk about this. Huh?"

The two women, as he had feared, smirked at each other grimly.

"OK?" said Jack, spreading his hands in a rather Jewish gesture and looking from one to the other, like a small referee in a heavyweight flight.

"OK," said Annie, very slightly amused.

She handed Egbert to Lucy. Lucy took him as if she and Annie had been passing babies backwards and forwards between each other for the last twenty years. Then, with Annie leading, they went through to the sitting room, a cold, neat sort of place, which always reminded Jack of the front rooms of his childhood.

The two women remained standing and Jack went to the window to check if Snaps' car was still there. It was. Snaps was in it too, drumming his fingers on the roof and staring ahead down the quiet street. Jack swallowed, swung round and found himself saying in a boyish, yet tortured sort of way –

"I've behaved like a shit. Like an absolute shit. I've broken every single one of the rules I live by."

The only one of the company at all impressed by this line was Egbert, who opened and closed his mouth several times, obviously under the impression that Jack was going to sing, something Egbert enjoyed. Instead of bursting into song, however, Jack said, rather stodgily –

"I've lied to you, Annie, and to you, Lucy. I mean I've tried to be two people, and all the time I don't add up to one. You know?"

"We know," said Annie. And she gave him a lopsided grin.

This was bad, thought Jack, but it wasn't absolutely disastrous. They hadn't burst into hysterical laughter or thrown things at him. Yet. So far, he *sounded* like a man coming clean, and if it was embarrassing/boring/repetitive, well, people coming clean tended to sound that way. Warming to his confession, Jack started to pace up and down in front of the window, keeping half an eye on Snaps, who was now keeping a close watch on the house, from the security of the driver's seat.

"The point about me is," said Jack, "the whole point about me is that I'm a fantasist. I won't own up to things. I'm a series of masks, right? A series of, well, impressions of other people."

Jack thought this was (a) pretty honest, (b) pretty modest and (c) moderately well put. More importantly, however, he felt himself lifted up from the dead ground of self-examination, bearing up towards something natural, new and interesting.

"OK Lucy, when I met you I was trendy Luke Danby the TV guy, you know? And when I met you, Annie, remember? It was dogged old Jack Warliss, the lefty worthy, but actually none of those people is the real me, you know? The real me isn't Jack Warliss or Luke Danby."

Who, the look on the women's faces seemed to be saying, *is* the real you? And is he going to come up with any better lines than this?

"The real me," said Jack, not quite sure whether this was a figure of speech or the literal truth, "is a guy called Peter Simmons."

Jack sat at the table, partly to establish narrative flow and partly because he was aware Snaps had got out of the Cortina and was looking insolently up at him from the road as if to say . . . "Come off it, Jacko . . . I would say, come *off* it, squire . . ."

"My mother's name," went on Jack, "is, or *was*, Simmons. I've never told either of you this. Isn't it surprising the amount I can conceal? Well, even after she married my step-father, who was called Warliss, she kept her name, or rather she *mentioned* it, I mean she kept her name the way she kept her hair blue-rinsed and smoked and left lipstick on the filter tips and did all the things that made my step-father hate her. Yes, I mean hate her, you know all about *that*, Annie. Mr Warliss hated Jennie Simmons. He hated her phoney love of culture, her phoney Scottish accent, the phoney coffee mornings and I shouldn't wonder phoney sex and all, which I always told myself wasn't the way it was with my old man, who died about the day I was bloody born and didn't leave me even his name, or rather she made damn sure I didn't use it, well, officially anyway I was handed Warliss."

He had never really talked about his father before to either of them, and, rather to his surprise, he found that talking about him didn't make him any more real – a man called Simmons who had worked in the City and was now dead, a man who had only left the shadow of his name, who was resurrected, occasionally, by his mother, usually by the extravagant use of cliché ("Your father was a wonderfully reliable man", "Your father would have wanted you to be a decent citizen"). He continued, however, in the attempt to make both of his parents real – to them, if not to him.

"Anyway. My middle name's Peter. I don't really use it. But till I was about sixteen I sometimes used to call myself Simmons. Peter Simmons. I mean at parties I'd introduce myself that way. So that was me. And Peter Simmons was . . . I don't know . . . bent-backed, terrified of women, dreamy, loved the country, wanted everyone to love everyone else and . . . anyway . . . screwed up sexually, that's for sure."

, No one in the room recognised Peter Simmons. Indeed, Jack had difficulty in remembering the boy he was describing. But a picture kept coming back to him, something suggested to him earlier on the hot, empty road in Barnet where he had encountered Snaps, a picture that had not been part of the self he had created at Leeds, a picture of a boy in a blue silk shirt, holding a guitar, looking down into the street at another boy who looked back up at him, mocking . . . it must have been September because the gutters were choked with leaves, and . . .

"The thing you ought to know about Peter Simmons, who was calling himself by his father's name, which was really his *mother's* name, and who wouldn't go and watch trains with his father because his father was his mother's husband, was that he had this . . . fierce . . . er . . . relationship with this other guy . . . and . . . anyway . . . if you see what I mean" (Jack was now twisting his fingers together tightly) "hasn't been able to forget that . . . well Jack can't forget Peter and really keeps telling himself that things are a fucking mess and maybe he's . . . queer or something."

Then, partly because he couldn't think what to do next, Jack found that he was crying. Whether the story was true he could not have said, but the tears appeared to be real. His face worked and he looked away from Lucy and Annie and towards the neutral grey of the carpet.

Both women seemed embarrassed and vaguely disappointed that the disclosures hadn't been more sensational. Jack, who'd stopped crying almost as soon as he'd started, began to wish he had made them more sensational, and revealed the fact that he was a Cuban spy or was dying of a rare blood disease. Lucy's face, as always, expressed bottomless sympathy for him and anyone else who might be in need of it, while Annie, serious and appalled, said:

"Er . . . I suppose everyone goes through a phase of that, I suspect."

Jack looked back to the window. He felt empty and lonely and silly. Snaps was now pacing up and down on the pavement.

"I don't know," said Jack, "maybe it's just that I can't handle relationships with women. I mean maybe it's just I'm fucked up."

"Maybe you are," said Annie, in her House of Doom voice. Things, as things often did, had started to strike Jack as humorous, rather than tragic.

"So what do we do?" he said to both of them.

"We work it out," said Annie, "the three of us."

Or, thought Jack, four. Counting Egbert.

Snaps was now marching up to the front door bell. He too looked like a man about to make a clean breast of things.

Five, thought Jack, five. Counting Snaps.

Then the doorbell rang.

T he reception committee for Snaps filed out into the hall. It seemed wrong for any one person to deal with him – it was somehow apparent to everyone that no one person in the company should be left alone with anyone else. Lucy led the way, stooping slightly, preparing to avoid her unwelcome visitor's eyes (eye contact was always a problem for Lucy). Behind her was Jack, back straight, step relaxed, brain in turmoil, and, bringing up the rear, Annie and Egbert. Egbert was now in high good humour. He was sitting up on Annie's shoulder, making whipping gestures with his right hand and crowing with pleasure at the way things were going.

Immediately Lucy had opened the door, Annie said to a rather po-faced Snaps –

"Jack says he's a poofter and his real name is Simmons."

"I said *might* be," said Jack, "I said – "

"Might be a poofter," said Annie, large and bluff, "might be a poofter called Simmons. Might on the other hand be a TV character called Danby. Might on the other hand be called Warliss. *Might*, you never know, be called Griddlebaum or Toastswitch. Might be a lesbian in disguise. Might be from another galaxy."

Snaps looked at Jack rather sympathetically.

"Problems, squire," he said.

"Yes," said Jack, "problems."

"Come in," said Lucy, "I'll make some tea."

Into the kitchen they trooped, this time Egbert and Annie leading the caravan – Egbert shouting and reeling like a football hooligan whose team has just won an away match.

As they were sitting down on Lucy's kitchen stools, shabby steel and shabbier red plastic, and looking out over Lucy's garden, five yards of wilderness, Snaps had started on *his apologia pro vita sua*. Unaware that Jack had been going through precisely the same routine minutes earlier, he paced (insofar as the kitchen allowed him to pace) and sawed the air with his hands in an agony of simulated honesty.

"Look, folks," said Snaps – he was, Jack decided, rather more cool than he had been – "look. I *would* say that I have boobed fairly badly. And I would say that I have intruded the Snaps nose in where it was not required. Squire, I would say."

As Jack remembered from a long time back – although from when precisely he could not have said – the strangled chic of Snaps' delivery and the intense circumlocutory slang he employed gave his speech a quality of originality that had been rather too painfully acquired, or anyway, acquired for no better reason than that it is, or may be, original.

"Fact *is*, Annie?" he went on, deliberately emphasising another off-centre word, "fact *is* I should have kept the Snaps nose out of it and not landed Jack in it. Squire. I would say you are a fairly desirable woman, Annie, and there was an element of that in it as far as I was concerned. But I just wanted to say that toe-holds-wise I don't seem to be too well provided for at this particular stage of the board meeting and that development-wise I'm into problems. Squire."

30

Jack found this a heartening, if incomprehensible, speech. But, sticking with the tone of what he had said, Jack felt it might be leading towards a confession not dissimilar to his own. Snaps was perhaps about to admit that woman-wise he was into confusion, and that his real name, squire, was not Snaps at all but Googlehof or Labrador. Before anything of the kind could happen, however, Lucy spoke for the first time at any length. Her face white, her eyes banked up with fury, she used the deadly, inward-looking whine that Jack recognised from the rows they had before, after and during sexual intercourse –

"You two," she said, "you two are just playing tricks. I think I mean as far as you two are concerned you – "

She started to cry again, bleakly. It was like the North Wind across her, her shoulders hunched down and her ragged eyes became red and ugly. There was misery in her every movement as she said –

"You two," (Jack noticed the housecoat rucked above her knees), "You two, you Lukey, you said you came to that poetry reading where I was reading my poetry and you said you were from the television I'd never seen anything as beautiful as you before and you said you'd make that film of me because you made documentaries well it turned out you didn't make documentaries but you kept talking about it and you were always around and then you had sex with me and after that – "

What? thought Jack. Was she going to give a blow by blow account of their affair over the last few years?

"And then it was a lie because you said you loved me but you didn't love me you didn't love anyone you're not capable of loving anyone you're all so clever and rich and important and beautiful you went to the right schools and the right Universities and you don't love me why should you love me I'm not attractive or interesting I'm dull and my face is all blotchy now and all I've ever been is a housewife poet that's what you called me because you patronised me and you're the same" (this to Snaps) "you're all the same you're hateful shitty little self-important horrible ugly ugly ugly little men and you don't care about women and babies you were once babies Christ you never stop being babies you think women just change nappies and you don't realise you're so ugly and shut off from the truth and the real way things are and I hate you I hate you I hate you – "

Lucy picked up a butter dish, and, as a kind of afterthought to her monologue, hurled it at Snaps' head. Snaps backed away muttering something about not going over the top, squire.

31

Lucy, without pausing for breath or looking at either of them, whirled up other utensils, cutlery, plates, bits of old food, one of Egbert's plastic pants and hurled them at Jack and Snaps as she talked. The two of them started to retreat into the hall, but Lucy followed them, unstoppable, keeping up her fire with anything that came to hand, an umbrella, a heavyish book, one of Jack's old shoes. Annie and Egbert followed her. Egbert had gone red and was screwing his face down into his neck while making grunting noises.

" . . . why do you do it? Why do we put up with it day after day? Is it because we haven't got anything else to do is it because we're chained to this rock it's true our bodies are a rock and we're chained to them it's endocrinology it is really our bodies make things but you you're just machines you go too far you break things and we wait but nothing happens don't you understand you stupid, stupid man I love you do you get pleasure from watching me suffer get yourself out of here get yourself out and let me suffer get yourself out go on go on go on – "

Things were getting quite dangerous for Jack and Snaps. Arms up to shield their faces, they reached the front door with as much sang-froid as was possible. Jack, crouching behind Snaps, with his right hand up to protect his head, started to slip back the bolt.

"Darling – " he began.

This was too much for Lucy. Uttering a Maenad-like screech, she picked up a large jug of flowers from the hall table and threw it at Jack's head. It hit the lintel of the door, shattered, and, under a rain of flowers and china, Jack and Snaps ran for the street.

Lucy stood at the door as they climbed into Snaps' car, screaming four letter words at them. There was a tragic quality about her, Jack thought, as they turned out of Lucy's street and up towards the Finchley Road. He put his head in his hands and shuddered briefly. So much for Plain Man and Plain Speaking.

"Pub?" said Snaps.

"Fine," said Jack.

A pub was a pub, even if you were drinking with Snaps.

"**L** ook", said Annie, as they went back into the house, "I don't think you should be by yourself just now."

"No," said Lucy meekly, stroking Egbert.

It was odd the way Lucy seemed to accept this suggestion. Passive. That was what women were supposed to be. That was their stereotype. It made Annie feel uncomfortably butch to be opposite this frail, damned creature (complete with baby) – she suddenly got the idea that her bum had become a vast, naval affair, and, to reduce its notional size, she got up and shifted her dress over her hips.

"I'll stay with you tonight."

"Oh. Oh would you? Oh ye-es," said Lucy, looking up at her with grateful, spaniel eyes.

Annie got the impression that had she suggested pulling out Lucy's arms by the roots she would have got a similar response. That was it. Lucy responded to a companion's hidden mood, not to their attempts to conceal it or their doubts about it. She was like a radar device, picking up signals she didn't understand. Poor Lucy, eh. Poor, troubled, passionate Lucy. She knew, somehow, in spite of everything, that Annie liked her, and that, in its turn, softened Annie's brisk, near martial style.

"Shall we get drunk?" said Lucy timidly.

"Er . . . "

"There's a bottle of Gordon's in the bedroom. And two of Teacher's. And some dry sherry. And four cans of Guinness. And some red wine. And some Tequila Ron left when he cleared out, back in Croydon."

"Fine," said Annie, trying to picture Lucy in Croydon with someone called Ron. It was surprisingly easy. Once again Lucy answered Annie's thought and not her spoken response.

"Ron was my husband. He was a Judo instructor. And I'm a housewife alcoholic. Sort of, anyway."

"Me too," said Annie, "there's thousands of us."

33

Her respect for Lucy increasing by the minute, she went out into the narrow hall, up the stairs and on to the even narrower landing. Here she had a choice of three rooms. On one door was a sign saying "THIS IS IT." Through the second she could see a white coat, a large teddy bear, a picture of a goat under which was written "A GOAT" and, hanging from the ceiling, a merry-go-round of what looked like monkeys, cut out of brown felt.

In Lucy's room, the bed was unmade, there were a lot of paperbacks, mainly poetry or works on the hazier fringes of the women's movement. They had titles like *Women's Bodies and Themselves* or *Sexual Aggression and the Female Role in Society*. There was a pre-Raphaelite poster, a lot of underwear scattered around the floor and, below the window, a pile of bottles and dirty glasses. One of the bottles was labelled MACON LUGNY 1975, underneath which, in scrawled pencil, was written MACON LOONY. Also (temptation) on the dressing table was a manuscript of some kind, several hundred pages in length, and faultlessly typewritten. From a distance it looked like poetry. On closer inspection it turned out to be a series of propositions, rather in the manner of Wittgenstein or Spinoza, although to Annie the resemblance to the work of these writers seemed to be almost exclusively typographical. She checked that Lucy hadn't followed her up the stairs and read the following fragment:

1341. Women who adopt the role of servants to their children are usually attempting mastery over their children.

1342. Children are strangers to their fathers, and friends to their mothers, for their first nine months of their lives. What is the answer to this? Careful introduction of friends and strangers.

1343. No political movement (and certainly not socialism yet) has succeeded in liberating women from the fatal consequences of their own biology. In Russia women who have been granted the enormous privilege of being sheet metal workers have not been robbed of the duties of creating and being the *primary* educative force in the lives of children.

344. Who gets the kids ready for the State Nursery (cf. Vozhensky op.cit.)? Is it male sheet metal workers? Not on your fucking life it isn't!

Annie wondered whether a person called Vozhensky could possibly exist. She flicked on through the manuscript, finding evidence of a Lucy that she had not expected and, perhaps, had not wanted. There was a huge section headed simply BIRTH. Interestingly misguided as Annie found much of this, it was the stray remark on the subject of Jack (Luke) that caught her attention, recalled to her the meaning of what she had just seen, that her husband had a mistress, and that the mistress had a child by him and that she, Annie, had nothing but her own mind, racing miserably on nothing, sending gusts of jealousy to her head. She let the manuscript fall back to the table, thought about Jack's weirdly unconvincing confession downstairs and read, out of the corner of her eye:

963. Luke is, in all important respects, homosexual.

Not knowing whether to laugh or cry, she picked up a bottle of Gordon's, two dirty glasses, and headed back downstairs.

There was nothing to drink with the gin.
  In the end Lucy discovered a fragment of Rose's Lime Cordial under the sink, and they poured two or three drops into the clear white liquid, watching the green crystals swirl and snowball across the glass. There was no question of bringing down the sherry or the Macon Loony. Gin, both women felt, was the only drink.

Annie set about trying to pump Lucy – a more difficult task than she had anticipated, even though she had gained control of herself on the journey downstairs. What she really wanted was more information, not about Jack Warliss or Luke Danby, but about the violent, curious creature she had glimpsed in the pages of Lucy's manuscript. Peter Simmons maybe.

"Ur – "

"Ye-es?"

"Do you and Jack – er – Luke . . . row a lot?"

A long pause. Lucy with her chin in her hands.

"Oh all the time. You?"

"No,t really."

"Oh."

This was true. Annie and Jack had, so far at least, always managed to find a verbal method of resolving their differences. There was another long pause. Quite a lot of gin was drunk. Then Annie tried again –

"Ur – "

"Ye-es?"

"Why do you row then?"

Lucy looked up at her shyly.

"I don't think he loves me enough."

Love, eh. Hmm.

"He's so . . . beautiful."

Annie had never thought of Jack as beautiful. Beautiful men, anyway, belonged on the pages of *Cosmopolitan* or *Honey*, and bloody boring they were too, those beautiful men with their dungarees and their Gauloises, leaning out of telephone boxes and trying to not to look queer. Their expressions learnt on holiday in the South of France, their –

"I think I know what the heart of his problem is – " To stop any more turquoise prose on the subject of Jack's mind and body, Annie said, finishing her first glass of gin and pouring them both another, this time neat –

"If bloody Snaps hadn't – "

But she didn't get any further than that. Lucy sat up, nose a-quiver, like a rabbit staring down a double-barrelled shotgun.

"Snaps, did you say?"

"Yes," said Annie, "Snaps is the man you threw the butter dish at."

Lucy had gone white.

"What about him?"

"Er . . . nothing . . . " said Lucy unconvincingly, " . . . nothing . . . "

Or, thought Annie, something. As the case might be. Lucy was now looking as guilty as a Dickens villain – not only did she seem unable to control her feelings, she seemed unable to hide them. Annie decided the mystery – if there was a mystery and it wasn't simply that the name of

36

Snaps had some kind of mystical significance for the girl – would be better investigated in the pages of the mysterious manuscript upstairs.

Annie went back to their earlier conversation, this time looking for a way to start Lucy off on some tremulous confession.

"He's a very frightened man in many ways," she said.

"He's a boy," said Lucy dreamily, "a lost boy in the wood. When I met Him first," she went on, voicing the capital letter in a way that made Annie want to bang her on the head with a soda siphon, "He was on the other side of a crowded room in Croydon and I" (the first personal pronoun was given slightly less glamorous treatment, but still managed to suggest that both Lucy and Jack, or Luke or whatever you wanted to call him, were characters in an Arthur Rackham fairy tale) "I was reading some poems I looked up and across the faces I saw Him come through the door of the pub and He was wearing a leather jacket and looking very slim and vulnerable and dangerous and wicked and He looked at Me and I looked back and suddenly I was reading the poem for Him and all the other faces melted like petals on a wet bough and then We" (the first person plural carried Lucy's speech into *Gone With The Wind* territory – it was pronounced as if the entire contents of the room were ascending to heaven) "We were lovers and then He was never here and He told me He was married and I said why can't We love Her and She love You and I love Her and You and – "

At this point, Lucy, bewildered by the glamorous, impossible creatures she had created, burst into tears again. It was astounding, thought Annie, to watch her effect the transition from Constance Spry to Gertrude Stein, and even more astounding to reflect how much better she wrote than she talked. Perhaps she'd had more practice at writing. However grudgingly, Annie found herself admiring the woman. People who thought of the world in terms of mediaeval romance were scarce and getting scarcer. She crossed to her and put her arms round Lucy's trembling shoulders.

"Why are we women?" said Lucy. "Why are we born to suffer like this? Why do we go on this pointless bloody journey?"

Annie had no succinct answer to these questions. They did not, however, seem to require one, for her charge leant into her new friend and, hugging her, buried her face deep into Annie's breasts. Annie, catching sight of the two of them in the mirror opposite, decided that they looked like a bad Victorian engraving, *The Sailor Who Did Not Return. Love Betrayed – A Sister's Grief. Away At the War.* Annie

37

didn't like this. Was it the passion Lucy had tapped in herself of which she was afraid? Or simply gin and undirected anger that made her pass through the hall, up the stairs and back to that manuscript? In the untidy room, on the edge of the bed, in the gathering darkness, she read on and on. Presently she was back at BIRTH.

Q uite early on, among bon mots such as –

821. The child is father to the jerk.

and

824. The world is divided into parents and children. Could anything be more hopelessly masturbatory than Wordsworth's obsession with Childhood as a state of grace?

Lucy had embarked on a detailed analysis of Jack and Snaps' relationship, the first statement of which reminded Annie of something that, for some reason, she had so far failed to consider in the Jack, Snaps, her triangle. Proposition 893 went:

893. Luke and Snaps were at school together. I can never understand that part of their life.

That was certainly true. So far did Annie fail to understand the workings of the mind of public schoolboys in later life (she herself had attended a grammar school in Lewes) that, for all practical purposes, she had forgotten that Snaps and her husband had not only gone to school together, they had also lived two streets away from each other.

896. Luke and Snaps were lovers.

It seemed funny at first. Annie scanned the page for the rest of the
sentence, viz. Jack and Snaps were lovers of *Match of the Day* or Jack
and Snaps were lovers of Five Card Stud, but the rational subject of this
otherwise palpably absurd sentence was nowhere in evidence. Jack and
Snaps lovers indeed. Snaps was the man known all over Leeds
University as the nearest thing to a goat with three A Levels. Annie
feasted her mind on visions of Snaps and Jack removing each other's
underwear, of Snaps and Jack in the pub over a pint of draught Guinness, and of Jack saying, "I love you, squire," and of Snaps replying, "I
would say this was true in the interpersonal sense for the moment at this
time." Wonderful wonderful wonderful. There was a grim intellectual
satisfaction to be derived from the fact that Lucy's apparent obsession
with personal relationships had led her inexorably, not only to making
suspicious generalizations about them, but also to committing herself to
even more suspicious (not to say barmy) specific statements. For Annie,
human behaviour was a science, and those who treated it as an art were
fated to a view of the world that was not simply irrelevant but also,
worst of all possible criticisms, inexact. Lucy had a pleasant enough
way with a phrase, but no coherent grip on theory. She might have a
baby but she was wrong, dead wrong about Jack. Sorry, Luke. Annie
clicked her tongue at herself. She had stayed long enough in this house
with her and her irritable son.

She got to her feet, letting the manuscript fall to the ground. The
pages fanned out like a deck of cards. It was time to go.

"Oh," said a small voice from the landing, "you're reading it."

"Er . . . sorry . . . " was all Annie could find to say, by way of reply.

"It isn't finished yet," said Lucy, stepping shyly into the room.

No, thought Annie, it isn't.

"What did you think of it?" said Lucy.

"I thought it was a wee bit far-fetched," said Annie, pacing. This
immediately struck her as rather harsh.

"I mean," she added, "I haven't yet read a book on the care of
children that has a feminist perspective. I thought that aspect was . . .
er . . . "

Lucy looked at her blankly. She felt she had been describing a different book.

"It's a bit bonkers really," Lucy said in the end, beginning to unwind
one of her rollers, and balancing Egbert, asleep on her shoulder, with

the other hand.

Annie found this remark reassuring.

"It is a bit," she said.

Then she went to the window and looked out over the tiny garden, the house opposite, the railway line beyond that, the bridge and the nearly dark sky. Lucy, with her infallible instinct for divining others' thoughts, said:

"It's true enough."

"What is?" said Annie, unnerved.

"About him and Mike Snaps."

Annie turned. Mother and child were turned away from her, practically in silhouette. They looked curiously strong and curiously vulnerable. Annie decided that she had been wrong about Lucy. She talked better than she wrote. She had, there was no denying it, presence. Of course Jack had had sex with Snaps. They went to bed together. They screwed each other. They were lovers, always had been. Lucy's bent shoulders made it so.

"Look," said Annie, "we'd better find them. Now."

"Ye-es," said Lucy, "ye-es."

Nelly Hortobagyi was thirty-five and at last she had a home of her own. Well, she wasn't Hortobagyi any more but Snaps now, although it was difficult not to think of herself as Hortobagyi, what with the blooming difficulty of the English language, which had a nasty way of sounding right when it was wrong and wrong when it was right. Home at last though, even if it was a basement flat in Paddington with a kitchen the size of a skunk's bum, squire, was better than the flat in Novi-Sad, which had walls so thin you could hear Papa Hortobagyi on the lavatory in the morning like he was the first world war or something. Christ all bloody mighty.

Thinking about Papa Hortobagyi set her teeth on edge. It was like she was having another bloody argument about the Partisans, with Papa Hortobagyi saying what heroes they were and her saying that she was fed up with the films where they blew up bridges every ten seconds and never got hurt and Papa Hortobagyi bursting into tears and asking her didn't she care about this new country Yugoslavia, so many races, so many peoples, but One Nation.

One bloody nation. Papa Hortobagyi had spent the war selling sausages to any invading army that seemed interested and was in possession of negotiable currency. I'm well out of *that*, she decided, stamping back from the sink and reflecting that even at seven thirty on a hot June night there was a lot to be said for the British way of life, not to mention the packet holiday that had winged Mikey to her all those years ago. He would be home soon, and tonight he would eat his dinner for certain.

She went through tonight's menu.

Serbian Sour Soup
Pancakes with Paprika and Vegetables to Choice
Cake

It was hard, but she could think in English now, although, in the middle of a perfectly decent English sentence, the odd phrase in Hungarian, or maybe even in Serbian, would claw at her, so that she faltered, stammered, and, aware of the disapproval in Mikey's eyes, would say . . . "I'm sorry . . . in Hungarian we say . . . "

She started to pour double cream into a large white bowl. A whole pint. That made her feel better.

Thinking about her English, however, had started her off, and she practised in melancholy. It was almost with a shudder of pleasure that she considered the possibility that Mikey would *not* come; he was drunk with someone from the Company; he was alongside a prostitute, and she would have to sit alone at the table in the damp front room, alone with the bowl of flowers, the check tablecloth (her aunt had given it to her), alone with about a gallon of Serbian Sour Soup, thirty pancakes with paprika and a cake the size of a car-wheel. I'll be fat as a pig, she thought, and found, to her surprise, that the idea of being fat cheered her up. Fat like her mother, or those women with black headscarves in the market. A fat peasant. Fat as butter. No more to pretend she was like these English girls who did not know their arse from an aeroplane.

Steady, Nelly. Steady on. Think in good clear practical English now. Mikey will be home soon.

After she'd put the double cream on one side she took a pinch of paprika (her mother's cousin had given it to her) and added it to the onions frying in the heavy steel pan. With her hair tied back in an Alice band, her strong hips and the neat, black dress she'd brought from home, she could have been a peasant girl and not the wife of a Ford's Junior Executive. Not that Mikey would ever be a *big* executive. For that you had to live in those houses like some of the others lived in – all glass and garage, in places like Sevenoaks or Tonbridge. They didn't trust Mikey with his flat in Paddington and spliced up to a bloody foreigner.

Nelly smiled. She liked to think of herself as a bloody foreigner. Next to get ready the mixture for *palancinke* – *Next I will get ready the pancakes*. No. Wrong. *Now I will do the pancake mixture.* She repeated it out loud to the wall calendar of the only interesting building in Novi-Sad (her brother had sent it to her for some reason). *Now I will do the pancake mixture.* She narrowed her mouth and the vowel sounds came out, rich, plummy and surprising. That made her laugh out loud. Really you could go mad waiting for Mikey with his bloody habits.

From the fridge came the milk. It was getting hot in the kitchen. She wiped her forehead with the back of her hand and caught sight of herself in the mirror above the sink. Old. Old and fat and foreign. Mikey wasn't going to come. He would never come back.

Now in a panic, Nelly switched off the gas under the onions, poured the milk into another bowl and hurried through to the front room. She could worry in the front room undisturbed. Yes, and why should she cook another meal for Mikey when he would be drunk for sure just like her bloody father with her bloody mother, why? He was with some bloody woman, no question about it.

Only one question to be answered, mate. Which woman?

Nelly went through her husband's pockets as a matter of course. It was simple self-protection. Married to someone like Mikey you had to. It was the only way you ever found out anything about him. If she wanted to know what he earned, where he'd been, even what he was feeling (or who he was feeling, squire, which was usually a lot more blooming pertinent) she would have to try and put together the story from scraps of letters, restaurant bills, theatre tickets . . . She was expert at knowing the places Mikey went to with men friends, the places he went to with girl friends and even the places he went to when he was by himself to "give himself a treat". Maybe there would be a new phone number or address. Something she'd missed. Nelly's great fear was not of Mikey's affairs but of the fact that he might be concealing one from her successfully. And he was concealing one, there was no doubt.

She started by the telephone. He often left scraps of paper between the pages of the telephone books and sometimes scribbled numbers in Pentel pen on the wooden shelf next to the directories. Most of the numbers and addresses here were familiar. There was 748-9001, that was Albert Neve, the spidery clerk from the sales department who had let out that huge fart at the cocktail party they had given last year. There was an Ealing number which was of an Older Woman called Radin, who had nearly got serious, and next to that a jumble of letters that were the extension numbers of Mikey's boss and a couple of other scrubbers who didn't count for anything at the end of the day. Underneath it was the name she had looked at a thousand times over the last God knows how long, and bit her lip in fury. ANNIE WARLISS. 435-9601.

She had never rung the number. She had never taxed Mikey with it. Half of her did not want to know. There was something so cruel and public about the neat capital letters, with the numbers to them. Oh Annie Warliss was important all right. She had heard Mikey on the phone to the bloody woman night after night saying things she could only half understand. That was what was so awful about Annie Warliss 435-9601. Mikey wanted her to know and she wanted it to be a secret. She was probably a thin girl with one of those walks like she was grating cheese with her thing disgusting fat chance poor Nelly had, eh squire? Oh, he would suffer. Tonight he would suffer on account of Annie Warliss 435-9601.

For a kick-off she would not give him this delicious dinner.

He could eat *sausage*. Cold sausage and pickle that he hated. He could − . She was just about to pour out the mixture for *palanc* − for *pancakes* − into the bin when she heard a burglar. She knew it was a burglar because he was coming down the stairs outside the flat one at a time, and waiting after every step to see if anyone had heard him. It wasn't Mikey's step, that was certain. Nelly, frying pan in hand, tiptoed out into the hall, from where she could watch from the shadows. Luckily the phone was towards the back of the hall, at the dark end of the flat, and she could phone 999 without he might see her.

43

The burglar was a tall, thin man with straggling hair and a big, curved nose. He was wearing a green corduroy jacket that could have done with a dry clean and an ant flea spray too probably, and, as he tip-toed his way towards the front door, he held his hands out in front of him, pointed. He looked like a conductor helping the orchestra through one of those bits when everyone plucks at the strings of the violin and makes faces like they had just sat down on a bucket of ice. Nelly had got almost halfway to the edge of the hall when the burglar stopped and peered in at the darkness of the flat. Without thinking what she was doing, Nelly darted for the nearest cover (a wall cupboard in which the linen was restrained) and climbed in, jerking the door shut after her. She stood in the darkness, holding her breath.

"It's OK," she heard the burglar say, "coast's clear. Out."

The other burglar then fell down the steps. He did not shout or cry or make any other noise apart from that of falling down the steps, from which Nelly deduced that he was probably wearing some special kind of burglar's clothing or was else so drunk he didn't notice. She wondered whether both or one of them were anything to do with the Balham rapist she had been reading about in Mikey's paper the other day. Mikey had laughed at her when she had mentioned the Balham rapist and said they were "off limits" for the Balham rapist. But what did "off limits" mean? Was it the same as "close season"? – the word Mikey had used about fish once. The Balham rapist, the article had said, winkled women out of their homes and attacked them with shears. Nelly froze against the wall, listening for the sound that might be discovered from shears. Then she heard the key in the lock.

"I would say, squire, that in terms of the face to face marital ones on this project as of now I am due for what we in the Department refer to as a pretty high scale interdepartmental bollocking."

The man with the straggly hair, who wasn't a burglar, but something much worse, a male friend of Mikey's whom she didn't know, replied –

"Why be frightened of your wife? I'm not frightened of my wife."

"How about your friend, equipped with the plate-throwing facility?" said Mikey.

"Not only plates, mate. Plates aren't fucking half of it," said the man with the straggly hair, gloomily.

Nelly peered out at the two of them. They had both removed their shoes, a thing Mikey sometimes did if he was prowling off somewhere.

"I couldn't face a bollocking," said Mikey, "I mean I would say in that respect it wouldn't even be up to a bollocking in our terms. It'd be sausages. Sausages with fucking pickle. Hundreds of them."

The man with the hair gave Mikey a funny look as Mikey said this and Mikey's nose went all stiff, the way it did when Nelly played his stereo and crunched up the needle on her old '78 of Magyar Dances which were a lot more fun than his rotten old pop music which wasn't even popular any more. They seemed to like the hall. Mikey slid down the wall, his back against it, his knees wide apart, and the man with the hair lay on his back and yawned. Nelly, who was finding all this a lot more revealing than going through Mikey's pockets, shuffled up to the crack in the door to get a better look. They were drunk for sure. Men always were drunk when they came in so blooming late. She peered beadily at Mikey, looking for signs of drunkenness.

"Annie and Lucy," said the man with the hair, "don't understand us."

"This is true, squire," said Mikey.

"Men are men and women are women," went on the man, "and never the twain shall meet."

"Confucius hath said this thousands of billions of years ago," said Mikey.

There was a pause.

"Annie Warliss," said Mikey, after a while, "that woman is wasted on you, son."

Nelly squeezed herself even closer to the crack. Looking out at Mikey from cupboards, she decided, was paying big blooming dividends.

"By tomorrow," said Mikey's unknown friend, "I have to decide. To Wheeble or not to Wheeble. By tomorrow."

Mikey didn't seem at all interested in this remark, although Nelly wondered whether the man could be referring to *The Wheebles* who were on every Tuesday and Thursday and were really good because they all spoke nice and slowly not like the American programmes or some of that blooming sex rubbish that made you puke to think about it.

"Look," said Mikey, "Annie asked me to."

"I don't understand," said his friend, "how she could keep something like that from me. Christ, for *two years*. You know? Spying. I mean for – "

"You managed to keep friend Lucy fairly well buttoned up," said Mikey. "I would say that deception-wise young Annie does not exactly win all the available awards in your immediate family situation context, squire."

"And what about you and fucking Lucy," said Mikey's friend, "come to that I'm not exactly bananas about you and her swapping cosy chats on the subject of me. I mean for God's sake is nothing secret any more? You were never as bad as this in the Modern Remove."

"I would say," said Mikey, "that there is a Guinness facility now available in the short term respect, fridge-wise."

Both of them now seemed to cheer up considerably. They got to their feet like old men and hobbled off towards the kitchen. Nelly heard thumping and clattering and the noises of things being broken, or narrowly avoiding being broken. They took up their earlier positions.

"We have never told," said Mikey's friend, "of the wondrous times we had at the old school. We have never spoken of these things."

"I was going to ask a few nasties on that front, squire," said Mikey, "in connection with the revelations vis-à-vis the . . . "

"Now – "

Mikey's friend paid no attention to his interruption.

"Now," he went on, "the fact that you and I know each other, in a way, so fucking well that we don't have to tell each other or anyone else about it sums up my point. Which is. Which is. That no one knows anyone. Really. Least of all themselves. The whole fucking thing is an unplumbable mystery."

"Aieeou," said Mikey, "I would say this is true, squire."

So this was one of Mikey's school friends, was it? Mikey had never introduced her to one of his school friends, indeed, to hear him talk, you would think he had never had any. But men just told you rotten lies all the time, and as to what they got up to when they were out of the house,

46

you were about as well informed as if they were on the blasted moon, so what they had got up to out of the house before you had even got them into the house, so to speak, was any bloody person's guessing game. Mikey's friend was now snorting through his nose and kicking his legs in the air like an insect, while Mikey shook his head in that helpless, don't-ask-me-anything-about-anything way he had.

"If only one could do without women," said Mikey's friend, "if only one could dispense with women. Eh?"

"According to reports recently received from the Finchley area," said Mikey, "you are in a full-time sense dispensing with the alternative sex scenario on account you are, not to put too fine a point on it, as bent as a nine bob note."

Mikey's friend looked embarrassed.

"Look," he said, "I get carried away. I mean you and I . . . you know . . . at school, right? . . . liked each other . . . and . . . I don't know . . . Annie, Lucy . . . they don't *understand*. I mean . . . "

"Say no more," said Mikey, giving his friend the thumbs-up sign, "the matter rests. Between members of the sex I would describe as male, it is not necessary to talk over questions that could well be described as I would say emotional."

"*Right*," said Mikey's friend, and on this, to Nelly, totally incomprehensible note, the conversation seemed to finish for the time being. It was pretty clear that one or both of them had been doing it, not only with the person called ANNIE WARLISS 435-9601, but also with a new, and probably even worse, prostitute called Lucy. In fact it was conceivable that they had all been doing it in the same room or something my God why had she married him he was sex-mad when you came to think about it.

"We," said Mikey's friend, after a long pause, "are the doomed generation of the sixties."

Mikey allowed his tongue to loll out of his mouth at this remark, so that he looked like Charles Laughton in the film of the Hunchbacks of Notre Dame by Victor Hugo. Otherwise he said nothing. Nelly watched them, brooding on their conversation.

Lucy. Annie. Sausages indeed. Why *should* she anyway? Why should she take all these doings on the nose? Tightening her grip on the frying pan, she edged close to the crack in the door until, with Mikey in her sights, she found her anger turn to shame and self-disgust, choking her throat, making her breasts burn and her eyes water. Unable to stop herself, yearning her way out of the cupboard, almost, almost but not quite giving away her hiding place, she said, in a low, throaty voice:

"Mikey. Oh Mikey Mikey Mikey . . . "

Both men froze. The man with straggly hair kept his head very still and rolled his eyeballs around like a lizard for some moments. Mikey screwed up his face as if in pain. Then, before either of them had a chance to do any more, Nelly staggered out of the cupboard, tear ducts starting up like billy-oh because the world was such a gigantic place really when you came to think about it, and just listening to him had made her feel even smaller.

Arms at full length (the right arm still carried the frying pan but it was now part of her arm, as much a part of what she felt as anything else in the room) she burst through the cupboard door, stepped towards Mikey and said, in a low, thrilling voice –

"Mikey. Oh Mikey. Oh Mikey, Mikey, Mikey."

Mikey looked as if he was about to sneeze. Trembling very slightly, he said:

"I would say that at this time I am feeling embarrassment."

I t was difficult to kiss Mikey while holding the frying pan and it was made a lot more blooming difficult because he did not seem to want to be kissed in front of his friend. Also, when Nelly had her arms around him tightly the pan was banging against the back of his head and so the only way she could keep on to him was to lower her arms and go gobble gobble at him with her lips. He backed away and suddenly she had a vision of herself pecking away at thin air like he was a flock of geese who have wandered away from the farmyard. The whole thing was ridiculous. She left him alone and said:

"Vell Mikey. Vart eez called your frien'?"

She could hear herself sounding foreign as she said this but she didn't care. In fact she decided to sound even more foreign, just to embarrass him.

"Carm on Mikey vot he called your frien' 'ere then hey?"

Mikey did not reply. Snapping her fingers, gipsy style, Nelly struck a Carmen-like pose in the middle of the hall, her left hand on her hip and the frying pan, now translated into a fan or a pair of castanets, held at a saucy angle above her head. She rolled her r's even more ridiculously, and did a kind of peasant shout, just to spite.

"Carrrm along then Mikey! Vat 'e a bloody well a callin' 'isself a den your frien'?"

The voice was now so ludicrous as to be incomprehensible to everyone present. Even Nelly wasn't quite sure what, precisely, she had said, but it was obvious from the now craven expression on Mikey's face that she was well in control of the situation. Mikey's friend, who had remained flat on his back during her appearance from the cupboard, lifted his head from the floor. He looked like the pictures of the people doing exercises to lose weight in Nelly's booklet − free with her last copy of *Beautiful Homes and Kitchens*.

"My name," he said, "is Jarlsberg. Terry Jarlsberg."

"Jarlsberg," said Nelly, still Queen of the Gipsies, "eez norra name. Eet eez a cheese. Jarlsberg. Hey!"

"Yeah," said the man, "a lot of people think it's really funny. I get a lot of jokes about it. It *so* happens that my name is also the name of a well known cheese. Big joke. But it is my *name*. OK? And there ain't a lot I can do about it."

"Hang on − " began Mikey, but Nelly interrupted him, imperiously.

"Let your friend speak," she said, "let heem talk!"

As well as intensifying the foreign accent, Nelly decided to like the man with the straggly hair and the unfortunate name. There had been something really from the heart so that you knew it was for real after she had made that stupid joke about him being a cheese. It wasn't his fault he had a name like a cheese and anyway, from what she had gathered listening to the two of them, they seemed to be having some kind of bust-in about bloody ANNIE WARLISS 435-9601, so she could really needle Mikey by smarming up to his bloody rival. Plus to that she rather liked the look of him − he had a scruffy, lost-dog look that she had always had a soft place for, in spite of his big, red nose and his eyes, which were not too big and a bit on the fishy side. He spoke in a weary, matter of fact sort of way, as if he was always telling people about his name and what he did.

"My name is Terry Jarlsberg," he said, "and I'm a fairly typical member of bourgeois society. I'm an account executive with a small advertising agency in Kensington. It's a boring but well-paid job. Nothing much has happened to me or will happen to me in the future, come to that. All I really want to do is to do my job and to keep a wife and family in reasonable comfort for a few years and then to die, if that's all right. I don't want to argue with anyone about anything. I just want to tick over without worrying too much about the state of the world or the state of my soul."

Mikey had started to bang his head against the wall.

"Aieeou!" he kept saying, "Terry Jarlsberg! Aieeou!"

Nelly thought it was rather unfair to keep mentioning the man's unfortunate name, so she said, giving her sexy, bedroom look –

"Would you like to stay for some suppair, Meestair Jarlsberg?"

"That," said man, "would be absolutely great."

Without waiting for further discussion, Nelly pushed past Mikey into the kitchen. She didn't feel all moved and Hungarian any more. Just plain bloody fed up with his conjuring tricks, oh she would make a meal, yes, such a meal, but the choicest bits would be offered to nice Mr Jarlsberg and if anyone got the benefit of her big black eyes (which were her best feature according to those men who had tried to rape her at the swimming pool outside Zagreb) it wouldn't bloody well be Mikey. Thoroughly pleased with the way things had turned out, she started to bang pots and pans together, pouring out cream, paprika, white wine and God knew what else. She hummed to herself as she did this, an old song, turning the words into English as she went because it made them sound so stupid –

> "Chop off Granny's head
> Put it in a basket
> Come it is market day
> Come come come!"

Outside she could hear the self-important but purring sort of noises that men made when they knew some woman was in the kitchen getting ready to fill their bellies. She heard the clink of the Slivovic bottle, the thump-thump of Mikey's feet as he sprawled on the sofa, practically lying on his back he would be by now, with his hands clasped to his stomach, staring at the ceiling. Pissed off. *Peesed* off. Then – the way men talked when they were alone – the same thing over and over again with long pauses in between but very pleased all the same –

"*I* dunno," from Mikey, "Jarlsberg! Jarlsberg!"

A whinny like a horse. Then Mr Jarlsberg, being very polite in spite of all the bloody rudeness –

"Watch out for Jarlsberg, Mikey. He might be the one."

More thumping and, probably, Mikey making a sour face as he downed his Slivovic in one and afterwards she would bet that shrewd look of his.

"And would you be able to explain that, squire?"

"I get a feeling, Michael, that Jarlsberg's the one. The breakthrough. And seriously, Snaps, I think he could mean a lot of trouble for you. After all, he's operating in the same area."

It was very odd. When Nelly heard Mikey's friend say this she was, all of a sudden, frightened. As if she was involved in something she didn't understand.

T his particular blighted midsummer day, Jack decided, had only really started to look up with the appearance of Terry Jarlsberg. Previous to Jarlsberg's unprompted entrance on to the scene, everything had, when you came down to it, been a bit of a frost. People had been getting hideously close to the soft mushy bit at the centre of what could be laughingly described as his personality. People who he had never intended to meet had met, had indeed, it seemed, been meeting for months and had discussed him and each other in his presence, just as they had been discussing him and each other, unknown to him, for the last two years. Bits of his unremarkable past life had come floating back at him, fragments of an undistinguished

51

shipwreck, and, worst of all, he had actually had a stab at describing his own corner in world grief: he had spoken in public of his sexual doubts and fears.

He blushed now, as Mike and he waited for their supper, to consider that he had actually admitted to lurking homosexual feelings. It was, somehow, such an obvious thing to admit to. Anyone with any spark these days had lurking homosexual feelings. You were considered plain dull if you didn't have lurking homosexual feelings. The only decent thing to do for any self-respecting man about town was to get on and bugger the man next to you with all convenient speed.

Talking about his mother, too, had been a mistake. There was nothing interesting or surprising in the fact that, as an adolescent, he had been obsessed with his mother, or that, as a boy at school, he should have been passionately fond of the man who now, it appeared, was attempting to seduce his wife by the unlikely stratagem of introducing her to his mistress. None of this, Jack decided, should have been mentioned, because it was dead history. We should bury each day, each brief attempt at a new character, with as little ceremony as possible.

But Jarlsberg. There was a man. Terry Jarlsberg. With a name like Jarlsberg you could go places. Norway for instance. Ssssh.

There were obviously going to be teething problems with Jarlsberg. Problems such as the fact that only half crazy foreigners, whose speciality was hiding in cupboards with frying pans, would possibly believe that his name *was* Jarlsberg. Terry Jarlsberg, to the casual observer, might look like the final positive proof of the fact that Jack Warliss had lost his marbles. But, to set against that fact, you had to put the unarguable truth that, for the first time today, Jack felt good. He felt in control.

He had a good, clear picture of Jarlsberg too, which was more than could be said for Warliss, Simmons or Danby. Jarlsberg was a man who, in a quiet way, was making something of his life. Jarlsberg wasn't one of those advertising men who moaned on about how awful it was in advertising. He just got on, quietly and firmly, with the job of advertising things. He wasn't particularly shabby or particularly flash. He wasn't a failure with women, nor was he a desperate stud. He wasn't married, he wasn't single. Jarlsberg had a series of satisfactory, deeply felt and meaningful affairs, which ended after seven or eight years. The women in Jarlsberg's life parted from him with a vague autumnal sense of loss, as they departed for foreign parts or other, even more fulfilling

52

relationships with people not unlike Jarlsberg. They never sent him letters with things like, "Let's meet for a drink sometime!" or "You have ruined my life!" after the affair was over. Jarlsberg's parents were dead. They had fallen into a fjord some three weeks after Terry's birth. A beautiful couple. Terry would like to have known them better.

Jarlsberg was a serious man, essentially. That is to say, people took him seriously. They didn't say things like, "Good old Jarlsberg!" or "Nice one, Jarlsberg!" when he passed comment on some question of note. Neither did they call him by nicknames, such as "Jarls" or "The Berg" or "Cheesey". He had a sense of humour, yes, but it was kept in check — it didn't leap out at him, causing him to giggle violently in the middle of political meetings.

"Food is ready, Meestair Jarlsberg!" said a curious foreign voice behind him, breaking in on his reverie, and, for a moment, Jack could not remember who he was. He turned to see the mad foreigner carrying a huge bowl of soup and grinning insanely.

"In Yugoslavia" she said, "we call thees soup Serbian Sour Soup and we eat it till eet comes out of our ear-holes!"

"We do in Paddington an' all," said Snaps, getting to his feet wearily.

"Terrific," said Jack, in a quite authentically easy Jarlsberg tone, "Terrif!"

"Terrif" was exactly the sort of non-word Jarlsberg might employ in such a situation. It concealed a wealth of reservations about what was happening, transformed an awkward social scene into an everyday business conference, where, after all, some awkwardness is to be expected, with the simple loss of three letters.

There certainly was a lot of soup. And Snaps wasn't entering into the spirit of the thing at all. He prodded at his morosely with a spoon, muttering something about salt. Jack, however, vaguely conscious that this was expected of him, and reflecting that Jarlsberg probably ate three expense account lunches a day, grasped his spoon and leaned forward in his seat like a prep school boy eager for pudding. To his horror, he noticed that in the middle of the soup (which was clearish grey in colour) floated what looked like a raw egg yolk. Coming to the conclusion that the mad foreigner must have made a mistake, he tried to roll this to the edge of the eating area, but, before he had time to stop her, she had pronged it with her fork and bright yellow viscous material was spreading in all directions, like the cloud of smoke observed after a nuclear explosion. Snaps had been secretive about his wife in the pub,

53

not even mentioning that she was a mad foreigner; he now sat, staring at his soup as if it were an old, unpardoned enemy. Jack started to eat. It tasted slightly of vinegar. To take the taste away he began to eat a piece of bread that had been thrust into his hand.

Occasionally the mad foreigner would stick her face into his and ask him whether he was enjoying his soup. She stared deep into his eyes as she put this question, a long, lingering, amused and yet soulful look, from which Jack deduced that his attitude to the soup was pretty important to her. He tried to be, in response, both satisfied and larky, as worldly-wise as only Jarlsberg could be.

MAD FOREIGN WOMAN: You laik thees soup?

JACK (WINSOMELY):   Yes. Yes. Yes.

MAD FOREIGN WOMAN: Eet eez good, yes?

JACK (STUNNED BY THE FACT):   *Yes.* Yes it is. God. It's . . . amazing. (LIFTING HIS SPOON AND LOOKING OFF CAMERA, AS IN ONE OF JARLSBERG'S MOST SUCCESSFUL ADVERTISEMENTS) *Inc*redible.

MAD FOREIGN WOMAN: Eeet eez traditional.

JACK (SERIOUS):   Traditional. Yes. In your homeland.

MAD FOREIGN WOMAN: On Sundays I weel eat thees soup until I am sick. Yes? So-o-o much *zoop!*

JACK: Indeed. In your homeland. Yes.

MAD FOREIGN WOMAN (THROATILY):   Eat. Eat. Eat.

Jack's mother had always described him as a "small eater". On top of a half a bottle of whiskey earlier in the day and three pints in the pub with Snaps, he felt as if the description fitted him perfectly, but, partly out of professional politeness, of the kind usual with such as Jarlsberg, and partly to cover the lack of meaningful conversation, he managed to swallow four bowlfuls. By the third bowl, Snaps (who had made no attempt at eating whatsoever) placed his head in his hands, and, halfway through the fourth bowlful, sounds of snoring were heard as Snaps slumped forward on to the deck. The mad foreign woman seemed undismayed by this performance. She told Jack how the soup was prepared, at what times of the year she and her mad foreign relations were prone to eat the soup, and she spoke of strange garnishes that could be used for the soup, how toast or croutons or fresh white bread all enhanced its flavour. Then she went on to tell him how the soup could be reheated, warmed with goose stock, added to sauerkraut, poured over stale breadcrumbs, refrigerated, not refrigerated, treated and mis-treated a thousand different ways. It seemed a shame, really, that all they were doing to the soup was eating it and talking about it. It didn't seem fair. Somehow, Jack felt, the soup deserved more than this.

At length, however, even the mad foreigner seemed satisfied and Jack pushed back his chair, preparatory to getting up and staggering across to the sofa. But, before he had time, the mad foreign woman got to her feet, and, gathering up the dishes, sped off in the direction of the kitchen. As she left, for a panic-stricken instant, Jack thought he heard her say something about pancakes, but dismissed such talk as a nervous tic of his auditory processes, a manifestation of his unconscious fears. In the brief pause occasioned by her departure, Snaps raised his head from the table and stared blearily at Jack. It was the sort of look travellers give each other on a bad sea crossing – blank, hopeless and yet compassionate.

"Pancakes now, squire," he said, "fucking pancakes."

And, slowly, replaced his head on his fore-arms.

He was correct. In due season, from the kitchen came the mad foreigner, black dress now slightly rumpled, black hair askew with the heat; she carried a dish about the size of a ladies' writing desk. On the dish was a shoal of little brown parcels, packed together tightly, like commuters. Between each parcel were gherkins, bits of red pepper and fronds of a strange, off-green vegetable that Jack had never seen before. Lapping the edge of this display was a dark, brown-red liquid. Gravy. Was gravy an adequate way of describing anything connected with such food? For a while Jack was lost in admiration, until the heart-stopping fact was brought home to him that he, the mad foreign woman and Snaps were expected to eat, as well as look at, this offering. And Snaps was out of the race. There seemed to be other things on the table as well. Beans in a sauce that looked like old plaster of Paris. Roast potatoes sizzling in an open dish. A jug of cream. More bread. Salad. And the mad foreigner was eating, knife and fork whizzing from mouth to plate, elbows going like the clappers, talking, this time, of pancakes, the history of pancakes, some other kinds of pancakes (Jack was eating too by now, with the thorough neatness of Jarlsberg), of how these particular pancakes had been made, of how they contained not only meat but something called Mother's Paprika which was not like the rubbish they sold in the bloody shops here but blew the roof of your mouth off the way paprika was supposed to (this Jack discovered to be no less than the truth). She was talking of batter and onions, of ways of tossing pancakes or of not tossing pancakes, of the pros and cons of pancakes *per se*, of whether pancakes were the best way of wrapping meat, of their existential validity, of the past, the future and present of pancakes, the way forward and the way back. And, mercifully, the pancake horde was thinning. Beans were being swallowed too, dunked in the hot, salty gravy, and roast potatoes were being split open, white and sweet, oh Jesus Christ this was an awfully big meal, a really awfully big meal indeed.

They were on the home straight – about fourteen pancakes down – when Jack felt it would be necessary to find out whether this person intended to force him to eat pudding. Jarlsberg was not the man to come out with feeble English suburban lines like, "Not for me, thanks," or "I'm full to bursting, thanks." In the mad foreign woman's hometown, moreover, it was fairly obvious that refusing a woman's food was tantamount to spitting on her father's grave and jumping up and down on her kid sister with hobnailed boots. Jack pushed back his chair and, on pretext of heading for the lavatory, went out, through the hall and into the kitchen. There, perched on the edge of a small wooden table, was a cake.

It was the kind of cake you eat with a knife and fork, or rather, the kind of cake you eat with a forklift truck and ten men in uniform to manoeuvre each slice into position. It looked like a giant display cake, made out of foam or polystyrene, an unreally huge item of confectionery, that only recent experience implied might actually be intended for human consumption. It was Supertuck and then some – its surface a mass of crazy whorls and turrets, studded with angelica and sprayed with the fine dust of hundreds and thousands that brought Jack back memories of tamer cakes made by Jack's mother in the drab, tiled kitchen at Mill Hill. It was obviously a layer cake as well, the culinary equivalent of a tower block, each floor concealing a wealth of individual experience behind the bland surface. On some there would be cherries, on others brandy and cream, sponge, chocolate, strawberries, raspberries, fruit in and out of season, kummel, kirsch, Grappa, sherry . . . It was about two foot in diameter. Jack stood looking at it, gleaming as if for someone's wedding, somehow shaming the underground gloom of the kitchen.

Suddenly he felt an arm slide round his waist. He looked down, and there, below his face, at shoulder level, was the mad foreign woman, her dress now showing a considerable portion of her suntanned breasts, her Alice band lost, her shoes kicked off and two wide rivers of grease across her chin. She wiped the back of her left hand across her mouth with offensive Continental thoroughness and looked up at Jack, pertly. Together they looked at the cake.

"Thees, Meestair Jarlsberg," she said, "eez the Nelly cake."

It was at that moment, Jack decided afterwards, that he felt the first stirrings of desire for his improbable hostess. Or, to put it another way, it was at that moment that he decided to seduce her. "Seduce" wasn't a word that Jack Warliss used very much, it had overtones of coldness and calculation about it, but it was the kind of word Terry Jarlsberg quite often found best described his casual flirtations after long lunches. It went with the confidence and smoothness that Jack had felt rise in him since Jarlsberg's ride to the rescue.

It was also (he admitted this grudgingly) the kind of setting against which his sexual adventures tended to happen. It was late, he was rather drunk (he seemed to have been drinking Slivovic with the meal) and alone with a not particularly attractive girl who, for some reason best known to herself, seemed to have become attracted to him. She reminded Jack, as she leaned rapturously against him, of the thousands of girls he had danced with at parties in North London when he and Snaps had roamed around together – girls shaped like sausages, with hair like Brillo pads.

"Come, Meestair Jarlsberg," she said gaily, "we will eat some cake."

It was only then that Jack began to understand what he was going to have to do. Sexual sensitivity was not his strong point – Annie had always maintained that he would respond best to women who approached him with a large placard inscribed LET'S HAVE A FUCK, and anything that deviated from printed directions, was, for

Jack, puzzling and painful. Looks, after all, could be mistaken, while gentle caresses could be gentle caresses and no more than that. And of course women cheated at this game, as at so many others. Sometimes a caress was just a caress and you were bollocked if you tried to escalate matters into the genital region. Sometimes you were meant to escalate matters pretty damn quickly and woe betide you for a spineless weed if you didn't. With both Annie and Lucy, Jack had groped and stroked, kissed and assaulted, more or less blindly and cluelessly, but with this good lady, he saw, no confusing pretence of any kind would be required. All he had to do was to eat at least two slices of the Nelly cake. That, as far as he could see, would be for her the equivalent of hours of stomach rubbing, hair twisting, buttock squeezing and other tiresome limberings up to congress.

Blessing once again Jarlsberg and all he stood for, Jack followed her and the cake back into the front room. Snaps had not moved. His untasted soup beside him, he lay like some Borgia *faux pas*, a guest poisoned too early in the proceedings. Nelly, after telling him three times that the cake was named after her, began to cut two huge slices, dumped them on two plates and smothered them with cream.

The Nelly cake had a history too, but although they talked of it at length, Jack had now grasped the point that what was said was unimportant – it was the manner that counted. He nodded waggishly as she told him how once, at a picnic on the Danube, an earlier version of the Nelly cake had rolled away down a steep slope, pursued by Great Uncle Akos, how once, at a gipsy wedding, the Nelly cake had been stolen by a member of the traffic police, and he licked his fingers prettily as she gave him a blow by blow account of the ingredients, how they had been brought together, how transformed and how they affected the stomach and the nerves. But he didn't listen. He kept his eyes on hers, quizzically, learning how she wanted him to look at her. Wanted and yet did not want. She was afraid, of course; even as her black eyes glazed with lust, something in her was saying (as a similar voice was saying to Jack), "Hold *on*, don't, not *now*, stop that *looking*," but Jack, inebriated with his theory, with Jarlsberg, with Nelly and with her cake, kept right on staring at her, levelly, with the disconcerting cool of the seducer.

At some stage they got on to the sofa. Jack was, by this time, making exaggerated munching noises and generally behaving like Marcel Marceau doing an impression of someone eating. He gulped, he burped, he swore with the pleasure of it, ran his tongue ostentatiously round the inside of his teeth, and finally, when he was at fever pitch of swallowing, chewing and licking, he placed a hand on Nelly's knee and fondled it with some of the same enthusiasm.

"NAUGHTY Meestair Jarlsberg," said Nelly, "thees eez Nelly's knee!"

"Call me Terry," said Jack, leaning across her for the first kiss.

She had a kiss like a suction pump. It was the kind of kiss where you felt it advisable and necessary to hold on to your jacket, wallet and shoes in case they disappeared up the slipstream. It was, in a phrase Snaps might have used, a lip cruncher, squire. It was accompanied by a vigorous exploration of Jack's trousers by both of the Nelly hands. They kneaded his buttocks in a firm, practical way, as if assessing how long they would require in the oven; after the buttocks, the hands crabbed round to his groin and began to undo his fly, swiftly and efficiently. Jack, by way of response, tried to work out where, if anywhere, one undid the Nelly dress. It was a strange, foreign dress, that appeared to have been welded out of one single, seamless piece of cloth.

"Yes please," Nelly was saying, "bloody hell yes please some more please."

Jack pulled violently at a bit of dress in the region of the armpit. There were several small popping sounds, and, above her shoulder, the dress parted, raggedly. Her skin seemed very brown. Jack started to nibble, half-heartedly, at the base of her neck, as, down below, the Nelly hands eased his trousers over his buttocks and twanged his underpants lustily. It was all too swift and wholesome, he decided, redolent of an obscure Pentathlon event, and, which was worse, probably about as strenuous. Somehow, however, the usual combination of politeness, surprise and vanity kept him going.

There was also the question of Snaps. He was, clearly, fairly soundly asleep, but there was also the fear that he might wake halfway through the proceedings. Hence, possibly, the unseemly Nelly haste. In fact, although the Snaps question was worrying, it was also, quite definitely, aphrodisiac. Hadn't he read somewhere that gazelles and antelopes fuck faster than almost any other creature? Presumably because their congress is liable to be interrupted by one or other party being eaten. It was a feeling of delicious hurry, swamping the brief feeling of despair, that prompted the swift removal of the Nelly tights, the Nelly bra and the Nelly knickers.

She was rather fat. But that didn't seem to matter. It was too late to go back anyway. Impossible now to say to Snaps that they were removing each other's clothes preparatory to lying there and talking about the weather. He was now, at this point in time, technically committing adultery, no longer contemplating it, for the Nelly hands were cramming the Jack penis into the Nelly vagina with speed and accuracy. Could you be said, Jack wondered, to have committed adultery if you had not actually ejaculated yet? After all, marriages could be annulled on the grounds of non-consummation, could they not? If simply sticking your penis into someone was adultery then you might as well say licking their ear was adultery. Or taking them out to dinner, for God's sake. No, adultery was, had to be, the whole caboodle.

Nelly didn't seem to be concerned with any of this. She was pumping and groaning and rolling her eyes up into her head like a woman demented. If President Tito himself had walked in she would probably not have noticed. But, for Jack, the unseen but felt presence of Snaps behind him was now passing beyond titillation and into the realm of serious worry. As the brief excitement stalled back once more into despair, he became increasingly conscious of his and her body, of the fact that he seemed to be thudding into her for no good reason other than that of exercise. His stomach had started to hurt as well and he began to thud slightly less gamely.

When he had slowed his stroke to practically nothing, Nelly too started the long climb down from the lower slopes of ecstasy. Her arms flung out behind her, she grunted narrowly at him as he lay sprawled across her, now violently depressed at what had happened.

"Vot eez eet, Terry?" she said.

"I think," said Jack, "it is the fact that your husband is about two yards away."

The expression in her eyes altered from pique to stark terror. Her head started to tremble violently.

"Oh my God," she moaned, "oh blooming God."

Hadn't she noticed him? Jack wondered. Or was this part of a strange *Who's Afraid of Virginia Woolf*-style ritual? A regular feature of the Snaps' summer evenings? Whatever her motive, she seemed to be wasting no time about getting out from under him, and, with one eye nervously on the figure at the table, slipping on knickers, bra, tights and dress. Jack too, impressed by her decisiveness, followed suit. In less than a minute they were standing, fully clothed. Nelly wrinkled her eyes with worry as she looked at Snaps and, bashing herself on the

60

forehead with the heel of her palm, said, while pacing to and fro –

"Oh my God my God. Vot ve are doeeng thees for, Terry?"

Jack did not attempt to answer this question. The awful thing was, now she was fully clothed, that prickle of lust (made up, perhaps, of suppressed bitterness towards Snaps) had woken in him again, only intensified by the unsatisfactory nature of what had just occurred. It was now plain, however, that nothing of any significance was going to happen while the Nelly husband lay, head on arms, within auditory range of the kind of screaming, sobbing orgasm Jack intended he and Nelly to share. Somehow or other he would have to get her out of the flat and into a place suitable for sexual intercourse. A hotel? No. He could not see him and Nelly checking into a hotel at this stage in their relationship.

She sat on a chair that looked as if it had been bought with the Yugoslav equivalent of Green Shield Stamps and blew out noisily, her legs set wide apart, then she tilted her head and stared at the ceiling through half closed eyes, allowing her mouth to hang, slack and open. She was muttering in the foreign language again, a soft, fluent sound, broken by the occasional, jagged vowel. Jack leaned forward and, in a bright, easy Jarlsberg-style voice, said –

"Look, honey. How's about you and me going for a stroll-io?"

She did not ask him why Jarlsberg expressed himself so badly, or why he used dated forties slang, which was as well, because this aspect of Jarlsberg's character surprised Jack quite as much as it might or might not have surprised Nelly. Instead she said:

"My God, vot a good notion."

And, together, they went.

I t was hotter and closer outside. In the street (one of those sham boulevards that abound between Paddington Station and Lancaster Gate, lined with tall trees and taller hotels) the citizenry were sitting on benches, strolling arm in arm and trying to pretend that they were in Aix-en-Provence rather than West London. The lamps were lit, their neon upstaged by what was left of the day, and, over to the left, people were spilling out of a pub to stand with their drinks on the wide pavement.

It all seemed so much easier now that they were out of the flat. They walked, a yard or so apart, quickly and decisively, as to some appointment already agreed. In a sense, thought Jack, something had been decided between them. They felt like a conspiracy, for, without anything having been said, it seemed clear that they were now looking for Somewhere To Do It.

"I thought," said Jack, "we might stroll towards the park."

Nelly replied with a half nod. She had gained something in the transition from joke foreigner to serious proposition; there was now a look about her, sideways, casual, that Jack found both scaring and exciting, and, shyly, like a teenager on his first date, he grabbed for her hand in the half light. It was curious how having her hand in his raised the whole tone of the proceedings.

They were now walking past a large modern hotel, busy with the arrivals and departures of the wealthy and, ahead of them, to their right, Jack could see the Bayswater Road, where taxis, buses and private cars scudded through to Marble Arch. They crossed two roads, threaded their way through a party of Arabs and found themselves at Lancaster Gate Tube Station, facing the darkened spaces of Hyde Park.

There was something attractive about the idea of Hyde Park. "Welcome!" the shadows and the trees and the grass seemed to be saying. "Welcome! Come out of the noise and the hotels and the bright faces. Walk a little deeper into the mauve light of our deserted spaces. Stroll out, illegally now, after the hour of sunset, and in the quietest, emptiest, darkest region of the park, on a patch of grass that by day is marked by office workers and office workers' litter, lie you down, remove your clothes and hammer away unmolested by the forces of the law!" Attractive, thought Jack, and yet not irresistible, for the railings that barred them out were at least five foot in height and the pavement opposite was dangerously busy. Trying to look unlike a man contemplating a serious breach of the by-laws he took Nelly's arm and set off, right, towards Queensway. She still did not speak, but, as if to acknowledge the fact that this was no ordinary walk, she slipped an arm round Jack's waist and squeezed him warmly, suggesting that she was behind any move he might dare to make. Jack, meanwhile, kept an eye over to his left, hoping for a miraculous break in railings.

About halfway between Lancaster Gate and Queensway the road suddenly seemed to get quieter and Jack steered Nelly over to the Park side, where the trees grew over towards the pavement. There was no one about. After a quick look over his shoulder, Jack pulled himself up on to the bar of the railings and succeeded in jamming his right foot in a gap roughly three feet clear of the ground. He scrabbled on the polished metal with his left foot and, rather to his surprise, managed to work the rubber sides of his shoes up the surface until he was lying more or less parallel to the ground. This was an extremely unpleasant feeling.

Nelly, bless her, was supporting his back and with her help Jack slipped his right leg over the railings and lodged it in a similar position on the bar, this time on the Park side. It was then that things started to go badly wrong. The plan had been to flip his body over the crest of the obstruction and then lower himself, leg by leg on to the forbidden grass. But as he brought his left leg over to follow the right he felt the right foot start to slide; a horrible vision of himself, impaled on the railings of the Bayswater Road and left there by the police as a warning to others, flashed across his mind as Nelly, in a still greater panic (partly because someone official-looking was approaching on the other side of the road), flipped his body up and over. Jack changed hands, slithered, squawked and finally fell to earth, swearing dully to himself.

"Oh my God, Terry – " said Nelly, "are you breaking a leg?"

"Not at the moment," said Jack, "right now I am breaking an arm and a leg, a head and an arm."

"Oh my blooming God," she went on, "eet eez too high thees fence!"

And it was. She tried jumping up. She tried winching her leg over. She tried tackling it inch by inch, as if it were a rock face, but several

63

decades of pancakes, goulash, home-made bread, farm-fresh cheese, recently killed pork, red wine, white wine, Slivovic, not to mention cakes, Nelly cakes, Serbian Sour Soup and cream, double, single and whipped, had left Nelly unsuited to almost all forms of physical exercise. Her best chance, reflected Jack bitterly after about five attempts, would have been to run at the railings in the hope of flattening them.

The problem was not eased by the fact that Jack had damaged some small but vital muscle in his back, and, as well as not being able to give her much assistance in getting over, was not now capable of returning to civilization by the route whence he had arrived. He cast nervous glances over his shoulder back at the interior of the park, wondering what the hell he was doing there; lust had proved not only bloody extreme, rude, cruel and not to be trusted, but also impossible to satisfy. He thought, with a twang of nostalgia, of the post-coital blues, as Nelly and he faced each other, limply, through the railings of Hyde Park.

"Look," he said in the end, "this isn't much use. I'll drift off up towards Marble Arch and see if I can work out an escape route."

"Vell," she said, "*I* don't know."

"I really don't know how long I'll be. But you stay here and wait for me. If something fouls you up then I'll see you back at the flat, OK?"

"Mikey – "

"Will be spark out."

"Terry, thees eez so *stupid*!"

"Yeah. I know."

They kissed then, rather tastefully, through the bars, and Jack backed off into the shadows, leaving her looking after him as if the two of them would never meet again.

This might well prove to be the case, thought Jack. He was fairly sure that horrible, nameless things lurked in Hyde Park after the gates had closed – he had always imagined it to be a kind of witches' Sabbath of flashers, foreign students and hideous, Tolkien-like creatures, who were probably even now sliding the grassy lids off their caves and setting out for their nightly ration of human flesh.

In fact it was pleasant and not a little soothing. Way over to the left he could make out the lights of Park Lane and Marble Arch and straight ahead, much further off, Kensington and beyond that, presumably, Victoria. It was curious to feel the grass under his feet. He felt thoughtful and calm, the excitement of the recent encounter faded, the sparks of fantasy almost out.

Jarlsberg, thought Jack, *Jarlsberg*. I don't know. Whatever next? Jarlsberg, who had seemed so permanent and useful back in Snaps' flat, who had seemed to be about to open new high roads of the self, the free, the anonymous, the gift-horse Jarlsberg now seemed to warrant Snaps' reaction rather than any other. "Aieeou! Jarlsberg!" Jack was beginning to have the feeling that Jarlsberg wasn't even in the class of Warliss, Danby or Simmons. It was worrying really. His identities seemed increasingly lacking in staying power.

Nelly was looking away from him; she had moved some way down the road and was standing, artlessly, in the light of a street lamp. She resembled an inexperienced prostitute. She looked up and down the road twice, then started to walk back towards Lancaster Gate. After about ten yards, she stopped and retraced her steps. Jack didn't call to her. He wouldn't have known how to address her. He lay back in the grass and watched the sky.

N elly hadn't been standing for more than five minutes before a very shabby-looking car screeched to a halt about twenty or thirty metres down the road. From the driver's seat came a man in a suit almost as shabby as his car; he went to the back door and opened it with as much fuss as if it had been the Royal family and their bloody Borzois inside.

Two women got out. Two women and a baby. The dearest little baby she had ever seen in her life. Even at this time of night it wasn't asleep on its mother – it was looking around it with big dark eyes, bigger even than Béla, her aunt's friend's grandson, bigger even than those babies you saw on the television crawling around and saying how much they enjoyed the stuff on their behinds. Nelly, as always a sucker for babies, and telling herself she was being a goose for looking when it was only another baby which she would get Mikey to give her one by hooks or by

65

crooks before too long, wandered a little closer towards the group, hoping for a better look. The swarthy man, who looked like the kind of dodgy Serbian she had come across in Germany, or maybe some bloody Turk, was waving his arms around and saying how it was good to know them and he was sorry he had been sick on the lawn. As Nelly watched, the baby gave a little yawn (such a sweet little yawn) and its mother, a big woman with a hat like you imagined them wearing at garden parties or something, said:

"It's round here somewhere, but I've never actually been allowed back to the Snaps' retreat. They must have gone there. Sure to be."

Nelly quivered with shock. At first she assumed she must have been hearing wrong. Often she did hear wrong because of her English. But before she had more than a chance to consider the possibility the big woman said, in a loud voice:

"Trust the Annie Warliss Find Your Rat Service. Eh? It'll be back to Snaps' flat for a few beers and a moan about the world if I know anything about men."

Nelly quivered with shock. That she could not mistake. ANNIE WARLISS 435-9601, the new one, the one who . . . oh my God, thought Nelly, oh my blooming God. This baby probably was bloody Mikey's, probably this was his bastard with this Warliss, bet you anything. My God, she thought, as, without thinking, she followed in their footsteps, it probably was too, with those ears. If they weren't Mikey's ears she was a Dutchman.

It was rather frustrating following them. The reverse of those detective films, in that she knew where they were going but they didn't. The Annie Warliss woman kept leading them up wrong turnings and stopping at traffic lights to look this way and that. The girl with her seemed to be half asleep; she kept her eyes down at the pavement and dragged her feet like a child who does not want to join in the fun. Keeping her head down, Nelly followed them until, a good hundred metres from the flat, they stopped and started going in close to the houses, calling the numbers to each other and which way they were going.

When they reached the flat, Nelly let them go down the narrow stairs, then, when she felt safe, she tiptoed to the hedge that shielded their basement from the road. The light in the front room was on and Mikey was standing by the remains of the food, his arms folded, his head to one side and his tongue pushing his lower lip, the way it did when he was embarrassed and didn't want to show it. The other woman was now holding the baby close into her while ANNIE WARLISS 435-9601 said something, probably blooming sex things most likely. Not that Mikey looked as if she was saying things he wanted to hear. For most of the time he avoided her eyes, shaking his head and trying out sniffy little laughs that were done by jerking his head and bending his body forward at the waist like he was the Crown Prince of Romania.

When she had finished propositioning him, *he* started. And the way it looked he gave her what for. His finger jabbing away like crazy, he shouted, too, and Nelly almost wished they hadn't had that double glazing put in last year. She did catch some words (or thought she did) but not enough to make sense. He seemed to be going on about somebody called Jack. But then you could never tell, it might not be a person at all but another kind of Jack (or was it Czech?), the Jack you used for a car when you had a puncture, or Jack, like in the box, or Jack, the rude word that was something to do with sex (Jack in? Jack off?), oh any bloody thing with this English that usually meant the exact opposite of what it said it did. Buggerholes, thought Nelly to herself, using the rudest word Mikey had taught her, that made him laugh. Buggerholes and other things too numerous to mention, squire. The little girl had taken out her breast and the little baby was having a drink. Maybe she was a wet nurse, thought Nelly, remembering that awful course she had had to do about Esther's Waters. Typical of bloody ANNIE WARLISS 435-9601 to farm the dear little bastard horrible thing out.

When the wet nurse had finished, that seemed to be it. Mikey sat at the table and began to pick at bits of the Nelly cake and stuff them down his throat. He always did that. Ate her meals when her eyes were turned the other way. She heard the front door click and the two women clatter up the stairs. Ducking away from the hedge she crept, her back bent double, hugging herself to herself, rolling her eyes up into her head and twisting her mouth into the Naughty Nelly expression. Yes. It was going to be funny facing Mikey with all these cards up her jumper.

When they had gone, she was quite posh the way she walked down the stairs and gave a short, sharp ring at the doorbell, as if she was a policeman. Quite posh also when a bleary-looking Mikey opened the door to her.

"Wadd*you* want?"

Nelly cocked back her head and looked at him archly.

"Iss not me you want to worry about," she said, "iss wart *you* bin up to, Mikey darleenk!"

"Oh yeah?" said Mikey in really rather a nasty way.

She pushed past him and into the hall.

His bloody rudeness did not touch her now, though; she knew too much from looking through windows and she turned to him now with the hauteur of Nelly the spy, who was always looking through cupboards or windows and who was well aware that he had had his last waltz with ANNIE WARLISS 435-9601. To her surprise the awful thing she hadn't quite done with Mr Jarlsberg did not seem to matter as, disdainfully (if she had been wearing gloves she would have peeled them off), she said:

"I think Mikey has bin a naughty boy."

She said this in an extra saucy way, to let him know she didn't care, cocking and reloading her head for a series of nods like she had seen someone do in that production of *Oklahoma!* that they had visited at Enfield with Mikey's mother. As well as the nods, she put her arms akimbo (akimbo?) and straddled her legs wide, the way she had seen such girls do. As Mikey didn't respond to this, she pulled her right shoulder round in line with her chin and squinted along it dangerously.

"Mikey does not know something his little Nelly knows," she said.

"Oh yeah?" said Mikey, even more nastily than before.

Really! Did she have to spell it out for him? Couldn't they have a civilised row, like people in that play at the National Theatre, all speaking in long sentences and walking about between speaking? What did he think she was anyway? Some blooming peasant, probably, from the back of beyond, most likely.

"Mikey's little Nelly sees quite a lot when she looks through windows and she can put two and two together."

"Oh yeah?" said Mikey. Really he was not trying at all, when you came to think about it.

Nelly stomped up to him and looked up into his face, Nelly the Girl Shrew. She released her right hand and shook her finger, half serious, half larky, under his nose, as, for the third time of asking, she put Mikey on the spot and serve him right.

"Mikey theenks that Mikey's little Nelly eez stupid but Mikey's little Nelly is not so stupid as some people including some weeth babies, eh?"

S he converted the finger-wagging into jabbing and pointing and telescoped her lips at him as rudely as she could.

"Why you making raspberries, eh? I know about you, mate, with your tricks up your jacket!"

"Sleeve," said Mikey, "up your sleeve."

"I would say," he went on, "that sexual intercourse was attempted."

Yes, but by whom on whom? Mikey out of Annie out of ANNIE WARLISS 435-9601, or from Mr Jarlsberg into Nelly?

"I would say," Mikey went on, "that in point of fact there is a sense in which I could be said to be described as unasleep with reference to certain activities that could be alleged to have taken place at this venue."

Nelly stopped. She could feel her heart clenching and unclenching as she said in a light voice:

"Asleep when?"

Mikey got up and went through to the kitchen. He re-emerged a moment later, carrying a large jar of gherkins; speaking like one of those nice young men you saw on *Playschool* he said:

"Aieeou!" said Mikey, "so I am." And now, looking more like a man

He seemed surprised and pleased to be pronouncing Mr Jarlsberg's name; as he came further into the room he took out a gherkin between thumb and forefinger and, playfully, threw it over his left shoulder as if responding to some ancient folk tradition.

"Mikey," said Nelly nasally, unable to stop herself, "you are throwing a gherkeen ovair your shouldair."

"Aieeou!" said Mikey, "so I am." And now, looking more like a man planting seeds, he started to lift more gherkins neatly out of the jar and send them in all directions. Nelly found it impossible to concentrate on the awful news he had just imparted.

"Mikey," she said, "you are throwing all zer gherkins all ovair the place!"

"Yes," said Mikey brightly, "I am looking for the perfect gherkin."
He came close to her and pushed his face close to hers.

"But," he added, "it isn't here!"

Then he set the depleted jar of gherkins down on a chair and went back into the kitchen in a businesslike sort of way.

What was he up to? Had he gone crazy? She felt somehow that he was not going to let her talk about her brief and frustrating affair with Mr Jarlsberg, and that, bad as she had been, it was almost worse not to talk about it than to let it all hang down from the window. She was forming a good, clear English sentence in her mind to show him that she bloody well had a life of her own and that he bloody well had better watch it when back he came with a length of traditional sausage, smoked by old Mr Horvath and his brother.

"Mikey – " she began, but he interrupted.

"Now what you have to remember about Mr Jarlsberg," he said, still sounding like a child's television presenter, "is that he isn't Mr Jarlsberg at all. But somebody else entirely."

As he said this he broke sections off the sausage and tossed them up towards the ceiling. Nelly was about to try and stop him, but decided that unless she stuck to the point she would get nowhere. Puckering up her lips and wobbling her head in irritation and puzzlement, she leaned on the mantleshelf. If he thought she was going to have a nervous breakdown just because he was throwing sausage and gherkin all over the place then he had some other things coming. Just to make sure there was no doubt about this she said:

"Eef you will think that I go to the funny house because you throw sausage and gherkin to the roof then you have some other things coming, mate!"

"Not sausage and gherkin," said Mikey, "sausage, gherkin and noodles."

"Wart eez thees?"

"It's a concept meal!" said Mikey and went back to the kitchen. Nelly shouted after him, really cross.

"You have a reason to be bolshy with your bloody Annie Warliss 435-9601, eh? Eh?"

Mikey showed his head round the door.

"Warliss," he said, "this is, I would say, the *thing*, squire. Warliss is a name to be committed to what might be described as the old memory facility."

70

And he flicked a noodle at her head. She dodged from it, flapping it away from her face.

"Wart *eez* thees?"

"Eet," said Mikey, mimicking her (something he only did when he was really angry), "*eet* eez that hees name eez not Jarlsberg."

"Vart eez heez name?"

"Heez name eez Warliss."

"No Mikey, *her name eez Warliss.*"

"*Heez name eez Warliss too.*"

Mikey poured the noodles into a small heap on the carpet at his foot and ducked back out of sight. What was he going to do next? The soup? The bread? The chicken for tomorrow or the cheese for Wednesday? In fact, he came back with the butter and set about smearing it on the chair-covers, the wallpaper and the watercolour of Split that had cost God knows how many dinars all those years ago. Nelly didn't care about what was happening to her larder any more.

"You are telling me that Meestair Jarlsberg eez really Meestair Warlees?"

"I'm telling you that he is in a married situation vis-à-vis Mrs Warliss and that Jarlsberg is, in our terms, none other than a pseudonym or alias, indeed a false name, squire."

He was obviously enjoying smearing the butter on the picture of Split. He stood back, the better to admire his handiwork, and then went in close to retouch a clump that was obscuring the chapel of St Gregory the Bald, that the monks still kept up as an attraction for tourists.

"Thees eez not true."

"It bloody is."

"Eet bloody well eezn't."

"It bloody well is."

There seemed little point in continuing this conversation without consulting Mr Jarlsberg, or indeed his alleged wife, so Nelly kept a dignified silence. Then she said, as Mikey went back into the kitchen singing to himself,

"Vy you throweeng food all over the shop, hey?"

Mikey brought some carrots back with him, snapping bits off them as he came.

"Food is what it's all about, wouldn't you say?"

So did he once like to eat filled pancakes, courgettes with mince and noodles, and veal stuffed with ham in tomato sauce, the way Nelly had

had it done once in Dalmatia, so did he once like to drink with her and eat cevabcici at that open air restaurant in Dubrovnik, and so, once, did he not disdain the Nelly cake. For how long, though, had it lasted, she wondered, as he bounced tomatoes off the printed rug they had bought at Hvar? For how long? A month? A year? Oh, if she had been honest she would have known that this was not love, that Nelly was not lucky enough to be loved by any man this side of heaven. Did it matter anyway whether his name was Jarlsberg or Warliss? Did any of this matter? (Mikey was now skimming French toasts at the windowpane as if they were playing cards.)

These English people did not know what was a home and a family. They did not kiss or quarrel in public. They told cold little untruths to each other over the breakfast table and blooming horrid little meals except on Sunday when they had a blooming horrid big one. They had houses, these English, but not homes. A home was a filled larder and a warm fire and her holding on to the pig's tail at Christmas while her father killed it.

"A home," she said aloud, Jarlsberg, Warliss and the rest forgotten. "Is that so bloody much to ask?"

Mikey stopped in the middle of decanting a tin of tuna fish on to the sideboard, and turned towards the window, staring at something or somebody over her shoulder, glassy-eyed.

"Well. A home. Mikey? Is that so bloody much to ask?"

He didn't answer, and, following his eyes round, she saw two faces at the window. The Warliss woman with her baby and, next to her, her friend the wet nurse, who looked now like a child and now like a much older woman.

"A home. Thees eez all I . . . "

The little woman with the drab curls, the wet nurse with the cast-down expression, had pressed her face to the glass and was staring into the room without any shame.

"A home . . . " faltered Nelly.

And the drab little woman smiled, as if she understood what Nelly was thinking.

O nce the two women were in the room, Nelly found her eyes drawn to the little woman (Lucy they had called her) who sat on the sofa, hands folded on her lap as though she had a transistor radio plugged into her earhole and was listening to some jolly interesting talk about knitting like they had in the afternoons occasionally. The woman was watching Nelly too, ignoring all the backchat between Mikey and Co, and eventually, when there was a lull in the conversation, she leaned forward to Nelly and said in a soft voice—

"It's my baby, Mrs Snaps."

This put the kiboshes on the attempts to sort out exactly who did what to whom when they were pretending to be someone else. Everyone looked in different directions. Then Lucy went on, in a serious sort of a voice—

"Did he come to you as Jarlsberg?"

There was a short pause while Nelly wondered what this meant. Then Lucy said, "Did you make love to him, Mrs Snaps?"

There was a horrid sort of pause then, like on *Mastermind* when the world expert was asked a real stumper about the early Pharaohs or something. Finally Nelly heard herself saying, in the tones of someone repeating a difficult lesson—

"Yes. I have done thees."

"Your husband said he was in the room."

Mikey nodded as if someone had just said something about wages policy or whatever it was called.

"He voz in zer room while we have been doeeng eet," said Nelly.

Lucy met her eyes.

"I think," she said, "that he is in love with your husband."

Nelly was, to say the least, intrigued by this. No one had ever called Mikey a bloody queer before. She got up and crossed to the sofa to sit next to Lucy, narrowly missing a damp patch of ratatouille as she parked her hampton as bossily as she was able, under the stares of

Mikey and Co. She like this funny little woman. She talked straight anyway. She decided to ignore Mikey and bloody Annie Warliss and get to know this lady better, also discovering if Mikey was indeed the father of the lovely little monster. Somehow she did not feel any more certain of this, and, even if she was not up to talking about Mikey being a bloody queer, they could probably find some common grounds.

The little woman looked up at her in a friendly fashion.

"Where is he?" she asked.

"Who?"

"Your Mr Jarlsberg."

"Een the park."

A respectful silence greeted this observation. After it, Mikey said in a rather over-patient way:

"What kind of park? A car park? An amusement park?"

"A Hyde Park," said Nelly, and stuck her tongue out at him. The little woman's head drooped and she said sadly:

"We went to the pub. We thought you might be in the pub."

"What on *earth* is he doing in Hyde Park?" said bloody Annie Warliss in a loud voice.

"He's with a friend," said Mikey, "called Wensleydale. And a bloke he knew at school called Cheddar. And a French girl called Camembert."

"He eez not a cheese," said Nelly, deciding to defend Mr Jarlsberg and his name, even if his name was sounding increasingly silly.

"He is," said Mikey, "of course he's a cheese. And *we're* COLD MEATS. We're all cold meats. I am, at this time, in name terms going under the description of David Saveloy."

"And I'm Salami," said bloody Annie Warliss, giggling stupidly, "Doris Salami!"

"Imagine it," said the little woman, "being a piece of food. Imagine it."

They all looked at her with vague respect. Nelly tried to imagine being a piece of food. She could not. For some reason an English phrase came into her head and without thinking about it she said:

"I feel like a gherkeen!"

Mikey and Annie just sat looking at her like a couple of goldfish. Christ, thought Nelly, surely they could tell what she was on about! They were English, weren't they? And she was talking in English, not blooming Hindustani.

"What you must understand," said Lucy suddenly, "is that we're all victims of a system that condemns two people of the opposite sex to live out the major part of their productive years in the same house or room. No wonder there are betrayals and evasions, when we're all trying to own each other. Why, we're pretending to be adults when we haven't yet had our childhood or adolescence. We're not ready for the responsibility of another. Not ready."

Annie got up, crossed to the window and slid the inside pane back; you could hear the distant roar of the traffic now. Annie slid back the outer pane and the volume climbed as if someone was operating it from a hidden switch.

Nelly watched Lucy in case she said anything else. This time she didn't want to miss any of it. She would listen really closely and then sneak away for a quick butcher's look at a dictionary, because she had never heard anyone talk English quite like this before. She felt honourable, really, to be in the same room as the remarks. She couldn't help noticing the little woman's hands, too, rather common hands they were, with stubby fingers, playing at cat's cradle, interlocking, breaking and twisting back to each other again, signalling some message to Nelly about something, about Mikey or her mother so many miles away or about this English that was so confusing. Then, quite unexpectedly, Lucy grinned widely.

"It's going to rain," she said.

And, far away, as bloody Annie Warliss stared up at the lights of the street like a tragedy queen, Nelly heard it—the angry, military noise of thunder.

J
ack heard the thunder as he strolled in leisurely fashion up towards Marble Arch in search of a convenient exit. He was thinking, as he often did at moments of crisis, about politics. He was thinking about

politics (of course) because that seemed to be the only area of his life untainted by Simmonsry, Danbyism or Jarlsbergese.

Start with the positives. Build up. Don't destroy. What had he actually *got*? What could he point to if he was going to call himself Jack Warliss, political activist? Man of the Left?

Not much.

A few memories. Being in the back of the family car in some street in Mill Hill and Warliss Senior, immobile in the driving seat, hands at the base of the wheel as the old Hillman croaked home. They had passed a group coming out of a synagogue and Warliss Senior, for no apparent reason, had muttered, "I don't like Jews." Jack's mother, in the warning tone used when the old man tried to put his arm around her − "Oh Daddy!" And Jack? Jack in the back, small, ferret-like, and identifying not with Mummy or with Daddy but (no question) with the Jews.

Being in the Corner House at Marble Arch, seated next to a black man. A waiter approaching. The waiter asking Jack what he wanted to drink and, from nowhere, a thin black finger jabbing the waiter in the chest while a thick black voice said, "How come you don't want to serve *me*? Because I'm too black, huh?" Jack's sympathies were with the black man (naturally) but also with the waiter, a tiny, overworked Turkish person with gravy stains down his jacket, incompetent rather than racially prejudiced, Jack felt.

"A lifelong hatred of oppression."

This was beginning to sound like a consistent personality. Or at least the beginnings of a consistent personality. *Brought up in the fearsomely prejudiced white ghetto of Mill Hill, young JACK WARLISS passed through a public school education to enter Leeds University, at that time, in the late sixties, a hotbed of STUDENT UNREST.*

Not in the Engineering Department it wasn't, reflected Jack, tacking back towards the Bayswater Road. As far as the Engineering Department was concerned, Engels were things you measured with a protractor and Marx were what you wanted to get plenty of in Finals, but, to be fair to this new Warliss, this simple but essentially decent human being, capable of absorbing the contradictions offered by his recent past, he had done something. He had joined something called the International Socialists. He had jumped up and down outside somebody's office demanding to see his File, only to be told by a world-weary University official that he hadn't got a File.

And now. Now. Hadn't he reached the stage when some action was

called for? Some glorious, liberating action that came out of his harden-
ing sense of the hopelessness of the system of government under which
he lived.

He felt the first drops of rain on his cheek. He was now almost up to
Marble Arch. Still no sign of a door, ladder or other means of exit. In a
minute he was going to get very wet.

As he stared out at the night traffic like a rustic on a gate, he became
aware that someone very tall indeed was coming towards him from the
Marble Arch end of the Bayswater Road. A head was bobbing up and
down against the line of the iron fence. A huge, kewpie-doll-like head,
stuck all over with mousey curls, and transfixed by a pair of gigantic,
staring eyes that were not like human eyes at all, but the plastic
simulacra sold in joke shops, in which the pupils rotated independently,
at will. The eyes were not the only doll-like feature of the head. The
nose, beaked and aggressive, like that of a vulture or eagle, and the
teeth, huge, yellow and set in a metallic grin, were spectacularly non-
human, rendering the whole – eyes, teeth, nose, hair and *tout
ensemble* — wolfish, troll-like, at once immeasurably old and colourfully
adolescent. It belonged to Jake Spielman, thirty-three-year-old wild
man, owning up to no school, no home address, no immediate family or
any of the things Jack usually used to get a fix on people. About the only
personal detail Jack could remember about Spielman was that, at some
stage of his life, he had attended a progressive school in Somerset, and
that, at a later stage in his career, he had worked on a building site. His
voice could have been that of a proletarian who has learned the language
of his masters or that of a radical member of the intelligentsia determined to sound at least a little Cockney. He could have been over-
educated or self-educated, ridiculously healthy or suffering from some
undisclosed terminal illness; he was, without doubt, a figure of contrasts – contrasts that remained inexplicable.

"Jacko!" said Spielman, stopping some yards from him.

"Spielman!" said Jack.

They looked at each other. Spielman snapped his fingers and started
to double up, as if Jack had just cracked a particularly good joke, or
staged some *risqué coup de théâtre*.

"Fan*tastic*!" said Spielman, "fan*tastic*!"

In his right hand he carried an important-looking canvas bag. he held
this aloft, like a Chancellor on Budget Day.

"Blast from the Past!" he said.

S pielman had been editor of a magazine that was to have done for Jack what *Lyrical Ballads* did for Coleridge and Wordsworth – concentrated his ideas, clarified his intentions and made all subsequent work a luxury. It was a magazine called *The New Democrat* and working on it had occupied most of the hopeless, bleak years immediately on leaving University. The sight of Spielman brought back (unwished for) the text of Jack's first article for the paper.

"Football: A Socialist View"

It had resembled one of those mad specialist papers in which all the events of the real world are filtered through the distorting lenses of the enthusiast – about as relevant to the mass of the population as Bee Keeping Journals or Conjuring Trade Papers. And, of course, the big fight had been to make it "relevant". Every week, football or *Crossroads* or Caravanning would be subjected to merciless Marxist-Leninist analysis, usually by Spielman, Annie or Jack. Every week, lengthy diatribes on the state of play in Northern Ireland, Chile or Vietnam would be hammered out, usually by Jack or Annie or Spielman. And, every week, the back numbers would multiply, damp piles of yesterday's news in the corridor of Spielman's house in Islington. People gave money – writers, artists, agents – but they were never the right people and they never had enough money. As Spielman said, on the day *The New Democrat* folded — *"What we need is a few thousand from Woolies or Taylor Woodrow's."* They had, in fact, succeeded in conning a thousand pounds out of a major industrial concern, until someone high up in the company stumbled across a few thousand words of merciless Marxist-Leninist analysis of the company and its dealings.

"I haven't seen you," Spielman was saying, with the display of Jewish grotesque gestures that he used to emphasise even the most casual remark, "haven't seen you since we *dumped the Democrat*."

"Right," said Jack sheepishly. "Right."

Spielman always made him feel as if he was suffering from a particularly dangerous kind of political deviation.

"The *Democrat!*" said Spielman, clicking his fingers and doubling up with laughter at the memory, *"The New Democrat!"*

They were both laughing now. Spielman was talking about Hovis, the Leeds Maoist, who had contributed a three-thousand-word essay called "Towards Building a Revolutionary Base Area in Croydon". Hovis, it seemed, had disappeared into the wilderness of the extreme left, showing signs of an imminent nervous breakdown. Jack felt tears (they were presumably of laughter) as he joined Spielman in the shot-in-the-stomach pose his old editor considered necessary for this kind of amusement. They swapped other memories. Because it was impossible to rid oneself of the delusion that there was something better about all that than what was happening to Jack now. There had been something foolish, optimistic and decent in the air then, that, just at the moment, seemed impossible to recapture. The difference, Jack resolved, between being twenty-two and thirty.

"And don't forget," said Spielman, "don't forget *Annie Sansom.* Stalinist wizard from the Home Counties."

"Difficult," said Jack, "I married her."

This stopped Spielman in his tracks. And, also, gave Jack a chance to examine the changes time had wrought in his old companion. He did seem to have grown enormously fat. Spielman had developed a spectacular gut. It started just below his neck and swelled out in a pregnant curve, at present supported by his left hand. had the man taken to drink? Or contracted a horrifying illness?

"Great," said Spielman, in reverence for the change in Jack's marital status, "great!"

And he loosened the top button of his jacket, shaking his head against the now steady rain.

As he did so — his bulge moved independently. At first Jack thought it a trick of the light. Then he caught sight of a pair of eyes, bright and suspicious, watching him from the innermost recesses of Spielman's chest. A pair of eyes and a head, not unlike Spielman's — bat-eared, chock-full of quaint bumps, swoops and curves — a kind of phrenological joke. Teeth too, that promised to live up to Spielman's not inconsiderable gnashers — four of them, two above and two below. The eyes watched Jack mutely, impassively. Spielman looked down with mock modesty —

"Rude of me," he said, "Little Luke!"

"Hi!" said Jack.

Little Luke's expression did not alter.

"Hi!" said Jack again.

Little Luke peered off in another direction, snaking his head left as if on the track of a passing insect or a Grand Prix racer.

A baby. But what a baby. A jumbo baby. About the biggest a baby could get without being a person − a mine of undiscovered skills and tricks. Would Egbert ever get to be a baby like Little Luke? Or was Little Luke's obvious superiority in every way a simple result of his being Spielman's child? For there could be no question of the fact that he was Spielman's child. At any moment, Jack felt, he would be slipping on a miniature check jacket of his own and sorting Jack out on a few tricky points of revolutionary theory.

"Er . . . how old is he?" he asked.

"Ten months and six days," said Spielman.

"He's big."

"He's huge," said Spielman lovingly, "he's grotesquely large. That's why we call him Little Luke. Don't we?"

He wrapped his jacket around his son and looked speculatively at Jack.

"Any more of you?" he said.

"Where?" said Jack.

"Back there."

"Oh no," said Jack, "I was rather keen to . . . get out actually."

"Fine," said Spielman crisply, "fine."

Unlike Jack, Spielman enjoyed making decisions and acting on them. He moved forward and put his huge hands under Jack's armpits, lifting him, like a puppet, clear of Hyde Park. Spielman set him down on the pavement and then stood back to admire his handiwork.

"What actually were you *doing* there, Jacko?"

"It is a long story," said Jack.

But he wasn't thinking about Nelly or Annie or Lucy. As with Snaps this morning, he was picking up the fragments of a story he had presumed broken into pieces, and again, as with Snaps, feeling that residual sense of loss, as if he had betrayed Spielman at some point. Perhaps he had. There had been some question of carrying on the *Democrat* under another name, had there not? Except that Jack had lost heart for the fight.

His fight now, of course, was with himself − and with the three women who had become part of the day's complicated design.

The two men walked together up the Edgware Road – Jack now buttoned up tight against the rain and, from time to time, skipping sideways in the boyish manner he had sometimes formerly assumed when with Spielman. All the shops seemed to be selling hi-fi equipment – stereos and tape-decks, patiently alluring in the steely neon light of after hours. Spielman didn't ask where they were going. That wasn't Spielman's way. From what Jack remembered of him, he tended to follow you wherever you went, either until he met someone else he wanted to follow or until you thought of a place he could not possibly want to go.

"I've got a kid," Jack blurted out suddenly.

"Oh *really*," Spielman grinned.

"Yeah. Called Egbert. I mean Egbert isn't his name but we call him Egbert."

"How old?"

"Four months."

"*Really*."

Spielman was obviously enjoying this conversation. As they threaded their way up towards Paddington, past more hotels, unlikely-seeming food shops, endless parking meters and cars glistening with rain, he gave Jack the run-down on babies, with particular reference to his own son, Luke's, bowel movements. He did seem somewhat obsessed with Little Luke's bowel movements. What made the whole thing even stranger was that, through the gap in Spielman's jacket, from time to time, Jack caught glimpses of two bright eyes, watching the world cautiously, as their owner's most intimate functions were discussed in public. It was going to be a bit embarrassing trying to fit Spielman into the Snaps/Nelly combination, but, as Spielman didn't seem to have anywhere to go, Jack felt it incumbent on him to provide a destination for their walk.

They reached Sussex Gardens, and, crossing the road, they dodged under the shelter of the plane trees while a dog, depressed at having to be out, waddled past them to the traffic lights. Beads of water rolled off Spielman's huge head and onto his shoulders.

What really perplexed Jack about all this was that, so far at any rate, Spielman had not mentioned the word "politics". When they had worked with Annie on *The New Democrat*, everything had to be given what was known as a "political dimension".

They were now drawing close to the black railings that curtained off the stairs to Mike and Nelly's flat. With Spielman in full spate behind him, Jack eased open the gate and looked down into the room. What he saw, at first sight, inclined him to run back towards Paddington at all convenient speed. There – ranged around the front room in various statuesque poses of gloom and despair – were Mike, Nelly, Lucy, Annie and Egbert. The lot.

"You OK, Warliss?" said Spielman.

"Fine," said Jack, "just fine."

It was too late for any form of protest or any attempt at escape. In a sense it would be a relief to face the ten years in jail or the stretch on a desert island they had all probably agreed would be best for him. So long as they didn't kill him. That was all he asked. Or, if they did – let it be by some gentle, narcotic method, something that blurred the borderline between sleep and death.

Snaps answered the door to him and then he was in among them, blushing bright red. No one spoke. Outside the rain, setting in for the night, bounced on to the pavement yard, smacking at the rickety windows and gurgled, slurped and poured through the landlord's inadequate gutters.

"My name," said Jack, "is Bin-End and I've come to read the meters."

Nobody laughed.

PART TWO

W here was Snaps? He had been in − that was obvious. There was a baked bean plate and a mangled sausage on top of the lavatory. For some reason, the landlord of the particular hell-hole in which Jack, Spielman and Snaps were living had not considered that they were in need of a self-contained kitchen. The gas-stove was next to the bath and, although there was a kind of ludicrous lid that was supposed to cover the bath when the room doubled as a kitchen, nobody except Spielman bothered to use it. The result was that when one bathed one bathed amidst bits of lettuce and bread, or − if you were unlucky enough to use the bath within two days of Snaps using the place for cooking purposes − amidst cigarette ash, bacon, sausages, and, on one occasion, recalling a meal with Snaps' estranged wife, half a fried egg, a lone fragment of Snaps' eating habits, that had rolled through the scum, brushing against Jack's thighs like ectoplasm.

Fucking Snaps.

There was something to be said for women. At least women didn't leave packets of chips on the landing or puke over the banisters at four in the morning. Even if they had babies which puked all over you and −

Jack's right foot trod in something unpleasant. Little Luke had not altered his rate of shitting since Jack had first made his acquaintance, although now, instead of doing it in his trousers, he did it in a yellow plastic potty. Jack rather wished he still did it in his trousers. At least one was not expected to applaud when he did it in his trousers. And there was something more flagrant about faeces in a potty − number ones *and* number twos, coiled shyly in wait for the unsuspecting foot.

He wiped his right foot and re-sited the potty nearer the door, where there was a working chance that Snaps would fall over it, and started to run the bath. The other danger in the bathroom was that most of your activities were clearly visible to a select group of Notting Hill flat dwellers, unless you kept to an area (about a square foot in size) where you were shielded by a towel that Spielman had pinned to the wood-work as a gesture at curtaining activity. The towel read, HOTEL DES BAINS, ROUSSILLON.

Jack backed up against the wall and started to work his brown Levis down his legs. The last time he had disrobed he had been whistled at by a large black man and, flattering as this was, Jack did not feel that his love life could accommodate a large black man. When underpants, trousers, shirt, socks and jersey were in a heap at his feet, he ran, head down, for the bath, feeling the eyes of thousands boring into his naked rump. Right foot hit water. Hot. *Hot.* He screeched and withdrew, standing naked and clearly profiled at the empty window. Cold tap. This was getting ridiculous. Abandoning all pretence at shame he waltzed, in faggy fashion, back towards the cold tap, one hand behind his head, twirling his buttocks satirically. Dum dum *da* di dum dum *da* dum dum *da* di dum dum *da* di dum dum dum di dum dum *dum* (whoops!).

Whhooops! The large black man was at his window opposite, eyes wide and mouth open in a friendly grin. Jack, overcome with shame and horror, fled back to the shelter of the wall.

Why had he ever got involved with all of this? Why had he agreed to a scheme designed to plunge all three of them back into the nightmare of adolescence?

Shutting his eyes, he marched to the bath and levered himself in. Tonight would come the major decisions. All this was going to stop. He was going to choose.

The bath was gritty and smelt like a tube station. Jack lay in it, studying the ceiling, wondering why the landlord had devoted such care and attention to its curves, twists and decorations, while completely ignoring the areas of the flat you stood on or looked at. Perhaps he was a man with a terrible disease of the neck, condemned to feel his way forward, staring vertically above him. Perhaps he just liked ceilings.

Enough of the landlord. Thinking about the landlord wasn't going to get him out of yet another Talk tonight. Thinking about the landlord wasn't going to remove the certainty that the Talk was, yet again, with Annie, or the fact that Annie would be (shudder shudder) pregnant. Even more pregnant than the last time he had seen her. Even more like an Elizabethan galleon in full sail, stomach ahoy, wearing flowing red robes from Eastern hippy-style shops with names like Forbidden Fruit or Jasmine Garden. Even more assertive, confident, charming, left-wing, glowing, rational and bossy than usual.

Lucy. Perhaps she would be there. Perhaps she, too, had joined the Communist Party. Perhaps Egbert was a member. There was, probably, an organisation called the Very Young Communist League and Egbert was a member. Annie and Nelly would have been indoctrinating him. The last time Jack had seen Egbert, Egbert had been talking. He had said things like "Glop" and "Flob" and "Blap", without any apparent attempt at meaning. But this *Beano*-style of conversation was probably a blind. When Jack wasn't there, Egbert was discussing him with Lucy. And Annie. And Nelly.

He levered himself out of the bath and stretched, unashamed. The black man was still at his post by the window opposite. He waved and smiled enthusiastically. Jack allowed a waterlogged baked bean to roll down his leg.

And waved back.

T hings were no better in the front room. There was an absence of Little Lukeana, but Snaps' collection of underpants (ranging from a racy item in electric blue, with the words FAMOUS BALLS tattooed on them, to serious, corset-like affairs in white cotton) was strewn across the centre of the room, as if he had been wearing all fifteen of them at the same time and had stripped off in sequence one crazy, drunken night. He had indeed worn all fifteen of them, as was obvious from their texture and smell, but they had been removed over a period of some three months and allowed to lie, undisturbed, as if in readiness for some underwear archaeologist, who would evolve complex theories about Snaps from their position on site.

Theories like – Snaps was not fit to share a cage with a reptile. Snaps was a blot on the face of humanity. The only thing to be said in Snaps' favour was that he was not (at the moment anyway) a member of the Communist Party. He still somehow managed to grope his way into

Dagenham, looking like a middle range Ford's executive – the blue suit and smart blue shirt giving no hint of the horrors that lay beneath.

Jack began to dress. Why had he been lumbered with sharing a room with Snaps? And why had Snaps got the bed? And why had he got the blue Li-lo? To be fair, Snaps had only got the base of the bed – the mattress was next door with Spielman, who could be seen asleep on it in the early morning, his huge horny feet protruding from the end of his grey blanket, like a vulture's talons, or the extremities of a badly concealed corpse.

Q. WHAT IS THE WORST THING IN THE WORLD?
A. SNAPS.
Q. WHAT IS THE SECOND WORST THING IN THE WORLD?
A. SPIELMAN.
Q. WHAT IS WORSE THAN THE FIRST AND SECOND WORST THINGS IN THE WORLD PUT TOGETHER WITH KNOBS ON?
A. LITTLE LUKE.
Q. WHAT IS WORSE THAN LITTLE LUKE, SPIELMAN, SNAPS AND INDEED THE WHOLE OF THE THIRD REICH PUT TOGETHER WITH BRASS AND GOLD KNOBS ON?
A. GOBBO.

Gobbo was the man upstairs. He had a habit of screwing his head down into his neck and staring at you from close range – at three in the morning on a deserted landing this could be disconcerting. Gobbo was, somehow, the symbol of all the disastrous things that had happened since that hot June night at Snaps' flat – that night of horrid frankness, that evening of unspeakable honesty at which Danby, Warliss, Simmons and Jarlsberg had melted back into the primal slime whence they had come, leaving a kind of early middle-aged jelly, a horribly unformed human being, best called by some science-fiction name like Drull or Throg or Kroton.

Thinking of the boil on Gobbo's forehead and the way Gobbo's mouth twitched when discussing much publicised sex-cases slowed Jack's rate of dressing. All this was bloody Annie's fault.

A gargoyle-like head peered round the door.

"Back again!" said Spielman, sucking his cheeks in and rolling his eyes towards his nose.

"Good day?" said Jack.

"Not bad," said Spielman. "Sued."

Spielman was now on the editorial board of a paper so left-wing that wags had suggested it should abandon publication on the grounds that actually going into print in a capitalist society was a bourgeois compromise sell-out.

"By?" said Jack.

"Some vicars," said Spielman, making his hands into an inverted spider and jamming the said spider into his face with comical ferocity. There was a thumping sound from the landing, and a high-pitched voice, with a strong West Country accent, could be heard saying –

"Oi is runnin'!"

It wasn't exactly West Country – more accurately a cross between West Country and Russian. It sounded as if its owner was surprised to be running, or, anyway, surprised to be able to describe the fact. Spielman slipped in through the half-open door and looked at Jack suspiciously.

"Going out?" he said in a vaguely accusatory tone of voice. Nobody at the flat was very specific about their movements – least of all Jack – especially when visits to any of the women who seemed responsible for their being there were concerned.

"That's it," said Jack. "Annie."

"Ah!" said Spielman.

Then –

"Fucking?"

"No," said Jack.

"Hopeless," said Spielman.

"Hopeless," said Jack.

This interchange seemed to give Spielman confidence. He sat on the bed as, outside, Little Luke ran into walls, fell, shouted, giggled and continued to tell himself, in a wondering tone of voice, that he was actually doing these things. Jack wondered idly where Luke had picked up the Russian accent as he watched Spielman, white and tired as he often was these days. It must be a strain running *Straight Talk*, as the paper was called.

, Jack moved to the mirror and tried to pat his hair into shape as a 52 bus roared past on its way to Ladbroke Grove, and Spielman peered at a speck of dust on the carpet. He seemed to have slowed up in the last year – his intense concentration on each surprising moment that he lived through having resulted in a sort of imbalance between him and

89

Little Luke, almost as if they could not control the way in which they took life from each other. What Spielman needed was a woman, of course, Jack mused, as on the landing Luke shouted, "Oi bengin' it!" in an accent that was now closer to Swedish than anything else. He was kicking the banister with his small but deadly shoes.

Jack trailed a tendril of hair across his right ear in an effort to provide a Grecian finish to his head. He sometimes, for brief flashes, thought he saw the beginnings of character and charm in his own face; then the spark was gone and he was back to the glasses and the big red nose. Why were all these women interested in him? Because he was such a jelly, presumably. It was a well-known fact that women liked jelly.

"Give her my love," said Spielman, "and tell her I'll see her at the racism demo."

He lay back on the bed, groaning.

The racism demo. So Annie and Spielman had been discussing a joint trip to a racism demo had they? Jack turned and looked at Spielman as he went out on to the landing. Spielman had clenched his right fist and, still supine on the bed, was holding it aloft in a satirical gesture of solidarity. Not for the first time this year, Jack wondered whether Spielman fancied Annie, and, if so, what he (Jack) made of it.

Nothing. He didn't make anything of it.

He walked out on to the grim landing and walked down the stairs to the grey street below.

Not only was he a jelly, he was also a hack. A hack jelly. And now, he did not have a single alias to stand between himself and the awful fact of boredom and jelly-dom – not even a miserable Smith or Jones or Cameron or a casual acquaintance in the street who was under the delusion that he was a tax collector or airline pilot, just him and himself alone against the pointless, lonely world.

No, he was now just plain Jack Warliss. Jack Warliss the Jelly. Author of Episodes 325 – 371 of *The Wheebles*, currently demoted from *The Wheebles* to a series transmitted at a quarter to eleven in the morning called *Herbert's Boys*. *Herbert's Boys* was definitely worse than *The Wheebles* – only the week before Jack had been sent a can of raspberries by the *Scottish Daily Mail* in their Raspberry of the Week for Worst Programme Voted by Our Readers slot.

He shouldered his way up to Notting Hill Gate – a black despair in his heart. A Jelly Despair. Wobble wobble moan moan wobble wobble. He turned left past a shabby newsagent's, past an overflowing dustbin and took the rainy pavement towards Queensway.

She had arranged to meet him in a wine bar. Annie had never, before the split, been what Jack's mother would have described as a "wine bar person". She was usually to be found in the public bars of sleazy alehouses, a pint of bitter at her elbow and a packet of Number Six never far away from her right hand. Her idea of glamour had been men called Dave or Ron, mournful fellows with white faces and donkey jackets, usually in some position of responsibility in the local Trades Council. The manner of these alternative Rotarians to Jack had always been frankly hostile – for reasons with which Jack had always sympathised.

Annie was now going through a glamorous phase. There were no longer reliable party workers and dour activists at her elbow, sprinkling their conversation with initials ("The UCATT General Secretary said to the NALGO and NUPE representatives that the meeting . . ." etc. etc.); instead there were attractive, denimed people with names like Sankia and Duveen, writers, artists, journalists, people who described things rather than did them.

The joke was that Jack found them fundamentally more depressing than the dour activists – both sets of people seemed to him unshakeably self-confident, purposeful and threatening, but at least the dour activists disapproved of him for what he wasn't, not for what he was. Annie's new friends, once they heard that Jack was the author of *Herbert's Boys* (a fact that Jack endeavoured to conceal for as long as possible), could hardly conceal their gleeful contempt for his position.

Annie was their tame Communist. They liked having a tame Communist around. In the middle of conversations about somebody's diary piece about somebody else's column, they would say, "Of course – being a Communist, Annie, you would disagree with all of this." And

Annie would nod magisterially, as if her disagreement was only a way of confirming the mutual understanding, respect and trust that now existed between her, Duveen, Sankia and the rest of the bright, satirical, hard-drinking, poker-playing ex-Oxbridge wankers who now made up her acquaintance.

Jack, in order to subvert Annie's position, adopted the posture of the hardline Stalinist at these occasions – wagging his finger, he would say, in a voice rich with cunning, "How do we know? How do we *know* that Stalin did shoot ten million peasants and half of the Bolshevik Party? What is your evidence, comrade?" The Sankias and Duveens were freaked by this approach, there being so much evidence that they had difficulty in remembering what it was.

He stopped by the entrance to the wine bar, about a hundred yards east of Notting Hill Gate Tube Station.

Perhaps he should have brought Gobbo along. Gobbo would have got on very well with Annie's current suitor, a man who wrote a gossip column for a Sunday Newspaper. Gobbo would have enjoyed staring at the gossip columnist's classical profile and liquid eyes. Gobbo could have discussed the Moors Murder Case with him.

A blast of hot air came at him as he went slowly down the stairs, listening for the sounds of Annie and Annie's friends. The place was called *Grapes* and, on the walls, the ceilings, the stairs, the floors, the tables, even in the lavatory there were – grapes. By a badly lit counter a woman in dungarees prodded some ratatouille malevolently. Next to her was a notice board on which was the word BRIE in big, raggedly chalked letters. Nothing else.

"Hi!"

Annie was smoking with both elbows on the table, turning her profile this way and that, to catch the light of her admirers. They all looked like admirers, although Jack recognised none of them apart from the gossip columnist.

"Hi!"

"It's Shakespeare!" said the gossip column writer.

"Where?" said Jack.

"Under the counter," said a girl with frizzy hair and a protuberant chest.

The admirers liked this remark. They curled their lips and rolled their eyeballs around, to indicate that, if they hadn't been so busy, intelligent and well-dressed, they might even have laughed.

"Oh fuck off!" said Jack.

This they did not like. To a man they looked wry.

"Lead balloonsville Shakespeare!" said the gossip columnist, addressing his glass.

"How are you, love?" said Annie.

She was, thought Jack, slipping in between two foreign-looking people, an almost completely different person now she was pregnant. She had taken to lifting her chin and smiling in all directions. Her face seemed to have been lit by an internationally recognised lighting cameraman and her nostrils were as publicly impressive as those of a bronze horse Jack remembered seeing in the British Museum. She touched him, lightly but carefully, on the lapels of his jacket, rich in eggstains, biro marks and other stigmata of bachelor life.

"Dreadful," said Jack. "Awful. Little Luke's shitting everywhere and I'm treading in it."

"Egbert shits in an absolutely splendid fashion," said Annie.

Why had she got this proprietorial attitude to his son? Egbert was his son by another woman. He was nothing to *do* with Annie. Annie had her own bloody baby, didn't she, although true to hardened feminist form she refused even to discuss the question of its likely father. Men were Annie's servants these days – the truly phallic mother, she allowed them to flock around her, including a few old duds like Jack for old time's sake. It had taken Jack an hour or so to establish the fact that he was even in there with a *chance* of being the father of Annie's baby, since the beginnings of pregnancy, the shadow outlines of new life, were a mystery hidden from men.

"We're drunk," said the gossip columnist, alarmed by what he took to be Jack's progress with Annie.

"Jack and I are going to have a serious talk," said Annie, "and then I've got to think about this play for Schooner."

Play for Schooner? PLAY FOR SCHOONER! AAAAAARGH!

"Oh," said Jack, trying to hold back the tears of fury, "are you writing a play for Schooner?"

"I am," said Annie, "he's all up-market these days. I'm doing something about South Africa for him."

"He's up-market," said Jack, "and I'm down-market."

"You," said the gossip columnist, "are off-market."

"Fuck off!" said Jack.

There was a pause while the admirers exchanged cigarettes and drank and looked cunning. Somehow, Jack thought, in the year or so she had spent away from him, Annie seemed to have succeeded in being politically active, fashionable, liked, rich, important, sexually desirable and pregnant. What had he got to put against that?

"Shall we go, Jack?" said Annie.

As he trudged out behind her, Jack could hear the admirers rustling with wonder and disapproval. What on *earth*, their silence seemed to say, does she see in him?

You tell me, Jack silently replied, as Annie banged back the door and bitter November, complete now with the beginnings of fog, tore at his throat and made his eyes smart, you tell me.

"Shall we go back to the house?" said Annie. "Why not?"

Well, firstly because Lucy, Egbert and Nelly would be there. Secondly because they would have to catch a bus (a precarious operation at the best of times) and thirdly because the last time he had been at the house he had been drunk and he and Lucy had thrown things at each other. Quite big things. He was also anxious in case Annie were to discover that he was still sleeping with Lucy. "Still sleeping" made their hurried, furtive attempts at sexual relations sound rather more glamorous than they were, but he suspected that Annie would be less tolerant towards his continuing affair with Lucy than Lucy was of his attempts to win back Annie.

"Who's at home?" he said, as lightly as possible.

"Not sure," said Annie, "I'm on the Egbert Rota."

Pinned to the back door at Sinclair Gardens, W.14, the current address of Lucy, Annie and Nelly, was something called the Egbert Rota. Its existence symbolised for Jack the awful talent for living women seem to acquire; when Lucy had been living at his expense, she had never gone out, never left the flat except to go to the shops, but now, thanks to the Egbert Rota, a complicated document, perhaps because, as Jack had pointed out on his last visit, Egbert was a complicated problem requiring the kind of security surveillance usually reserved for visiting American Presidents, Lucy was able to go to cinemas, theatres, restaurants and all the other places Jack was too disorganised to attend. Women had it sorted all right. Very soon they would grow in size and start eating their mates after intercourse.

"Let's walk," said Annie, "it's a lovely evening."

This was obviously not the case. It was, clearly, a repulsive evening, but along with the admirers and the television plays and the foetus, Annie seemed to have developed a kind of Nature Ramble approach to life. The last time they had met she had gone on about leaves.

"Look at that sky!" she said, "sort of dirty-red!"

"Sort of bus-coloured," said Jack wistfully.

Annie paid no attention to this but strode off towards Holland Park Avenue.

"Been up to Grunwick?" she said.

"Er . . . no . . . " faltered Jack, "I kept meaning to but . . . "

He could not tell her the awful truth that one morning he had set out for the strike-bound Grunwick factory with the vague idea that it was somewhere in Kilburn. On leaving Kilburn Station he enquired after its whereabouts. Everyone had heard of the place. Everyone knew there was a strike there. Some expressed their views about it with varying degrees of violence. But no one seemed to know where it actually was. At twelve o'clock Jack had repaired to a Cricklewood pub, where he had engaged an elderly local in a heated dispute about the Disappearing Strike (as he had privately christened it).

"Grunwick's only the beginning," said Annie, "they're out to smash unions, they're out to smash immigrants – "

An immigrant was passing as they spoke – a big, raw-boned West Indian youth with what looked like a tea cosy on his head. He certainly did look smashed, but not quite in the way Annie meant.

"I like immigrants!" Jack blurted out as they strode past expensive white houses set well back from the road, and the traffic crawled past them in the stern twilight *en route* for Shepherds Bush.

"You like everybody, Jack," said Annie, "and everybody likes you. Eh?"

"But nobody knows me," said Jack, "nobody knows who I really am."

He was beginning to enjoy this conversation. As Annie goose-stepped her way forward, lump at full tilt, he tried to keep it afloat a little longer –

"I'm confused, you see. I react with blind hostility to any power group I meet. I'm not interested in power. I'm only interested in dislodging it."

"And after you've dislodged it what do you do, Jack?" said Annie. "Phone your Mummy and ask her what to do?"

She clearly found Jack's position so uninteresting as to be worth no further reply, and whereas Jack would have welcomed a heart to heart on the nature of commitment (one of his favourite topics) she returned, implacably, to questions of the moment.

"The National fucking Front," she said, "that's the issue now. Fascism. That is the main issue."

Jack rather agreed with this.

"Right," he said, "I nearly went on a demonstration about that."

"*Nearly*," said Annie in genuine puzzlement, "how can you *nearly* go on a demonstration? Surely you go or you don't, don't you?"

"I was going with Snaps. I mean Snaps feels quite strongly about the National Front."

"He wants to join?"

To Jack's surprise she then stomped off at a fair running pace.

Jack had never seen a pregnant woman run before. It was an awe-inspiring sight. Her brown boots hit the pavement like an ack-ack gun, her head lowered and her fists clenched crossly, her blonde hair banged against her forehead, while un-pregnant passers-by stood back, aghast. Limply, Jack plodded after her as the pains traditionally associated with running began in his back, chest, legs and arms. She seemed to be pleading with the conductor to delay the bus on Jack's behalf. What was she was saying? – "Look, officer – my husband isn't pregnant!" Gasping, Jack grasped the rail, clambered up next to her and the bus pulled away.

"Why," said Jack, "do you bother to keep meeting me?"

An elderly lady stared at them, expressing frank, friendly curiosity about their conversation.

"Keeping in touch," said Annie.

"To what *end*?"

"Stick around," she replied.

Beyond and behind them the traffic jolted forward in the fuzzy, freezing evening – the shop windows were full of the desperate gaiety of November and the faces of the homegoing crowd were as bleak as the weather.

"I feel conspired against!" said Jack.

"Don't worry," said Annie, "you are."

Jack looked along the bus's gallery at the women laden with shopping and at the neutral faces of the men, at the breath of both, white and cloudy in the chill interior.

A tumbril, he thought, definitely a tumbril.

When they walked in through the door of Sinclair Gardens, picking their way past soaked, yellowing nappies, old copies of the *Morning Star* and a baby buggy that appeared to have been coated, carefully, with porridge, as if for some well-defined artistic purpose, Egbert was waiting for them.

He was being restrained by Lucy. He wore a white jersey, smart black dungarees and a tiny pair of white brothel creepers, and pawed the carpet with his right foot, anxious to be away into the fog, the traffic jams and the thousand and one other things that were capable of ending his life some sixty-eight and a half years ahead of schedule. He had also, in the last year, acquired hair, mousey, sculptured layers of it, that made him resemble a Roman senator. Beaming chubbily, he waved a small plastic bucket at them and shouted –

"Kabooka!"

This was not, Jack discovered, a Japanese war cry. Whatever it was or whatever it meant, Annie understood it, for she slammed the door shut behind them and grinned at Lucy.

"I know what *he* wants!" she said.

"You want Kabooka, don't you, little love," said Lucy, obviously well up on the language.

Both of them, in fact, began to speak in fluent Egbert, while Jack pressed himself against the wall, wondering whether his manner to either woman betrayed the fact that he was still in what Snaps would call "an on-going sex situation" as far as both of them were concerned.

"He always wants Kabooka, doesn't he?" said Annie.

"We've been having a go," said Lucy, "on the ha-ha!"

What on earth did this mean? The news seemed to please Annie, however.

"Did we have to be taken away from the ha-ha?" she asked with humorous concern.

"We did," said Lucy, "and we went Gop Gop a Gobbum and asked for our Kabroopkoop."

They were both clearly mad. Jack felt he could do with a Kabroopkoop. A large Kabroopkoop with ice and lemon and tonic.

"Kabooka!" shouted Egbert at Jack, as if willing him to understand.

"Right!" said Jack nervously, backing further up against the wall.

"He wants to go out in the car!" said Lucy.

"Ah," said Jack.

A pause. Then –

"But I haven't got a car."

"No."

"*You* haven't got a car."

"No."

Another pause. Egbert looked round at all three adults, wondering which one was going to make the first move.

"He went in one once, didn't you, Eggie!" said Lucy, "A few months ago. And he liked it."

"Obviously!" said Jack.

"Kabooka! Kabooka! Kabooka!" shouted Egbert.

Ignoring him, the two women went through into the front room, which was festooned with posters, slogans, toys, nappies and old wine bottles. Unlike Jack's and Snaps' and Spielman's mess, this was a mess with a purpose, mess that seemed wholesome and reasonable, like the occupants of the house. IT MUST NOT HAPPEN AGAIN, said one poster, featuring a picture from a concentration camp, over which was superimposed the phrase, NATIONAL FRONT NAZI FRONT! There were posters demanding the withdrawal of troops from Northern Ireland, posters demanding equal pay for women, fair treatment for lesbians, more schools, less bombs, international peace and brotherhood and all the other things Jack believed in or thought he believed in.

When they had finished discussing Egbert's immediate future, the two women looked at him. Jack could feel none of the slight tension evident in the Egbert-chat, and concluded he meant less to both of them than his son.

"I suppose Jack'll want some food," said Lucy to Annie.

"I suppose so," said Annie.

"He never eats, does he?"

No. He never eats. He never sleeps. He never talks. He just crawls about cluelessly from venue to venue, wrestling with Episode seven million and five of *Herbert's Boys*. Oh God, Jack thought, that was a problem too. Schooner had sent him a curt little note demanding to know why Paul the Postman had suddenly come down with cancer of the feet. Since Jack had been writing *Herbert's Boys*, the serial had been showing dangerous signs of developing dramatic tendencies, and, unknown to Schooner, Jack had plans to turn it into a cross between *The Dance of Death* and *The Duchess of Malfi*. People were going to die, horribly and in large numbers.

"And now," said a hideously familiar voice from the door, "we will have a leetle paprikash weeth some young turnips in butter, yes?"

Nelly was wearing a yellow T-shirt, on which was written OK I'M A LESBIAN. For one awful moment Jack wondered whether this statement was intended to be taken seriously, and then remembered that, every time he came to Sinclair Gardens, Nelly would be wearing some new badge, emblem or sticker relating to a campaign she could not possibly understand. Good old Nelly was simply entering into the spirit of things.

Last time it had been a badge saying WAGES FOR HOUSEWORK and when Jack had asked a keen, probing, let's-discuss-this-like-men question about the said movement, Nelly had replied "Eet eez true. Some of these bloody women dust over once and you could wallow een eet, eet eez so theeck!" to which Jack could think of no suitable reply.

She had lost weight though, and her ample breasts, jutting out cheerfully and distorting the chosen slogan, sorted well with the jeans, the stacked up shoes, and all the other things that had effected her transition, over the past year, from dowdy foreigner to swinging Londoner. Being a foreigner, of course, she played that out-of-date role with a zest and style no one else in the room could manage or aspire to. She waltzed in among the debris, a steaming bowl of something in her left hand, right arm festooned with plates and cloths, like a perfect young housewife, dressed and educated by J. Sainsbury's Ltd, serving a clean husband and two clean children perfectly; she no longer smelt of garlic. If she smelt of anything, it was of denim and formica. Only her accent, impervious, remained, even more bizarre in the light of her re-modelled appearance.

"Our vagabond eez here!" she said, and began dishing out plates, knives and forks with the speed and efficiency of a professionally trained waitress.

"You look a bit peaky, Jack!" said Lucy, as Egbert strutted around at the edge of the room, mouthing like Demosthenes in rehearsal on his pebbled beach. "Are you eating enough?"

"I'm fine!" said Jack defensively, "I'm just dropping through. I've got to meet somebody later."

That ought to throw them.

Nelly poured a heap of veal, potatoes, sauce, onions, peppers and carrots on to his plate. It smelt wonderful. Unlike food prepared by him, Snaps or Spielman, it actually smelt like food and not some test assault on the senses. He ate greedily.

"Yeah," he went on, "a fringe theatre group is putting on one of my plays."

This was not exactly a lie. About a year ago a man called Wetherby Lane had expressed interest in the idea of Jack writing something "committed". Jack could see him now, bearded, friendly, intense and vaguely biblical-looking. He ran something called the *Boot Theatre Company* and, shortly after meeting Jack, he himself had been "committed" – to a mental home. "Apparently," Jack remembered him saying, "I've got something called schizophrenia." Jack had not written the play, had not intended to write the play.

100

"Vell," said Nelly, whose ability to eat had not suffered in the last year, "that was blooming great anyway. We go to the meeting, Lucy?"

"Right," said Lucy.

And the two of them rose to their feet. Egbert, who was halfway across the floor to his mother, flung his right arm forwards in a yearning, eloquent gesture.

"Kabooka!" he said.

"That's right, darling," said Lucy, "only we're walking, not going in a Kabooka. We're walking. We haven't got a Kabooka!"

Oh yes we have, thought Jack. We've got a Kabooka and a Kabroopkoop and a Gop a Gobbum and a ha-ha. And we're going to take them all out into the woods and eat fairy meals off dandelion leaves and then we're going to go hoppity hoppity hop to see Wetherby Lane in the lunatic asylum.

Lucy stopped – her face suddenly serious.

"Egbert, you stay with Jack," she said quietly.

This was another feature of visits to Sinclair Gardens. Jack always got the impression that whenever Egbert (or Egbart as Nelly still insisted on calling him) was introduced to his father there was an atmosphere of gentle, sisterly sorrow in the air at the non-relationship between the two males.

Jack felt bad about this. He had discovered, over the last year, and more especially in recent weeks, that there were soft, mushy places in his heart capable of being stirred by his son's ludicrous attempts at speech and movement.

"We go, Egbart!" said Nelly, and they were gone in a flash, before Egbart had time to grab their clothing or otherwise restrain them.

"You're going on this demonstration," said Annie.

"Am I?"

"You are."

Jack was momentarily distracted from this proposition by the sight of a shirt in the corner of the room. It was a hairy, check shirt of the kind worn by lumberjacks or men on oil rigs, and was instantly recognisable as belonging to Spielman. Was he really indifferent to the possibility that Annie and Spielman might be having an affair, that Spielman's huge, tentacle-like hands might be roving about her . . . No, he wasn't. He still loved her then? He wanted her back? He certainly wanted her to want him back. And if Spielman *was* having an affair with her then –

"Now," said Annie, "let's have a drink and then you can shove off."

"Fine!" said Jack.

So this was all she wanted from him then. To her he was, before he was her estranged husband, or that necessary victim of Communists, a wavering liberal with doubts, a hopelessly individualistic bourgeois, just interesting enough to be a potential convert. In many ways that was easier to deal with than Lucy's uncritical admiration.

"Scotch you like, don't you?" said Annie. "Where's Egbert?"

"I'll check," said Jack.

He had last glimpsed his son heading for the corridor, whence there was now an ominous silence. He went to the door and peered round. No Egbert. Into the small back room. Up against the corner, squatting by Annie's desk, Jack's son was grunting to himself, a faraway look in his eyes.

"Hullo, Egbert!" said Jack.

"Nah nah!" said Egbert, rather formally.

Jack went back to the front room and picked up his drink.

"What's he doing?" said Annie.

"He's sort of crouched," said Jack.

"Is he shitting?"

"I don't know," said Jack, "he's wearing trousers."

"Did he look sort of . . . abstracted?" said Annie.

Jack returned to the back room. Egbert look abstracted. He looked abstracted, tense and thoughtful.

"Are you shitting, Egbert?" said Jack.

"Nah nah!" said Egbert.

Jack went back to Annie, who was sitting with her feet on the coffee table glaring at a magazine. He sat opposite her, noting once again the bold, Viking lines of her profile and the brilliant blonde hair of the kind usually found on SS officers in British war films.

"He says he isn't shitting," said Jack.

"Oh Jack," said Annie, putting down her magazine, "you didn't speak to him, did you?"

"I did – I said 'Are you shitting, Egbert?' and he replied 'Nah nah!' "

"Thanks a lot," said Annie peevishly, "now you've probably made him selfconscious."

There was a pause. They both sipped their drinks, while presumably, next door, Egbert continued to shit.

"I'll go then," said Jack.

"You can stay and put him to bed," replied Annie.

Jack thought of dismissing this proposition with a curt oath. It occurred to him to say that he had never put his son to bed while he was living with his (Egbert's) mother, so why on earth should he start now that he was living apart from the said mother? Let alone the fact that he would be putting him to bed with the woman to whom he had been married, the woman who had talked the said mother out of her relationship with him on the grounds that it was repressive, bourgeois, outdated and all the other things that made it so convenient from Jack's point of view, the woman who . . .

He would find it easier, he decided, as she sipped her Scotch, next to the gas-fire, if he could persuade himself that he didn't need her. Like his political conscience, she was an awkward piece of luggage, a constant reminder of his own inadequacy. And yet he could not let the thought of her go.

"Do you good!" said Annie. "Do you ever put Little Luke to bed?"

"No," said Jack, "but he helped to put me to bed once. When I was the worse for drink."

Little Luke's bedtimes, from what Jack had seen of them, were reminiscent of the nastier moments of Wagnerian music-drama.

"OK?" said Annie.

"Fine," said Jack doubtfully.

They went next door. Egbert was still crouching by the desk but now he was flapping a piece of paper, feebly, on the floor. They stood at the entrance to the room like jailers and Annie said –

"Bedtime, Egbert!"

"Nan nah!" said Egbert softly.

"Yes yes," said Annie.

Jack felt stirrings of sympathy for his son. Was Egbert too doomed to a lifetime of obedience to the unreasonable demands of women? He would have to stop coming to Sinclair Gardens.

If he wasn't careful he'd end up liking the child. He crossed to him and stood over him. Egbert's small, blue eyes travelled up the immense figure in front of him.

"Nah nah!" pleaded Egbert.

"Sorry, old mate!" said Jack.

He lifted him up and followed Annie up the stairs.

O nce upstairs, Egbert seemed to know what was going on. He had, in fact, a rather better idea than Jack – for he scampered to the edge of the bath and, craning his neck over it, said, quite loudly:

"Guck! Guck!"

From a string bag nailed to the wall, Annie took a large yellow duck and threw it into the bath, then, dodging Egbert's outstretched hands, she put the plug in place and set the taps roaring.

"Pa! Pa!" said Egbert.

As far as Jack could make out, the child wanted to hold or control duck, plug and water, for his head swayed between all of them, bug-eyed with reverence for their existence. None of what he planned, however, came to pass. As so often in Egbert's life, it was the thing he least desired that was visited on him. Annie sneaked up behind him and, rather smartly, pulled down his trousers.

"Nah nah!" said Egbert.

"Yes yes," said Annie, then to Jack, "Deal with the shit."

What did this mean? Presumably some sort of wiping. He had seen Lucy do such a thing in the past, but until now had never considered the possibility of doing it himself.

Annie passed him a wad of cotton wool and he took a stab at the infected area. Not daring to look at what he had captured, he thrust cotton wool, nappy and plastic pants on to an old copy of a magazine called *Woman's Voice* and, holding his nose, said –

"OK?"

Annie inspected the damage.

"Do a proper job!" she said, and, seizing another piece of cotton wool, she set to work scouring, digging and scraping with unholy relish. When she had finished her task she rolled Egbert down into the flood. This pleased him.

Her competence with his child increased his sense of frustration and impotence with Annie, sharpened to an almost unbearable pitch the feeling that she had access to a body of information denied to him; it was as if her very superiority with the boy made him hunger for an exclusive relationship of his own.

"Stop looking soppy at him!" said Annie, "and wash him."

"Right!" said Jack.

He sat on the edge of the bath.

"See much of Spielman these days?"

"A bit," said Annie.

"Isn't the Trotskyism a problem for you?"

"Oh Jack," said Annie, "*please!*"

"Sorry. Sorry."

Jack was making even less progress with Egbert than with Annie. Every time he approached his son with sponge or soap, Egbert writhed away coquettishly, frequently slipping sideways into the water as he did so. It was probably best to go now – back to the half-empty flat in Elgin Crescent with Spielman poring over his magazine's losses and Gobbo beckoning from the shadows. One more try before he went –

"Spielman," he said, "is on amazing form these days!"

"Is he?"

This seemed either the remark of someone who was not having an affair with Spielman (i.e. it was said almost without any emotion whatsoever); or it could, on the other hand, equally well be the remark of someone who was having an affair with Spielman and was being very careful to conceal it by sounding as if the name meant no more than "Smith", "Jones" or "Andrews".

"Yeah," said Jack phonily, "he's still into everything. Still making the revolution, ten years after the glorious sixties."

"So you think revolution is an accidental, local phenomenon, do you, Jack?" said Annie.

Egbert threw his plastic duck at the wall of the bath.

"I don't mean that," said Jack, "I'm talking about England and about politics in England. Ten years ago we thought that a few marches and a

105

few people setting themselves alight was going to sort out the whole of Western Capitalism. What we actually had in mind was a sort of Garden of Eden – a planned economy for hippies. What we're getting, ten years after, is lies and mess and muddle, with our private lives a mess and our public concerns in even worse shape."

"There were those", said Annie, "in the Student Movement with little understanding and less vision. It looks increasingly as if you were one of those. There were, however, some of us who saw ahead beyond the student pranks."

"You, of course," said Jack, flushing, "have the advantage of a simple-minded view of history – that blithely assumes that your lot will do more for the genuinely miserable than capitalist profiteer pigs, or whatever you call them."

"And you," replied Annie, "have the advantage of having no views whatsoever. About anything. My view of socialism isn't fucking graph paper and concentration camps. It's quite as 'human' as your timorous, bourgeois, oh-dear-isn't-the-water-cold *crap* that I put up with for all those years, thinking you'd see the error of your ways."

Egbert threw a small rubber fish, a green bakelite ball and a wooden spoon at the wall of the bath. Then he beamed at Annie. Time to go, thought Jack. Annie was right about one thing. His view of the world did not seem to encourage action.

"I've got to go now," he said brokenly.

"Put him to bed first."

"No no. I can't stand it. I can't stand any of it. I can't stand the whole thing. You, the big wide world. Everything. I can't take it, Annie."

"Christ, Jack," said Annie, "you are pathetic. You really are *pathetic*. You hang around me and you hang around Lucy. Neither of us wants you. You stand on the sidelines of life hoping someone'll take you into the game but that isn't really what you want either, is it? You want a hole to crawl into. You want your fucking Mummy, don't you, Jack? You are incapable of living as an adult, with adults. I sometimes wonder if any man is. No. You want your fucking Mummy."

Jack considered, briefly, his mother. Memories of Mrs Warliss shrieking at Annie – "You're a Communist! You're a card-carrying Communist!" and worse memories of Annie taking out the card and waving it above her head, shouting, "Yes, I fucking well am! I am! I am! I am!"

"Annie – " he began. Then stopped.

Egbert grinned, half fearfully, at him.

This was too much for Jack. Closer to tears than he cared to be, he turned, ran for the stairs and bolted back into the icy November night.

I t was impossible to see anything on the street.

It must, by now, be seven or eight o'clock and the fog slouched and swirled around the few available lights, a dirty rind on the Belisha beacon at the corner of Sinclair Gardens and Richmond Way, bumping and writhing at the window-panes like a sea monster, making home, any home, suddenly an impossible, private pleasure.

At the end of Richmond Way he took the underpass across the round-about at the end of the Green, and finished up on the north side of Holland Park; the fog seemed to be even thicker here, in spite of the lights from a small row of shops. Jack hurried over Royal Crescent and then turned up left through the maze of furniture shops, quiet pubs and council estates beleaguered by the gentry. He walked up Queensdale Road and stopped at the Prince of Wales, where the usual crowd of large, sinister, semi-professional men were playing darts and calling to each other across the crowded bar. Jack pushed his way through to the further bar, ordered a large Bell's and sat for a moment, morosely surveying this happy, well integrated group of people.

Why didn't he have a group to belong to? The women in his life wouldn't let him engage in anything so frivolous, time-consuming or essentially male. And the men he knew seemed as pinned down by women or causes as him: unable to rally against the collective loneliness of age, they stood their ground, muttering brave words about "sexism" and "women's rights" or (Lucy's favourite theme) The Caring Father. But what stared them in the face was the destiny of those blank-eyed Householders of Mill Hill Jack remembered from his childhood, poised over garden or half-plastered wall, a desperate empty plea in their eyes.

He gulped back his whiskey and, banging through the nearest door (why did he always imagine, when drinking alone, that people were noting and pitying him?), found himself in a Dickensian cobbled yard, on the other side of the pub. With the free-standing inn sign (more like a gibbet than anything else) behind him, and feeling now as if he was in one of those Hammer horror films in which prostitutes are disembowelled by men in tall Regency hats, Jack set out down the narrow street that leads, past Julie's Wine Bar, through to plusher houses on the edge of Ladbroke Grove and to the bleak wasteland south of the Westway.

He was halfway down one such street, genteel, quite deserted, when he saw a figure ahead of him, walking in the middle of the road, stopping every three or four yards to read the numbers on the houses. It was probably a woman, but at twenty yards it was difficult to be more specific than that. Then, just out of visual range, it stopped, put its hands on its hips and set its head on one side, pettishly.

"Oh my blooming God!" it said. "Vere are we, eh?"

Nelly.

"Nelly!" said Jack.

"Oh saints alive!" said Nelly. "Thenk the heavens for thees!"

"What happened?'

He came up close to her. Her clear, oval face was haunted with worry, and there was a touch of gamine gauntness about her, eradicating all suspicions of her peasant origins. Her black eyes scanned Jack's face suspiciously, as if to ascertain that it was indeed Jack and not some demon of the fog sent to torment her.

"I have left thees meeting early about Weemen in Bondage in order to get some cheecken on for Tuesday and whoops a bloody daisy I am lost, hein? Thees eez a real pea souper, squire, no?"

"Indeed!" said Jack.

There was a pause. She still smelt of formica and denim. It seemed, in the circumstances, a pleasant enough combination.

"Why don't you come back to the flat?"

"Ur – "

Nelly's eyes grew troubled. Something was telling her perhaps that Annie, and maybe Lucy (though who knew what Lucy thought about anything?), would not approve of such a move. The mood of the female collective, whoever was responsible for it, had appeared to be in favour of her having an affair with a huge Croatian physicist called by a name that sounded like Stinko.

108

"Nice to see you."

"Nice to see *you*."

She grinned.

"Meestair Jarlsberg!"

"Ah yes," said Jack, "I believe we have some unfinished business to discuss in that connection."

"Do we?"

Say what you like about Nelly's level of political consciousness, dress sense and her general resemblance to a creature dropped from another galaxy, you had to admit that when it came to ogling, fifties style, she was a winner. This last remark was delivered with a complex bump-and-grind body movement that enriched its simple interrogative to a point well beyond the unbearable.

"I think we do, Nelly."

Jack put his arms about her waist and she leaned back, allowing him to support her. The ogling was now reaching a point at which either laughter, flight or sexual intercourse would have to be attempted very soon. Nelly was wriggling her shoulders, turning her head to one side and leering and winking like a salesman of pornographic postcards. Giving new meaning to the term "bedroom eyes", she said, tapping Jack lightly on the nose –

"Naughty Meestair Jarlsberg!"

A lot of this kind of thing was, presumably, forbidden by law at Sinclair Gardens. Jack took her in his arms and allowed his hands to glide from chin to neck to brassière, as the two of them fell together in the awkward, urgent style of adolescent kiss that had nearly ruined Jack's early manhood.

Somehow, Nelly's Marks and Spencer's trousers were slipping down over her buttocks, and, somehow, her blue coat wrapped round them both, Nelly's white Marks and Spencer's knickers were joining them in an unholy ruck off her knees and somehow –

"Jack. Jack. Jack."

Her voice was tearful and far-away. She was buttoning herself up hurriedly, appalled by what had happened.

"Oh Jack, Jack, you – "

Backing away in the fog, she looked at him.

"Oh Jack, what the girls say about you is – "

"Is what?"

"Iss true. Iss bloody true what they say."

And then she was running, duck-like, awkward and bruised, away down the fog-drenched street, crying, perhaps, or something worse, suddenly a little girl, shocked and broken by what had happened.

Jack tried to shout something after her, but it seemed useless to call her back. He looked down at himself, open, rude, cruel, not to trust . . .

Christ almighty, he thought, they've turned me into a fucking rapist. That's it – a fucking rapist.

T hat was the root of it.

Jack gazed down at his cock. The root of it. All the posturing and the apologising and the "Am I a Homosexual?" could not conceal the awful truth that he was a boor and a rapist and a lout who did not understand women or at least was unable to think of them as human beings. Did he even *like* women? Not really. They were things you battered at, lusted at, cried on the shoulders of . . . but *liked*? No. No way.

An ugly and instructive encounter. The blindest of blind dates.

He heard footsteps behind him and his fingers, numb with cold, attempted to stuff his organ back into his trousers. SCRIPTWRITER EXPOSES HIMSELF IN FOG – "Had it not been for the appalling weather conditions, residents of West London might have been subjected to yet another 'flasher' incident last night. As it was – mercifully – thick fog made it impossible for the casual passer-by to get a good look at the penis of *Jack Warliss*, currently author of the successful early morning drama *Herbert's Boys* and now resident at number thirty-nine, Elgin Crescent, W.10."

It really was quite difficult getting the thing back in, though. The footsteps drew level with him and passed by on their way without stopping. Jack kept his head down, as if trying to find a lost coin. Then, biting his lip, he turned smartly in the opposite direction and walked back towards Spielman, Little Luke and Gobbo. Not to mention Snaps.

W hen he at last returned to Elgin Crescent, Spielman and Snaps (who was still in his Dagenham costume) were crouched over a convector heater. Little Luke was stretched out asleep on the mattress-half of the bed, clutching a teddy bear. He was wearing a kind of polar suit, and looked free of all human vices.

Feeling glad to be back (in some ways), Jack slid down the wall and watched the two of them dismember the heater. Spielman held each tiny screw between his giant fingers, acting out the business of committing their size and shape to memory for when the time came to reassemble the heater.

"I've been over at Sinclair Gardens," said Jack.

Neither of them paid any attention to this. Snaps, from the bowels of the machine, produced something that looked like a metal caterpillar — it shook to his touch.

"Aieeou!" whinnied Snaps. "It's got intestines!"

"The thing *about* your convector heaters," said Spielman, giving slow serious attention to this question, wielding his bum up into the air and lowering one goggling eye to the level of the machine, like a giant sussing out a pigmy's castle, "the thing *about* your convector heaters is that they're made by very old, very blind men. Hopeless."

Jack tried again. Getting a response out of these two was, on occasions, like dealing with the Girls.

"Do you get over there these days, Jake?" he said to Spielman.

"Once in a while," said Spielman ponderously, "for a fuck."

This was a fairly typical ploy of Spielman's. To state the thought in your opponent's subconscious, as if it were a well known public fact, was as neat a piece of one-upmanship as Jack knew.

"She rang, actually," Spielman went on, "Annie rang. Just now."

"Oh."

"Yup."

Snaps was enjoying this conversation. Crimson with suppressed

111

mirth, he looked from Jack to Spielman. Snaps was always able to enjoy the discomfiture of a close friend, especially one he suspected of being complacent.

"She phoned," went on Spielman, "about the racism demo."

"About the racism demo."

"Yup, Jack," said Spielman.

The convector heater was now on its back – its intestines strewn around it on the dirty yellow carpet. It did not look as if it would ever heat anything ever again.

"What about the racism demo?"

"Apparently she persuaded you to go on it."

For the first time since it had been mentioned, Jack started to think seriously about what his attendance at this dangerous left-wing function might mean.

It was, after all, a serious step to take.

When was the last demonstration he had attended? Eight years ago? Ten? And, from what Jack could gather, this was not going to be as cosy as a few young bearded persons demanding to see their files.

"Apparently, squire," said Snaps, "they are probably going to commit themselves to some sort of on-going stone-throwing situation vis-à-vis the heroic marchers."

"Yup," said Spielman, "this will be the case."

Did they supply you with helmets on these occasions?

"Where is it?" said Jack.

"East End," said Spielman, "the good old East End of London. Where Bengalis get clubbed to death and insulted in the newspapers and generally Nazified."

"Shit!" said Jack.

There was a pause. Snaps was looking more than usually thoughtful.

"She's writing a play," said Jack, "for Schooner!"

"I know," said Spielman. "Hopeless."

Outside on the landing there was a scuffling noise, as of mice. Little Luke turned in his sleep. Jack abandoned all hope of getting anything out of Spielman, and, deciding attack was the best form of defence, addressed his remark to Snaps, whom he took to be a junior member of the conspiracy against him.

"Hope you'll be there, comrade," he said.

"I will be," said Snaps, "I would say that a certain person not a million miles from the area of what could well be described as foreign, not to mention East European, has requested my presence at the said function."

There certainly was, thought Jack, a terrifyingly high degree of collusion between Sinclair Gardens and Elgin Crescent. What was even more worrying was that everyone, apart from Jack, seemed aware of it. An awful vignette exploded before Jack's eyes – Snaps, Spielman, Lucy and Annie crouched round Nelly. Nelly was saying – "And *then* he has flashed hees theeng at me!"

"I think," said Spielman, rifling through nuts and bolts in a leisurely fashion, "I *think* that Gobbo is at the door."

"Gobbo? What on earth can Gobbo want?"

"A head transplant," said Snaps, "or maybe a few earwigs to make a stew."

"Let him in would you, Jacko!" said Spielman.

Wondering why, in whatever group of people he found himself, people seemed to spend their time giving him orders, Jack got up and opened the door a fraction.

Gobbo was, indeed, lurking on the landing, nodding and smiling in the gloom.

"Do you want some money for the meter?" said Jack.

"Nlike to talk to you!" said Gobbo.

"What about?"

I am in love with you wife, Mr Warliss. We want to go away together.

"Nflat!" said Gobbo. "Come inside?"

"OK."

Gobbo slid in through the crack and, snapping his knuckles, nodded and smirked at Spielman and Snaps.

"Gobbo!" said Spielman, as if announcing the score at a tennis match.

"Gobbo," agreed Gobbo.

He seemed pleased at this riposte. Snaps stretched out on his stomach and looked up at him, quizzically.

"Why are you here, Gobbo?" he said. "Why aren't you in a museum or a zoo or something?"

"Flat!" said Gobbo, "nflat!"

Gobbo had found another flat. This was good news. They might even have a human being upstairs.

"Have you found a new flat, Gobbo?" said Jack.

"Nyes," said Gobbo, "yours!"

His smirk crackling up under his nose, he nodded, nodded, nodded at the three of them, his eyes glassy with merriment.

"Gobbo," said Spielman, "are you OK?"

"Nperfectly!" replied Gobbo.

"Go away, Gobbo," said Snaps.

"Mr Spaton sent me a letter."

Gobbo passed a grubby sheet of paper across to Spielman, who held it with the caution dictated by anything that had been in Gobbo's pockets. Jack crossed to the window and looked down at the bank of fog. Buses, cars and vans were now in two parallel lines along the street, immobile.

"Jesus," said Spielman, "Gobbo is buying us out."

"Nyes," said Gobbo, "for my wife."

This was too much for Snaps. Howling with mirth, he beat his head against the carpet, crying, "Mrs Gobbo! Aieeou! Mrs Gobbo!" It was indeed a sobering thought. Presumably he had found her through some sort of agency. "Young man with plenty of go in him and head shaped like a sprout wishes to meet similar with a view to marriage." That, or else she was in desperate need of British citizenship.

"Nbaby!" he said, simpering.

"Nkeep your ngreasy fucking hands off of him an' all," said Spielman, looking up from the letter.

"Is it true?" said Jack.

"Seems to be," said Spielman.

"Nfour weeks' notice," said Gobbo.

Spielman leaned his head on his hands and looked, long and hard, at Gobbo.

"Amazing," he said, at last. "Imagine what it feels like to *be* Gobbo. Imagine it."

114

Jack imagined it. It didn't feel so bad. After all, you were about to get married. You had somewhere to live.

"Nennyway," said Gobbo, "I thought I'd drop by and tell you."

"Thank you, Gobbo," said Snaps, "where's the wedding?"

"NSt Paul's fucking cathedral," said Gobbo.

Jack's jaw dropped. The three of them watched with new respect as Gobbo slouched back to the door. He had made a joke! Gobbo had made a joke! Anything, thought Jack, is possible. If someone the size, shape and texture of Gobbo could get married and crack a joke, then there was hope, even for Jack Warliss.

"Nin my opinion," Gobbo continued, "Mr Spaton gave me the nplace because he's a nfamily man himself. He believes in something. He believes that there's nothing more nbeautiful than a man and a person of the opposite sex settling down to raise a family together. My goodness! Nif you three nstopped behaving like adolescents and settled down to something the world would be a nbetter place. Nand don't think I can't hear the cruel things you say about me nand don't think I nhaven't got nfeelings. Three grown men nindeed. Nit's time you settled down!"

He slammed the door behind him and pattered off up the stairs.

"Strike a light!" said Snaps, slightly shamefaced.

"Gobbo," said Spielman slowly, "has nfeelings!"

A silence. Then –

"Whither Spielman?" said Spielman.

"Whither Snaps?" said Snaps.

"Whither Warliss?" said Jack, turning back into the room and attempting, probably unsuccessfully, to conceal his inner turmoil.

Spielman seemed to have decided that the convector heater was now to be re-graded as a sort of executive toy. He was arranging wires and ball bearings in neat rows on his chest as he lay back on the carpet, then flicking them up and out into the air.

"We'll have to find somewhere else!" said Jack.

"Bachelors Three," said Spielman distastefully.

Nobody, of course, wanted to pretend that they were in any way enjoying this thirty-year-old adolescence, this drunken, Bohemian, underpantless existence. Their nervousness with each other might mean that its dissolution was followed by separate lives in separate bed-sitters. Jack tried to imagine living alone in a bed-sitter. He didn't try for very long.

"What I need," said Spielman, "is a valet."

"We could find somewhere together!" said Jack, more brightly than was tactful. The other two looked at him sideways, as if they had only just rumbled his adolescent nature, his suppressed homosexuality, his general inability to face the world alone. They both looked eminently capable of living alone in bed-sitters. Somewhere outside, a motorist pressed his horn, a purposeless wail, muffled by the fog; there was not threat, only sorrow in the sound.

"I mean, it might be quite nice!" said Jack. Spielman balanced a washer on the tip of his nose. Still neither he nor Snaps spoke. Once again, thought Jack, IT IS ALL MY FAULT.

"Living with anyone," said Spielman, "is hopeless!"

A homeless suppressed homosexual rapist jelly with anarchist tendencies *cuckold*, thought Jack. That's me. I might as well go on this fucking demonstration. Whatever I do will make no difference to the downward slide. I will go, he added to himself, with the courage born of nihilism. I will go and the more violent, badly organised, politically extreme and dangerous the affair is, the better.

"Hopeless!" said Spielman, contentedly. "Hopeless!"

O n the morning of the demonstration Annie awoke, as usual, at six, to hear the sound of Egbert's morning chorus from Lucy's room across the landing – "Sowarrghntzaah!" – a kind of vocal equivalent of the stomach rumble. She awoke as well pleased with the last months as she had ever been. It was only afterwards she realised that the landscape around her was more threatening than she had supposed – capable, in an instant, of being transformed into something terrifying and strange. It was a day of action after all, and action had a way of making the unpleasant clearly visible.

She pushed back the duvet and looked at her lump.

It wasn't a bad lump really. Not one of those low-slung, effortful ones, or one of those ridiculous, high-stepping jobs that gave the impression that the baby was going to clamber up one's wind-pipe when the time came for his arrival.

She thought of the baby as "him". Odd, that.

From time to time certain areas of the lump would twitch, like custard on a low heat, as Annie's baby punched a signal to the outside world, circling, jumping and doing all the other extraordinary things that Dr Gordon Bourne said he did in his dark hiding place. Perhaps she only thought of the baby as "him" because of Dr Gordon Bourne, because Gord, in spite of his obvious talent for designing see-through sections of the Fallopian tubes, and his undeniable gift for reconstructing side elevations of the uterine duct, was, let's face it, a male chauvinist. You could tell from the mild, bespectacled face and the neat consultant's suit (at least the fragment of it visible in the dust jacket photo) that here was yet another man paid millions of pounds for peering up women's fannies and telling them they were going to have boys. The pregnant woman on the cover was a dead give-away, although to use the word "pregnant" in connection with such a vision seemed unfair. She was "awaiting her time" or "expecting a little stranger" or whatever other pathetic euphemism men had coined to ward off the beauty and terror of women doing something so fundamentally much *cleverer* than anything they had yet come up with. The woman was standing at a window, looking out through gauze curtains and wearing what looked like a gigantic pair of gauze curtains herself. What she was looking *at* was unclear — the little stranger himself, possibly, lolloping down the garden path, desperate to make it to the womb on time. That or else (as Lucy had suggested) an army of midgets in Lincoln Green who had stolen on to her lawn with armfuls of vaseline, layettes, scissors, vaginal pads and other things needful for pregnancy. From across the landing came the heavy thump of Egbert, who was throwing books at Lucy's head.

"Hub!" Annie heard him say, "Hub!"

"Ohhh!" came Lucy's nasal whine, "Eggie, I'm tired. I want to go to sleep now, Egbert. I don't want to get hub."

Egbert was implacable.

"Hub!" he said, "Hub!"

"I won't get hub," said Lucy, "I won't I won't I won't!"

"Hub," said Egbert, "Hub hub hub!"

Was Egbert like Jack? Seeing resemblances in people's children was,

117

clearly, an absurd pastime, but Annie fancied she caught a look of Jack in the way the little boy laid his head to one side and stared distantly at a glass, a chair or a book cover, as if to wrest some secret from it.

Was it Jack's child or Spielman's? They were both under the impression that she had, of late, been sleeping with half the bourgeoisie of London, as an act of principle, but she did not propose to tell either of them that they were the only two candidates for the position of father of the child now curling and crawling inside her.

Jack would want to know, of course. Jack, unlike Spielman, was lumbered with all the outdated apparatus of patriarchy, but these days, his kingdom dissolved, he seemed a lost soul. Even the consolations of fantasy had been denied. The problem with Jack was that, although he remained tender, intriguing, on occasions amusing, and never less than unpredictable, the last year had made his charm superfluous. The times were too hard for charm, and the only thing Jack had to his credit these days was a variety of the hopeless, self-destructive immediacy traditionally associated with the Celtic fringe. Lucy, poor sap, was probably still falling for it.

Annie levered herself off the bed and looked at her lump appreciatively in the mirror. There were times when she felt it to be an ugly, unsightly thing, but not so this morning. This morning it was clenched, streamlined, nicely made, wind-resistant. A small face peered round the door and beamed at her.

"Hullo, Egbert."

"Ung," said Egbert.

He usually called Annie "Ung". Sometimes it was "Ing" and sometimes "Erng-aah", but usually "Ung". Egbert, pleased to find someone who was up and about and capable of doing things, waddled towards her and grabbed at her knees.

"Hub," he said.

He was wearing what looked like a truncated eighteenth century frock coat, on which were pictures of small insects − his nappy, over burdened by the night's activities, had buckled down to below his knees. In order to cope with this disability, Egbert adopted a kind of Groucho Marx walk − bending at the knees he dodged her legs and headed for a suddenly more interesting pile of underwear by the window.

"Today, Egbert," said Annie, "you and I and your father and mother are going on a demonstration."

"Ohhh," came Lucy's voice from the other room, now a comic whine

118

of distress, "ohhh. It's going to be *awful*!"

"Death to Fascism, Egbert!" said Annie.

Egbert grinned.

Egbert couldn't know what Fascism was but, whatever it might turn out to be, he was determined to enjoy it.

From down below came a voice, carolling merrily, unspeakably cheerful for this hour of the morning.

"Hullo, happy campairs! I done some reesoles and a beeg pot of coffee for you lot and there is a fuck of a sight more where that has come from!"

Nelly had learned many things in the last year, but how to behave in the morning was not one of them. Annie heard her down in the kitchen, banging pots and pans together, and singing her own words to a tune that surely must be traditionally Hungarian. The words went –

> You take three pieces bacon
> You take four beeg hunk a' bread.
> You steek them een a frying pan
> And whirl zem roun' your head.
> You take four hundred reesoles
> An' srow zem at zer vorl!
> You add a leet'l beet gou-oulash –
> An' you sick all over the hall.

It was, in fact, a song written by Snaps, with intent to discomfort Nelly, but his wife (as she still insisted on calling herself) had committed it to memory and now sung it at all hours, especially in the early morning.

Next, Lucy, sounding waterlogged with sleep, began singing one of *her* own compositions. It went –

> Show me the way to Amarillo
> I'm in love with an armadillo.
> He likes the paintings of Utrillo
> And plays by writers like John Grillo
> Although he looks like a pad of brillo
> He is the only one for me!
> Oi!

They were good girls both, in spite of everything, reflected Annie, as Egbert got to work on the gas fire (mercifully, already broken).

Was it wise to bring the kids? thought Annie, then pushed that worry from her mind as well. Bad as the National Front might be, they hadn't got around to bashing babies. Yet, anyway.

I n time, Lucy herself appeared at the door, her once mousey curls now dyed black, and her big, violet eyes more dramatic at the centre of a face that was now, quite definitely, interesting and confident. She was wearing a long white nightgown and carrying her son's teddy bear.

"Loosh!" said Egbert dramatically, like a sailor who has sighted land after years at sea, "Loosh! Loosh!"

"Loosh" sat on the bed and watched Annie dressing with embarrassingly greedy absorption. She pulled one delicate leg up on to the duvet and allowed the other to trail wistfully down to the floor. Lucy was good at these faery gestures, an aspect of her that Annie found as irritating as anything else, apart, possibly, from Lucy's continuing obsession with Jack.

"Did you know – " she said, as Annie bolted herself into what must be the biggest bra yet worn, "did you know that women living together have synchronous periods?"

"Meaning?" said Annie.

"They have them at the same time."

"No," said Annie crossly.

Not for the first time she found herself wondering when, if ever, Lucy was going to get a job. As usual, Lucy answered her unspoken question for her (a trick that was beginning to irritate Annie).

"I sent the *Households* manuscript to a publisher," she said, "a feminist collective. Is it all right about my using Eggie's money to pay the rent?"

Lucy worried endlessly about whether it was "fair" to use her child benefit allowance in this manner. Annie, who wanted to avoid one of

120

Lucy's lengthy analyses of those nearest and dearest to her, tried to steer the conversation on to more practical things.

"Who's doing Loo Duty?" she asked, as she pulled on an expensive secondhand dress that fell in folds around her and started to brush her hair, in matronly style, at the cracked mirror.

"Whoever wants to, I suppose," said Lucy.

It might have been intended as a joke but, in her present mood, Annie read it as yet another declaration of live and let live from Lucy, already the theme of too many, too arid debates between the two of them. Annie wondered whether she had been wise to persuade Lucy to move with her into the new house. Lucy trailed one foot on the floor as Egbert watched her yearningly.

"Which means," said Annie sharply, "that no one does it. A good old anarchist solution."

Luckily Egbert provided a diversion. The sight of Lucy's toes was finally too much for him and, eyes bulging and wispy hair ablaze, he staggered towards them, arms wide, shouting "Tars! Tars! Tars!" At the same moment, from down below, a slightly irritable voice called:

"Reesoles weel eat themselves soon, you people!"

Picking up her boots, Annie fled, leaving Lucy and Egbert to their traditional *It's a Knockout* style of conversation – Egbert lunging with his teeth at Lucy's toes and Lucy shrieking with assumed horror.

Rissoles. It was curious really. In some ways she had had a profound effect on the lives of the other two girls – without those long conversations with her, neither of them would have been able to tear themselves away from Jack and Snaps, without her (and God alone knew how much she'd had to nag them) they probably wouldn't be attending women's meetings, rallies or even (once) Communist Party meetings.

But, in spite of Annie's marshalling and counselling and pleading, Lucy stuck to her writing and her anarchic feminism, while Nelly, well, Nelly stuck to her rissoles.

They must find Nelly a man. She had been closer to depression than Annie had ever seen since she had first moved into Sinclair Gardens a few months ago in order to "make herself interesting" to her absent man. She had been cooking eight-course meals, a sure sign that all was not well with her.

"There," said Nelly, as Annie came into the kitchen, "there is a breakfast for you. Blooming marvellous!"

"Great, Nels," said Annie, and sat at the groaning table.

If cooking was Nelly's only way of unburdening her heart then, lying before Annie, was an appeal to rival Isabella's to Angelo or Mark Antony's to the Roman crowd. Steaming jugs of coffe, *croissants* fresh from the oven, rissoles in hot sauce, smoked fish of some description, at least four different kinds of cereal and a bowl of freshly squeezed orange juice. On a side-dish were grilled bacon, grilled kidneys and a *massif central* of scrambled egg and anchovy fillets. Nelly was clearly close to suicide.

"You vont Bran Men?" she said, pouring Annie a slug of orange juice.

"Where are we meeting them?" asked Annie, more out of mechanical nervousness than anything else.

"At the station," said Nelly, helping herself to rissoles, bacon and kidneys. "My God, we're really going to put the wind up these Fascists, eh?"

"Oh, sure," said Annie.

Annie was perhaps the most depressed of the three. She had had previous experience of police behaviour on pickets and marches and expected today nothing less than an invasion of Special Patrol Group thugs, dedicated to bashing students and black men over the head. All freedom-loving, time-giving, bicycle-riding, baby-patting, tourist-guiding, fundamentally *passé* British Bobbies would be at home with their wives and children, preparing to read distorted accounts of the affair in the National Press.

T hey finished the breakfast in their different ways. Then Annie said –

"We go."

"Yes," said Lucy softly.

The three of them sat looking at each other in silence, then Lucy, as so often, returned without apology or explanation to an earlier conversation –

"I'll do the Loo," she said, "I don't mind."

"No no no," said Annie, crossly, "there's a Rota. We might as well stick to it. OK? It's fairer."

"I'd like to do it," said Lucy, with a hint of satire.

Annie, as usual, did not want this argument. She tried to deal directly with what she took to be a typical overdose of bourgeois scruple about getting off the arse and doing something.

"Look," she said, "*I* will do it. OK?"

"Fine," said Lucy, now openly satirical, "if you *want* to."

Damn the woman. Damn the fey, loopy, insidious woman. Why did she waste her time on her? Lucy stooped over Egbert and muttered –

"Poppet features."

"My God!" said Nelly, "all this talking about it is making me want to go."

And, putting back her chair, she proceeded to follow the advice of her own home-made proverb. They could hear her, grunting, groaning and urging herself on, from the ramshackle convenience next door – then the hectic rattle of the roll and the bravura flush, favoured by Nelly – "Hoop*la*!" In many ways, thought Annie, it ought to be possible to make a Communist out of Nelly. Essentially she was a materialist. Lucy put Egbert down and started to clear the things off the table. Nelly flounced past to the sink, where she began to make up a lunch basket more suitable for an Edwardian picnic than an act of political protest. Annie, unable to rid herself of that sense of doom, said –

"Look. Why don't we leave Egbert behind?"

"Oh no," said Lucy, "he wants to come."

"Lucy," said Annie, "he doesn't really know what's going on. And he might get hurt."

"Like us, you mean," said Lucy, "ideologically unprepared?"

Annie joined her friends in the task of preparation. At least she had tried. At least she could not be said to have inflicted her principles on a baby.

Getting Egbert into his pushchair was the next item on the agenda. Annie and Nelly each held an end, while Lucy strapped him in and Egbert, scenting the great outdoors, bucked, swayed and yelled at his tormentors. When he had been strapped in, like a lunatic in Bedlam, Lucy folded a large red plastic sheet over him – for a minute or so he wriggled beneath it, then, deciding on passive resistance, slumped forwards, eyes glassy with resignation. Then the three women, seizing

123

hats, coats, copies of newspapers and umbrellas, marched through the crowded hall and into the grey field of the November rain.

"You think," said Lucy, as they hustled up towards Shepherds Bush Green, "you think that I'm a hopeless individualist, don't you?"

"Er . . . " said Annie.

"I don't mind," said Lucy.

"No," said Annie, "you wouldn't. Being an individualist."

"I don't have any ambitions to change the world," said Lucy, "or other people."

"In that case," said Annie, angrier than she meant to be, "why are you coming today? And why are you bringing an eighteen-month-old baby on a demonstration that may endanger its bloody life, when you don't, presumably, think that things like politics matter?"

"They matter for me," said Lucy, "I don't think I have a right to say whether they matter for anyone else . . . "

She broke off. Lucy was becoming adept at censoring her tendency to rhapsodise. But although she spoke no more, afterwards, Annie remembered the way she had looked ahead of her, the translucent face and the wild, Cassandra-like expression that could still, after all this time, persuade Annie that she knew some awful secret only the future could reveal. Thinking back, Annie decided the rest of that ghastly, violent day could have been deduced from Lucy's troubled eyes, as she stared into the rain, her dream of revolution suddenly soured and halted.

All Annie said at the time was, "I still don't think Egbert should come." And then no one spoke as the three of them pushed their way through the crowds of shoppers, under the threatening sky.

A ldgate Station was not itself.

Normally a quiet, gloomy place, blighted by long pauses between the arrivals and departures of commuters and the dust-laden wind that haunts the Underground, it offered, at least, a sort of peace to those condemned to travel through it, but today there was a nervy, pre-Match tension in the air as the women disembarked.

Annie noticed a group of heavily built men by the barrier. One of them was carrying a furled red banner, about eight feet tall. Behind them, two or three policemen, a small group of Asians and a gaggle of youths. Curiously, she found she wasn't worrying about the demonstration or about Egbert.

It was Lucy who troubled her now.

She had not, until this morning, seriously considered the possibility that Lucy might still want Jack or that Jack might still want Lucy. Her involvement in their affair had been – for her anyway – so clear cut, so obviously "political" that she had never stopped to consider what either of them might feel for each other. Lucy had been criminally exploited by Jack – as had she – and therefore the connection must be broken.

She was jealous. She still loved him. She didn't love Spielman. Nobody could love Spielman. He looked like a sea monster. She hoped he wasn't the father. She didn't want a child who looked like a sea monster.

Annie tried out this idea on herself as they struggled up to the light, Egbert bumping up the stairs in his pushchair, pointing out things of interest on the way.

Spielman did *not* look like a sea monster. And even if he did, what was so wrong with sea monsters, eh?

"Where now?" said Lucy, nasally, at her shoulder.

They were standing by a crash barrier on the north side of the Whitechapel Road. Opposite them policemen in studded City of London helmets were standing, four or five yards apart, in a line that curved away down towards the Tower of London and back up to their left. On the narrow pavement they were jostled together with anoraks, donkey jackets, banners, knitted handbags, people selling newspapers (*"Morning Star!" "Socialist Worker!" "Newsline!"*), people giving away, or trying to give away, free sheets ("END THIS CHILEAN TERROR NOW!" "IRAQ: THE TRUE FACTS!"), white-haired, elderly revolutionaries with the expressions of young children, families of Trades Unionists, Asians, students and all the determined handmaidens of progress. Annie breathed deeply and grinned.

As they stood, unsure of which way to go, a black taxi swerved round the corner and halted in the middle of the road. Then, as cars hooted and drivers yelled, it turned about ninety degrees to the left, and crawled towards the kerb like a huge insect. Egbert had seen something.

125

He was straining at the complex array of leashes that held him to his chair and calling, " 'Oook. 'Oook." Annie followed the direction of his gaze and saw, at the back window, the bat ears, the perfectly formed teeth, the curls, the dungarees, the twisted nose and the huge brown eyes of Little Luke.

Annie found herself watching Jack and Lucy as the three men got out of the cab and clambered over the metal barrier, Spielman passing Little Luke into Nelly's arms. Lucy and her son were gazing at the newcomers with passionate reverence. Jack was behaving like a man with an over-full bladder – moving from foot to foot and jerking his eyes away from the group.

"Let us get Shanks' pony on the march!" said Nelly.

"No no," said Snaps with mock patience, "in England we say – 'let us put Shanks' pony in a first gear situation.' "

"OK," said Nelly, "let us put heem in a first gear situation so long as we blooming well get going. I don't mind."

They turned, and, following the movement of the crowd, began to walk down the Whitechapel Road towards Itchycoo Park where, so someone had said, the march was to assemble. Snaps and Nelly kept together and Annie heard him telling her that an even more idiomatic way of saying that you wanted to go somewhere on foot was to say, "shake it about a bit." She turned her attention to Jack and Spielman, who both seemed to be seeking her attention.

Jack turned to Lucy.

"Nice to see you," he said.

As he turned to her something happened to his face. It became tighter, nervous, disapproving. Annie recognised the expression. It was sexual desire. Shit shit shit. Where had she been all these months?

T hey were approaching the rallying point for the march, and still the questions nagged at her. She tried to concentrate on matters in hand.

On a battered piece of ground, separated from the main road by a low wall, a large crowd stood, silently, in the rain. Their faces shielded by black umbrellas, a solid phalanx of neatly dressed Asians waited for the order to march. Correct and well drilled, they gave the impression of being at a Mafia funeral or an open-air prayer meeting rather than a demonstration. Around them, less neatly dressed white socialists of all descriptions held their banners and behaved as if they were at a slightly *risqué* fairground. Few of the Asian contingent seemed to be talking. They looked like men (and they were for the most part men) who had come out on to the streets to do something specific. Their faces were carved, motionless, endlessly patient, like those of American Indians, Third World Peasants or of any other group for whom suffering seems to be the main business of life. Annie thought about faces different from these – those of politicians – fat, well-fed faces, talking about immigrant quotas and national identity and the historical importance of free speech. She thought about Labour Governments and Conservative Governments, *Times* editorials, *Daily Express* campaigns and *Daily Mail* exclusives on how Asian families stole council houses from decent English families.

Then, her face set in hard lines, she went up to join the solemn immigrants, standing under the rain with their black umbrellas.

The mood of her contingent had changed as much as her own. Spielman led the search for a suitable banner behind which to march. He announced that he was going to line up behind Southwark Trades Council. Why, Jack asked, Southwark? None of them lived in Southwark. Spielman did not live in Southwark. Spielman, it then transpired, had friends in Southwark. Anyway, he could see the banner, which was more than could be said for Hacks Against Racism or whatever organisation Jack was proposing to follow. Nelly said she didn't want to march with the Indians. Not that she was racialist, but the Indian round the corner had overcharged her by ten pence on a tin of tomatoes and she was off Indians. Annie tried to find the Hammersmith branch of the Communist Party and failed. Snaps asked her why she was trying to find it and she told him to mind his own business.

Eventually they found themselves in between a splinter group from the Anti-Nazi League and a lively contingent from the Gay Liberation Front. After a wait of ten or fifteen minutes (perhaps an attempt by the police at boring them into cancelling the proceedings), the head of the column wound down into Whitechapel Road. After a wait of another five minutes, Annie and the rest were jolted into motion.

"I don't see any Nazis," said Jack, rather nervously.

"Stick around," said Annie.

"We've been kicked out of our flat!" said Jack.

"Uh?"

"Me and Snaps and Spielman. Kicked out."

"Oh."

This was all she needed.

"When?"

"We've got to get out soon."

"What are you going to do?"

Spielman leaned into their conversation.

"Jack has designs on your very nice house, comrade," he said, showing his huge white teeth.

Annie tried to look neutrally cheerful.

"We'd have to vote on it," she said.

"Oh!" said Lucy, "wouldn't it be marvellous? All the people you love and trust. Together."

Nelly did not say anything. Perhaps, when it came to it, both of them would let her down, thought Annie. Women, true to their Freudian stereotype, are castles betraying themselves, never more vulnerable than when most fortified, yearning for their enemies. Perhaps, a prisoner of sex, she too had a hankering for gates to be opened and walls to crumble back into the surrounding countryside. Jesus, she added to herself, is Lucy getting to me? What is all this crap about castles?

She kept her eyes on the road, though, and did not speak of her concern to any of them. She shut back the growing doubts and fears of the day, and marched with the others, as the line of demonstrators, flanked by police, proceeded, by devious route, towards the derelict heart of Whitechapel, the centre of trouble, the place where trouble, if trouble was to be expected, would surely develop.

Conflict developed long before they reached their destination. Just ahead of them a group of West Indian youths in striped woolly hats had linked arms and set up a cry of "Seize the Day!

Organise!" which was having a very bad effect on the nerves and diges-
tion of the policeman nearest to Annie's group. He was a big-
shouldered man wearing leather gloves and, as the youths shouted, he
stole brief, violent glances in their direction. The two policemen ahead
of him seemed disturbed by their colleague's behaviour, the younger of
them occasionally looking back to monitor his colleague's discomfiture.
Beyond these two, however, was another policeman equally irritated at
the sight of young Negroes displaying public aggression – even if it
was purely verbal. He had worked his right hand into a fist and was
punching it into his left palm, his gooseberry-coloured eyes registering
some unseen horror.

It was just after they had turned into Alie Street that Hovis made his
entrance.

Annie wasn't at all surprised to see him. It was somehow a comment
on the dangerously peripheral nature of her involvement with politics.
Not that there was anything wrong with middle-class graduate Communists or, indeed, with middle-class graduates – the circle in which
she moved – but they were, essentially, a doomed and unglamorous
species. That, although it was an article of her political faith, had never
been clearer than when Hovis emerged from the doorway of the Half
Moon Theatre Club, rolling slightly from side to side, a half bottle of
whiskey protruding from his jacket pocket, and, in his right hand, a
large placard. The placard bore a picture of Chairman Hua Kuo Feng,
and, underneath it, someone had written,

CRUSH THE FOUR INSECTS, LADS!

For a start, Hovis had quite clearly lost the quality Annie had once
found almost attractive in him – the sense of certainty. He had never
been, by any stretch of the imagination, an attractive man, but there had
been a splendid, red-blooded refusal to connect with the real world in
his ultra-left dissident Maoism (or whatever it was called) that Annie
had admired as much as Lucy's indomitable obsession with the Condition of Woman. But now, now, there was a beaten look about him. He
had that bowed, shrugging wryness she had seen in Jack and Snaps, and
even, from time to time, in Spielman. A look of defeat, a suggestion of
too much thought in private and too little achieved in public. Hovis, in
his own way, had grown old, and the resignation he had acquired was
terrifying and perfect.

The sight of the march seemed to please him. His face (wizened when
she had known him at Leeds, now pitted and marked like an Aztec's)

129

contorted with mockery but not, as with Jack or Snaps, a graceful, being-observed emotion – something that recalled rather a Victorian clerk, denied all jokes save for private ones, or an undertaker whose delight has long since turned inwards from the light. As Annie watched, he began that strange, jumping movement that she remembered him using on demonstrations. His clothes had not altered – he seemed to be wearing the same desert boots he had worn at Leeds – but the impression they gave was of not having been removed at any time during the last decade. He had a blue combat jacket that reached to his knees, rich in tatters, and practically obscuring his forehead, ears, eyes and nose was a gigantic, green beret. As he began the jumping movement, the beret slid further down towards his mouth.

"Go it, comrades!" he croaked satirically, "Abolish Soviet Socialist Imperialism! Crush the so-called Communist Party of Great Britain! The Gang of Four Has Friends in The Imperialist Heartlands! Beware!"

What on earth had tipped Hovis over the edge? He seemed to have fallen victim to a kind of despair at the schisms of the Left (a despair with which Annie was familiar) but his own despair had become a schism of its own, trawling him into the select band of lunatics that haunt church halls and meeting places, small ad columns and street corners – Flat Earthers, Seventh Day Adventists.

"Blimey!" said Spielman as they shuffled towards him.

"A Chinky!" said Snaps.

"Fucking Hovis!" said Annie.

There was another reason why the sight of Hovis seemed, to Annie, of symbolic import. Jack's almost hysterical rejection of anything that could be described as a group had, at times, carried a certain amount of charm, but now, looking at that small, deranged figure hopping up and down in the drizzle, Annie saw, or thought she saw, the logical conclusion of many of Jack's habits of thought. What had drawn her to Jack was the hope of resurrecting certainty in him, but that certainty had probably never been there in the first place. What had passed between them was, for the most part, misunderstanding, at the time taken for tolerance of each other's positions. Looking at Hovis, mouth curved down in a frenzy of self-deprecation, Annie knew herself to be a serious person, like the Asians behind and in front of her. She could not afford to tie herself to a man who would, one day, come to act the part of a Hovis, sneering in the rain at things he once believed in, burnt out,

130

wasted, no longer of use to person or party.

"Well, comrades," Hovis was saying, in a voice lower than the one Annie remembered, a cracked, tremulous drawl, giving promise of serious mental derangement, "well, comrades. Glad to see you are on the streets marching against the Fascist Imperialist boot-boy lickspittle capitalist profiteer pigs especially the so-called Soviet Union hell-bent on hegemony and world domination not to mention the liquidation of big landlords and robber gentry, eh!"

There was little doubt that Hovis was barking mad, and possibly, as well as drunk, under the influence of some mind-expanding drug. What made the performance so eerie was that, years ago, Hovis had found the set phrases of Maoist ideology easy as breath – they had performed the same function in his life as cigarettes or sweets, suggesting a view of the world that was as unshakeable as change itself. What had thrown him off the rails? Was it, as the poster suggested, the death of Mao and a new Chairman? Had he failed to make the necessary adjustment to the Thoughts of Chairman Hua Kuo Feng? Or perhaps attempted to bring his ideological position in line with the majority around him and, in so doing, blown his mind completely? Whatever had caused it – it was wondrous to behold. It was as if someone had tied Hovis up in a cellar and had, over the last few years, forced him to read nothing but Orwell, inducing what could only be described as fanatical scepticism or over-zealous doubt.

For the policeman on the left, already rattled by the black youths' evident disregard for the superiority of the white races, the sight of Hovis was too much. He could have had no idea of the burden of Hovis' song, or of the fact that what Hovis believed in, at least by implication, was good old British common sense and a bit less of this ideological Marxist claptrap. All the policeman saw was a small, angry student waving a poster and shouting.

"Remember that the so-called Anti-Fascists of the bourgeois capitalist Labour Party, also the reactionary Trotskyist thugs and the dangerous landlord element of the soi-distant Workers' Revolutionary Party, must be lined up against the wall and shot through the bollocks! Remember the intrigues of capitalist roaders in our own party!"

Perhaps Hovis had become involved with fringe theatre? Perhaps this was an Event, designed to provoke soul-searching among the unthinkingly political? Another curious element in the performance – which reminded her increasingly of Jack and Snaps – was the fact that Hovis

131

seemed to be rehearsing the manner affected by many of his University contemporaries, as if, long after it had become possible, he had decided to be one of the lads.

The policeman with the leather gloves, as he came level with Hovis, looked down at him, trembling with fury at Hovis' respectably anti-socialist sentiments. Suddenly Hovis was dragged up off the pavement, flailing his picture of the latest Chinese leader at the winter sky. Hovis' voice screeched up four octaves to the high-pitched whine that had once struck terror into the hearts of the Leeds bourgeoisie. With some of his old *élan*, he shrieked: "Fascist Boot-Boys!" He did not get much further.

The policeman started to punch Hovis in the stomach, hard, and the line of demonstrators, as if impelled by some genuine communal will, snaked off the road, up the pavement and swamped the two of them. Annie had time to think something about hopeless ex-Maoists being better than most policemen, before the fighting started.

I t was worse than she had feared.
Before the policemen ahead of them had time to pull off their enthusiastic colleague, too many demonstrators had piled up against the walls of the houses. When the first few policemen went in to drag off gooseberry eyes, they ended up fighting demonstrators, an activity that both parties took to with some keenness.

Annie's first thought was for Egbert. Lucy was shielding him with her body up against a shop-front, and Annie drove her way through to her. Spielman, moving more quickly than she thought he could, had grabbed Little Luke off Nelly, who was being pushed by a policeman twice her size.

The demonstration was rolling on again – but, like a river split by an island, it had changed its identity; some were coming back to help, some, from behind, passed the fight quickly, hurried on by the Law. A

132

scuffle seemed to have broken out further down.

It was when the vans arrived that it got worse. The game, as often before on these occasions, was to sling everyone within a certain radius into the meat wagons, prior to charging them with assault and battery. Particularly suspect were black or brown men and women, but, in the absence of these, the police were making do with those who carried cameras and any comrade who showed signs of resenting a large hand grabbing him or her by the neck. Annie and Spielman, the only two expert members of the group, stayed motionless, as close to the wall as possible, shielding the two children and Lucy. She could see Jack, Snaps and Nelly fighting their way towards them.

They could not have been more than two or three yards away when, just in front of Nelly, arising from the pavement like a beast from the depths of the ocean, battered placard somehow miraculously in his hand, Hovis stumbled to his feet, his thin, pitted face awash with blood. Somehow he managed to scream something – quite unsatirically – about policemen being the maggots in the corpse of capitalism, which, under the circumstances, was little short of heroic. He narrowed his mouth to a small O-shape, and, holding aloft his banner, like St Joan repeated the phrase. Two very large of the said maggots in the corpse of capitalism then grabbed him by the hair and started to drag him towards the van, one of them aiming a shrewd kick at his thirty-five-inch chest as he did so.

"Vot a' you a'doin' of?" Annie heard Nelly shriek, and bowed her head as her friend flew at the larger of the two policemen, howling in a language that Annie recognised as Hungarian. Spielman got to his feet (by now they were squatting down out of range of the action) but Annie held him back.

"For Christ's sake!" she said. "The kids!"

Lucy was weeping.

"Eggie!" she was saying. "Eggie my poppet!"

Egbert and Little Luke wept with fright as two more policemen went to the help of the one under attack from Nelly. If there had ever been a distinction, in Annie's eyes, between good guys and bad guys among the representatives of the Law, it had, by now, been obliterated. Nelly seemed to be doing rather well. Kicking with both feet – *savate* – Parisian style – she was an Alice-band down, whereas her opponent was already a helmet, two buttons and a cheek wound to the bad.

133

Jack and Snaps were making feeble, aggressive movements in the direction of the fracas – mainly consisting of waving their arms around and saying things like "Watch it!" "Easy now!" and "For Christ's sake!" in deep, uneasy voices. But, with the arrival of another two policemen on the scene of the Nelly Hortobagyi versus City of London Police Force confrontation, they found themselves involved. As the three constables dragged Nelly away, one at her head, the other two holding a foot each, Jack went in after them. He ran, jerkily, in their direction, and, lowering his head, clasped the smallest policeman around the waist, from behind. It was not, in fact, a conspicuously aggressive gesture. Jack resembled a baby ape clinging to its mother, or a non-violent homosexual Rugby player, rather than a left-wing agitator.

The policeman, however, seemed to find something particularly offensive about the embrace. Letting go of Nelly's right foot, he attempted to disengage Jack's hands, twirling like a disco dancer as he did so. Nelly, her progress forward suddenly halted, flipped herself over and bit his ankle, while back into the fray, somehow or other free once more, the bloodied figure of Hovis clambered into Annie's field of vision. Snaps seemed to be having a strained, rational discussion with a senior looking officer in a peaked hat. His attempts to explain away his presence ("I would say at this time that I was simply exercising my in a sense legitimate, in my terms anyway, rights by going for what I would describe as in fact a *walk* with several others in the department that I seemed to be into") were having no effect whatsoever.

The sight of a still free Hovis roused the spirit of the enemy. From all sides they flooded in, as the tiny figure raised its partially destroyed emblem of Chairman Hua Kuo Feng – now a standard at Agincourt rather than a sick, off-centre joke, something worth fighting for, even if, like Annie, you were of the opinion that Hua Kuo Feng was basically an untrustworthy Oriental.

The stress of combat seemed to have brought Hovis nearer to his senses than at any previous period of his existence, and, from deep within him, yet another voice was heard, this time somewhere between Old Hovis and New Hovis, a voice to which he now perhaps aspired, to which he once had shut his face – Possible Hovis, it might be termed, or, The Best of Hovis. He did not embark on a cunning parody of *Krokodil* magazine or *New Left Review*, did not mention the reactionary state capitalist tendencies of the USSR or inevitable destruction of hegemony in the Imperialist heartlands. He spoke in words of one or two or even one syllable. Some memory of a time prior to his having been sent round the bend by the Sino-Soviet Split, the Trotsky-Stalin Split, the Eurocommunist Split and other factions and fissures disfiguring the landscape of the Left, surfaced in him and, in a voice that was not too high and not too low, a voice that made him, if only for a moment, indeed one of the lads, he yelled –

"Fucking policemen! Give anyone a helmet and a few buttons and they think they're God All Bleeding Almighty!"

Swarming up to the standard bearer, the blue uniforms fell on him again, and, now, like an integrated organism, the Blob from the Other Side of Mars or a huge amoeba, divided against itself, Jack, Nelly and the policemen pulsated, swayed and screamed their way towards the waiting vans. Hovis' banner was observable in the middle, a pin stuck in the map to mark the spot where a brave comrade had fallen. Snaps, laughing in a dry, forced manner, followed them, still explaining to the man in the peaked hat why it ought not to be necessary for him to accompany his friends to the station.

It was unfortunate that Annie's group had been stationed towards the rear of the column. In spite of the fact that several people had come back to help from further up the line, the inertia of movement forward and the swift nature of the police action had allowed most of the demonstration to move on as if nothing had happened. It was only within a radius of about twenty-five yards from Hovis that people were being arrested, and, within that area, no one was safe.

The street was almost empty. As Annie and Spielman watched, a big sergeant approached them. His left eye was badly bruised. He looked down at them, breathless. He didn't have an unpleasant face. He looked puzzled rather than anything else.

"How – " he said, "could you take a kiddie on something like this?"

"How – " said Spielman, "could you let something like this fucking *happen?*"

"Hop it," said the sergeant contemptuously.

Annie got to her feet.

"A police officer assaulted a perfectly innocent passer-by!" she said, hearing herself sound rather pompous, "and police officers assaulted and beat up perfectly innocent demonstrators!"

Her voice was close to cracking as she said this. They were throwing Jack and Nelly into one of the vans. Presumably they had already mashed Hovis to a fine Maoist pulp. The sergeant's face twitched.

"You want us to charge you!" he said.

"You bet!" said Annie, "you bet!"

He probably would have done nothing, Annie decided afterwards, if Lucy hadn't interrupted. She had been pressed up against the wall, head to one side, lacing and unlacing her fingers, seeming to absorb the violence rather than see it. Suddenly she snapped her head forward like a snake striking.

"You're evil!" she said. "You're evil. The most evil thing you can do is to have authority over people and you look for that violence violence all I hear is violence, violence on the streets you're violence on the streets you're why it's there with your fat black cars and your don't you look at me like that faces you're not normal you don't have families and you hurt and despise your children you smell of bad pub food and your eyes are quite cold and you say you believe in decency and order but that's a lie, decency and order are people loving each other and caring for each other and policemen belong in hell in HELL IN HELL IN HELL IN HELL!"

A policeman who happened to be passing, who was clearly unacquainted with Lucy's stream-of-consciousness debating technique, grabbed her shoulders. Then the fight started again.

I t wasn't much of a fight this time. Mostly noise.

Lucy/Egbert and Spielman/Luke were hurried towards the vans. The police seemed embarrassed at the fact that they were arresting one-parent families *en bloc*, but they seemed to feel that, if honour was to be preserved, there was little alternative. Perhaps, thought Annie, they suspected Egbert and Little Luke of being members of an infantilist revolutionary group – Toddlers Against Racism or the Pre-School Marxist League. Egbert seemed to be holding Lucy personally responsible for the unpleasant atmosphere. He scored at her cheek with splayed fingers, his mouth turned down with disapproval or unshed

136

tears. Mercifully, this halted Lucy's abuse of the bewildered sergeant, greatly to Annie's relief, since any physical violence near Egbert or Luke was, at the moment, her main fear for the group. Luke himself had stopped bawling and, after a slash at his father, became interested in the top of a nearby policeman's helmet. Suddenly nobody was angry any more. It was squalid, unpleasantly public and pointless, but nobody was angry. Annie saw a group standing by a café further down the road, watching with the same boiled, vulture-like neutrality that they might reserve for a car-crash or a pavement coronary.

They stopped at the van that already contained Jack, Snaps and a rather badly damaged Nelly. By now, there were no more than twenty or thirty policemen left on the street and the rest of the demonstration was out of sight. Spielman and Lucy, unresisting, clambered up among the others. Annie waited on the street, watching the street, watching the sergeant with unbelieving disdain.

"Get on," said the sergeant.

"You are *lucky*," said Annie, "you are *lucky* that – "

She turned from him, her brief gallows address forgotten, as, round the corner of Alie Street and Leman Street, in the shadow of the giant concrete blocks, shipping firms, warehouses or car parks that loom over that part of the East End, came, at a run, twenty or thirty very large men indeed – larger, certainly, than the average policeman. Miners? thought Annie wildly. This far South? Whatever they were, they weren't students or magazine editors or shopkeepers and they weren't – although they might look as if they were – construction workers out for a teabreak jogging session. They were wearing donkey jackets on which was written something in orange, some of them were carrying large sticks and all of them looked very angry indeed. Whether they were Right to Work Marchers or National Front Thugs, who had been barracking the demonstration further down the line, or simply demons of violence conjured up by the bleak encounters of the morning, Annie never discovered. There were no more than ten policemen on the street, but optimistically they fanned out away from the vehicles to confront the invaders (the rest of the march was now well out of sight). The policemen next to Annie grabbed her by the shoulders and hoisted her up to the others. Although she didn't resist he was in too much of a hurry to consider her manner, or her condition, and he threw her, hard, against the metal floor of the van. There were several policemen at the back – on an order they clambered over their charges

137

and spilled out past the sergeant, who, muttering something about little twerps staying put, slammed and bolted the doors on the ten or fifteen intellectual members of the vanguard of the proletariat, who between them, Annie reflected bitterly, would not have been able to hold down a good-sized St Bernard.

The van's driver at this point decided it was time to go, possibly at the sight of an army of giants approaching him (they were shouting something now about somebody or other getting out out out, although who or what was to get out out out, and where where where they were going to go, Annie never discovered) or simply because the crash of the doors was a recognised signal for departure. He engaged gear and accelerated down towards Leman Street. Annie's side hurt, and for a moment she thought of her baby, but stifled the concern as she had stifled earlier doubts and fears. She was, after all, much better at worrying about other people. It hadn't been a hard blow and babies are protected by a –

"Jesus!" said a voice to her left.

It was Jack who, improbably, was wearing handcuffs. Outside they could hear screaming. People were getting badly hurt. In here it was quiet. Nobody spoke. Violence, Annie thought, though occasionally necessary, is, in itself, pointless, ugly and demeaning to those involved. Jack looked like a scarecrow – his red-brown hair standing up in sheaves and his glasses to one side, he scratched his head, holding both hands up in a praying gesture in order to do so.

"Ford's", said Snaps, "will be unamused. Squire."

"Think of the headlines!" said Jack. "Think of the damage done to world capitalism by your defection."

"What defection?" said Snaps.

Annie watched him as Snaps said this, as her doubts of the morning, clarified by the appearance of Hovis, hardened into convictions. Asking herself now, in the swaying van, with cramp in her stomach, what she felt about Jack, she was only able to say that, whatever it might be, boredom, exasperation, love, hatred or friendship, she did not want to feel it any more. It was too painful to carry these things with her.

Spielman was whispering nonsense to his son. Egbert was grinning coyly at a demonstrator with a cut lip. Hovis was nowhere to be seen. What had happened to him? Perhaps he would emerge, like the Button Moulder in *Peer Gynt*, at the next crisis in Annie's life.

"Annie – " said Jack softly, "it's stupid, isn't it?"

"What is?" said Annie.

She hadn't wanted him to say this. She couldn't bear the idea of both of them feeling nothing for each other.

"I don't know," said Jack, "what love *is*, or is supposed to be. But I don't think we're in it. I don't think we ever were in it."

"Jack – "

What a bloody time to have this conversation. And how flat it all seemed. They might have been discussing the weather. What they seemed to be saying was that they had been wasting each other's time.

"Whose baby is it?" asked Jack, in the same toneless, casual way.

"I don't know," said Annie. "It can only be yours or Jake's. Isn't that a joke? Eh?"

"I thought you were . . . "

Jack didn't finish this remark. Mercifully, Spielman was still occupied with his son.

"Living apart doesn't make things easier, does it?" said Jack, "and look where we got to living together. I don't know."

"Oh, there's nothing to be said about that," said Annie, "men and women want different things from each other. Well – I want different things from men than they seem able to give."

"You're dealing with imperfect materials, love," said Jack.

"People," said Annie, "we won't be building a brave new world out of people. We'll have to invent something else. People are used up. People, well, they're . . . Hopeless."

Spielman looked up at her, disconcerted by the use of his catch phrase. But, unlike Spielman, Annie meant the word. She could not rid herself of the idea that Jack was dropping her. That was absurd, wasn't it? It was simply a closing of hostilities between them, a recognition that the cold war of the last year and a half would have, for her anyway, no satisfactory solution. The pain in her side came back, sliding down lower to the belly. Oh my God, she thought, am I losing him? But she couldn't have said whether she meant Jack or the baby.

"T his van," said Jack, "is going at one hell of a lick."

Indeed it was. And, partly because the van was being driven so lightheartedly, and partly because of the absence of fuzz, there

139

was an atmosphere of subdued carnival among the damaged comrades.

"Are you OK?" said Spielman to Annie, still tactfully ignoring her encounter with Jack.

"Fine," said Annie, not feeling it, "what's with PC49?"

She didn't want to think about herself and Spielman. Increasingly, in fact, she was finding it difficult to concentrate on anything, apart from her own physical pain. The driver was not helping. Whoever he was, he had evidently decided, not only to take them to a police station many miles from the scene of their arrest, but also to break the world speed record for a police vehicle loaded with suspects. He cornered with the abandon of a slalom champion and he cornered, or so it seemed, about every fifty yards. The comrades swayed, fell against each other and rolled helplessly about the floor, swearing and giggling to each other.

"This," said Spielman, "is sensory deprivation."

He pitched forward into Nelly's lap. Nelly howled. Egbert, miraculously, had ceased to cry.

From the cab at the front came the muffled sound of what sounded like (surely not?) singing. The demonstrator with a cut lip got to his feet – the consignment of prisoners, thanks to the intervention back at Alie Street, were imperfectly shackled, and, by now, recovering even more of their *joie de vivre*. The feeling of the meeting was, perhaps, closer to a privileged corner of Newgate or the Marshalsea. At any moment, Annie thought, someone will get out a bottle of wine.

"He eez a loony!" said Nelly, groaning and rubbing her head, which had been bumping up and down on the floor, seemingly divorced from her body's nervous system. "My God! Eengleesh police are not so bloody marvellous."

The man with the cut lip, dodging, falling and elaborately balancing, like a man on the roof of an express train in some film of adventure, had reached the tiny, barred grille that connected to the driver's cab. He squeezed his head against the toughened glass and gave a whinny of amazement.

"Ferkin' 'ell!" he said.

"What – " started Annie, but at that moment the van seemed to turn through a hundred and sixty degrees. Somewhere behind them Annie heard a siren. What was *happening*?

The man had collapsed against the far wall. He grinned in a lunatic fashion.

"It's 'im," he said, "the geezer in the beret."

"Sorry?" said Jack.

"The guy 'oo looks like a sparrer."

"Uh?" from Spielman.

" 'E's drivin'."

Hovis. Hovis driving. Hovis driving a hi-jacked police van. Hovis driving a hi-jacked police van full of left-wing demonstrators. Hovis. Hovis. Hovis. He-elp!

That seemed to be the reaction of most of the other members of the party. Death by Hovis, their expressions seemed to say, might be more painful than death by torture at West End Central police station. Did Hovis know how to drive, thought Annie? It would be surprising if he had actually passed a test of any kind, Old Hovis presumably considering them a bourgeois aberration and New Hovis being too cynical and despair-ridden to accomplish anything as positive as a State-organised test. Not that, really, she knew anything about Hovis, or the workings of the Hovis mind. What he had been doing since he left the *Democrat* was a mystery. He might have been attending a school for advanced road users (was she getting delirious?). Certainly the siren behind them seemed to have faded away, and, judging by the fact that they had not braked once since the beginning of the journey, Hovis was more in the mood for risks than his pursuers. God alone knew what was happening back at Brick Lane. The whole of the East End might be alight.

The pain had got worse. The movement of the van wasn't helping. Annie felt light-headed now, for certain, a light-headed, hard-headed woman, that's me. Jack doesn't love me. Jack loves Lucy. Jack doesn't know Jack loves Lucy. Lucy doesn't know Jack loves Lucy. Annie isn't going to tell Jack or Lucy that Lucy and Jack love each other because nobody loves Annie. Nobody does anything for Annie so she does it all for herself and she does it for Jack and Lucy too, she tells Jack and Lucy what to think. Why does Annie tell Jack or Lucy what to think? It is a private affair not a public affair. They are having an affair but it is not public. Public affairs are Annie's business not private matters, and private affairs don't matter to Annie. Do they? Do they?

Hovis, it seemed, had found a motorway. At least, he had found a stretch of tarmac along which it was possible to drive at a speed comparable with that of an Inter-City train. Without hitting anything. It might not be a motorway of course. It might be an aerodrome. It might be that they were all dead and gone to heaven.

Christ!

Suddenly the surface under the van altered and they lurched, bumped and rolled like a ship at sea. Grass of some description. Grass verge of a motorway? A ploughed field? Whatever it was, it wasn't stopping Hovis. Although they had slowed, they were continually moving forward in what felt like a straight line. Then the surface beneath them changed again, this time to what felt like cobbles. A sharp turn and they encountered an obstacle. A loud crash – a sound as of the ripping of giant's trousers – and then back on to the smooth surface – tarmac? – again. A siren. But not the siren of another vehicle. Their very own siren. Hovis was hooting.

In triumph? Annie wondered, and, for the first time, cried aloud from the pain.

I t wasn't Jack but Spielman who was first to her, and Annie recalled the way his physical nature had sorted with hers over the brief months of their almost wordless affair as, with some of the same humorous tact he used in bed, he leaned across her taking her left hand in his right.

"I'll cope!" he said and turned to the man with the cut lip.

"Hammer on that fucking window!" he said, "and get that cretin to stop!"

"What's up?"

"GET HIM TO STOP!"

"Can't you see?" said Jack softly. "She's pregnant."

"Oh Christ."

Imperceptibly she was moving from her social self to the dimmer outlines of a patient. There were faces bent over her, Jack, Spielman, Nelly, Lucy – the people she had, in spite of herself, become fond of, and she could hear the babies chattering or crying but she no longer felt in her own body. She was looking down at herself, a woman in a flowing dress, wearing a blue bandana, her blonde hair falling on the arms of a stranger.

Was the van going more slowly?

It seemed, once more, to be encountering obstacles – was as if waist-high in foliage – while the November rain had hardened and drove against the walls and roof in sheets. Hovis, impervious to the shouts and entreaties of his cargo, continued his eccentric, high-speed progress to his unknown destination. Perhaps they were headed for a retreat for lapsed Maoists, deep in the Essex countryside, or possibly an aircraft carrier of the People's Republic, stationed off Southend in order to aid the re-education of comrades who had been unable to take the pace. Wherever they were headed, they seemed to have reached it, for the van, quite definitely now, was approaching a normal rate of progress.

There was a colossal bang, impact waves shuddered through all of them and the wagon, at last, came to rest.

The first thing Annie realised was that they must be under cover of some kind, for the rain had stopped, or rather, could no longer be heard on the roof, while somewhere above them, in the horrified silence that followed their arrival, she could hear the hiss and gurgle of guttering. People started to hammer on the window. Annie heard the driver's door slam shut with a hollow bang and then the echoing footsteps of Hovis approaching the rear doors. There was a scuffling noise and they swung open in the half light.

They were, as far as Annie could see, in a warehouse of some kind, but one that had not been in use for some years. Annie could see crack-ed, mouldering boxes piled high against a far wall, and above them what looked like a grimy glass roof; above the glass roof were wooden beams, many of them encrusted with the kind of rusty tackle seen on the walls of disused dockland buildings. The place smelt of moss. Spielman and Jack covered her with somebody's coat. Perhaps because of the isolation from the proceedings forced on her by the frightening, ir-regular spasms that were shaking the lower half of her body, Annie was registering everything with unusual clarity.

Hovis was still wearing the beret. Close to, it seemed even larger than before. Its angle, poised at the tip of his nose and allowing only one bloodstained eye access to the light, might well have been a factor in their recent motoring experiences. He was also, and this struck Annie as being the most forcefully absurd thing to have happened so far, grin-ning in a lop-sided fashion. The grin was pure New Hovis, but behind the sceptical, glinting eyes, Annie saw, or thought she saw, more

143

misery, uncertainty and puzzled compassion for the condition of others. It was as if Hovis had had a vision of all the wretchedness of the world and had been transfixed by it. He gawped down at her as Jack and Spielman explained her condition and the need for a doctor, as if he was a part of her pain and as if, by being a part of it, he had abnegated all responsibility for action. Hovis, thought Annie grimly, had simply gone mad like everybody else. When Jack and Spielman had finished speaking, or, to be more precise, shouting abuse at him, Hovis turned his wizened face to them, like a priest about to hear a new confession.

"Fuck!" he said, this time in a fluting, sacerdotal voice – Medium Hovis, thought Annie hysterically. "Better phone one of the lackeys of imperialism who prop up our soi-disant system of socialised medicine, viz. the running dogs of the . . . er . . . 'National Health Service'."

Then he giggled, shyly, and ducked his head in an over-subservient fashion. There was a brief pause while everyone (and, from his puzzled expression, Hovis too) tried to work out whether this "joke", if joke it was intended to be, was intended as a deliberate insult to a woman (Annie, thought Annie, Annie, i.e. me) who seemed to be threatened with a miscarriage, or whether (this seemed slightly more probable) Hovis was unfortunately unable to stop speaking like this.

What made Annie suspect the latter was that Hovis' miniature, red-rimmed eyes were clouded with concern. He looked as if someone else had just spoken, or else he had been forced to repeat the lines against his will. The return of compassion to his eyes was followed by a moderation in the voice and, in a slightly lower tone, he said:

"Sorry. Look. I don't *see* people, you see."

Then,

"I'll phone."

"Where the fuck are we?" said Jack.

"Romford," said Hovis, "I think."

Spielman could scarcely contain his anger.

"*Move!*" he snapped.

"Indeed!" said Hovis, remaining motionless, as the dreamy look returned to his eyes, the suggestion that he was far away from all this. "Indeed. Revisionism has eaten its way into the fabric of my so-called body, comrades, so that I cannot tell the difference between the real and the non-real. This is dialectically logical."

Before Spielman had the chance to rise and hit him, Hovis hit himself hard on the side of the head, as if expecting fragments of malfunction-

144

ing clockwork to spill out on to the floor. Turning swiftly, he ran, or rather scuttled, towards a shabby white door in the far wall, wincing elaborately to himself at something – Spielman, Annie, the march, or, most probably, himself.

W hen she was suffering the pain, she pulled it across her like a cloak. It was in the brief periods of respite that she saw those around her. Some seemed to be leaving, perhaps convinced that at any moment hundreds of vans, not dissimilar to the one in which they had just arrived, would descend upon them. Perhaps Hovis would hi-jack these, thought Annie deliriously, and drive them out to the aircraft carrier. Perhaps . . .

Spielman and Jack were there, though. And Lucy. And Nelly too. Yes. Snaps of course. She hadn't known Nelly was seeing Snaps. They always came back though, didn't they? The women to the men who cheated and betrayed them. Her and Jack, of course. Same thing. Loved him, of course. Far as she was able. One man one woman. Jake a different matter. It was Jack for her. Not Jake. Jack. Jake. Is there a difference?

"He's calling a doctor!" someone said.

"Away from the van!" said someone else. "Away from the bloody van!"

Of course. Not good. Awkward in fact. "Excuse me, madam, is this your police van?" Outside. Would they take her outside? Hovis, knuckles cracking, was racing back across the floor of the warehouse, face puckered up with concern. He stopped in front of them, now a Boy Scout with a Mission. Arms akimbo, he said:

"Phone's no good. Fuzz anyway. Stupid."

He indicated the van and, for a moment, the shadow of a smirk played about his mouth. Then –

"I got wheels here. Quicker. We'll drive her."

For the first time he recognised her. Then Jack. Then Spielman. His sparrow jaw dropping, his head pecked forward over his combat jacket and he said, in the throaty, parody-jargon voice:

"Warliss, Sansom and Spielman. Revisionist swine from the so-called *New Democrat!*"

He stopped in mid-flow, as if someone had just pushed a long metal skewer through the back of his neck.

"Get the wheels, Hovis!" said Jack, "and fast!"

"Sorry – " said Hovis, "I – "

He seemed on the verge of tears.

"Look – "

Then with the same demonic access of energy he was off once more across the warehouse, towards a battered Dormobile parked among a waste of magazines and oil drums, empty bottles and broken footballs. There seemed to be fewer and fewer people around. Was everyone going? Perhaps she was the most dispensable of them all. Leave me here to die. I'm the heroine here. Annie the Head Girl. No one needs me, that's why they can't do without me.

With a blue roar the Dormobile started and shook over towards them. It was hand-painted with slogans, pictures of peasants, men with hammers, women with sickles. Sick women with hammers. Oh Christ, when it hurt it hurt, waves of pain like they had said it would be when the child came. The child. Was this the child then? She didn't know what it was. Never thought about the child, of course. Lucy always on about the child. Never thought about it. Too busy. What was it like when you had a miscarriage? Surely it wasn't like having a baby? Not even this far gone. They didn't ask you to go through all that just for nothing, did they? What did they think little girls were made of? Rats and snails and puppy dog tails. Sugar and –

Jesus Christ, make it stop. Please make it stop. Now. Please.

Spielman and Jack and Snaps got her up through the doors of the Dormobile and laid her on a dirty grey blanket in the back. To her right was a pile of magazines, yellowing, dog-eared, stained with urine, axle grease, cigarette ends and other things of which there were plenty in Hovis' car. With a tremble she recognised the title page of one of them as more people as well as her ("her" was somebody different now, still recording all this for some saintly reason of its own) climbed in around her. Unbelievable. She moved her head sideways and saw, twenty or thirty times, on the spines of the magazines, "THE NEW

146

DEMOCRAT." Ha ha. The New Fucking Democrat. Above her was a poster. Somebody else with a hammer. Or a sickle. Or both. Red. Red revolution. Watney's and blood. Half of blood, please. You can't taste the blood these days you might as well drink water, we do in our household. It thins down family quarrels. The pain waltzed up her, glorying in its ability to make her body twist and turn, master of everything (the pain was male of course), able to make her cry out when he wanted to, to cry out as she was supposed to when he was making love to her but had not or would not or could not for so many years because crying for a man oh Jesus what did they want from you, blood or something? The pain the pain the pain. Regular, like they said, and –

They were moving.

This time Hovis was driving in a relatively sane fashion. He seemed to know his way. They drove through High Streets, battered into anonymity by the passage of traffic, and down quiet, suburban roads, frighteningly empty, paler than the rain. Eventually he turned off a main road, past a statuesque gateway, set into high, iron railings, and slowed to walking pace. There was a bump as he encountered a low mound in the middle of the road, and then they stopped.

Annie remembered the plump, homely woman at Natural Childbirth classes, "When you feel your contractions begin, start with shallow breathing and move up through the levels." Move up through the levels. When you realise that you have not been able to love anyone because you have not thought about any of this and it is far too late to understand anything let alone your own bloody body just move up through the levels. When the vice grips your whole body below the waist simply move up through the levels and when you realise that there is absolutely no doubt you are going to miscarry just MOVE UP THROUGH THE LEVELS. Natural miscarriage. Unstoppable.

I don't want it to happen here, she thought – in the back of this van, surrounded by a derelict magazine, driven by a man who is the apparent wreck of everything I believed in, I want it to happen somewhere neutral, somewhere that will give me hope, somewhere that lets me believe that what I am suffering is not normal. Hovis was bending over her – his sallow face marked by concern. He looked like one of Dickens' suffering errand boys, pinched, white and ludicrously humble.

"Comrade," he whispered, "the . . . er . . . lackeys of imperialism are bringing a trolley."

Through her haze of pain, Annie decided that there was no such thing as Old, New or Medium Hovis, that, in fact, what she was looking at was a miracle, a man who, in the midst of wearing jargon like a facial tic or stammer, in the haze of unguessed-at mental damage that had swamped him since their last encounter, had learned how to feel as others feel and suffer for their suffering. It was the face of Hovis, not Jack or Spielman or Snaps, that shone down at her from the circle of sympathy.

"Oh Hovis," she said, "you shouldn't have. You shouldn't have."

For she was not listening to his words, paying attention only to the red-rimmed eyes, bowing and scraping on the perimeter of tears, full of the fearful apology of a very young child.

After that they got her out on to a trolley and she was being rolled across the concrete, the rain stinging her face as she looked up at the sky, low, murky and miserable between the empty trees. A rattle of doors and she was looking up at strip neon lights, and around her was the buzz of hospital conversations. Jack and Spielman were beside her now. Jake or Jack. What's the difference? The others seemed to be gone. For some reason she felt the distant whispers could be applying to her . . . "poor love" . . . "oh *no*!" . . . "Oh look!" . . .

Where am I? She thought. Casualty? Maternity? Where people are born or where they die? Is somebody being born? Or is it just that I'm dying and too stupid to tell the difference?

Jack had hold of her wrist. Spielman's large fingers were stroking her hair. The trolley rolled forward through patients and doctors, well and sick, visitors and sufferers. At six months, thought Annie, they sometimes live.

T hey never reached the ward or labour room or wherever they were planning to take her. At some point in the journey, under the cracked hospital roof, the pain stiffened and, against her will, she found she was pushing down into her pelvis. They had said something about that. You weren't supposed to do that, were you? People were giving her advice, telling her to breathe or push or pull or something. She wished they wouldn't give her advice. Her body didn't seem to understand it.

Somebody in a white coat was coming up and somebody else (Jack) was shouting while Spielman held her right leg. What in God's name was he doing, holding on to her right leg? People were still passing on either side of them. They had shifted her clothes away and something, good or ghastly, was pushing its way into the world.

I'm bored with all this, she thought suddenly. I'd like to go home now. Please. OK? And then, when she was least prepared, the pain hit her again, a shrewd opponent, biding his time. Look, I didn't want this to happen, she felt like telling them. A woman's right to choose. It's my body, isn't it? Isn't it? Whoever it was forcing their way through her didn't seem to think so. Neither did any of the faces around her – they coaxed and cheered her poor frame as if it were a car or a team or anything but her, Annie, her.

She only later came to think of it as a baby, and later still as a boy, because it was a boy. There was, at that moment in the corridor, certainly a sensation that she was being protected from what was happening to her, and, that, being an objective and polite girl, a girl who didn't like to make trouble – except in an organised fashion – she may have welcomed the opportunity not to see or consider it. Him. Not it. Him. Later, though, she still could not bear to confront what had happened, and that must have been because there was more than high-minded desire to save her unnecessary discomfort, there was, quite definitely, an atmosphere of fear, almost of hatred, an expression on the faces of the doctors and midwives and nurses that said, "Oh, we don't *like* this at all. We don't like you for making us go through with it." It was the faces of the hospital attendants and the eerie silence after the baby fell or was forced through her legs, splitting her in two, falling, so it seemed, miles below, miles over a cliff or something headlong into the waiting arms of someone completely different, someone or something that must have been like oceans of cotton wool, deep dark felt because it was the silence, yes the silence, that made her turn to Jack and then to Spielman, to Jack or Jake and shout or cry – "It's not alive, is it?"

And no, it was not alive (that was better than saying dead, because it had lived only inside her, which wasn't living really) – their faces and the continued silence said that. The silence that seemed to stretch on and on and on, an aching, stupid silence, an eternally missed cue for the cry of a child, the sound she had heard in so many films and imagined from so many books, designed to inform or prepare people like her for something which, in her case, had not occurred. If she had had any doubt at all that something was hideously, grotesquely wrong, a young girl in a blue dress, who might or might not have been a nurse, removed it. The girl rounded the corner, or came from a side entrance, entered, anyway, the rank of faces above and around her, and screamed with fright. Annie knew then that the girl had seen the baby and that it was dead. Him. Not it. Him. Him.

They explained it all afterwards, of course. How the stress of falling (had she been playing some game or carrying on some argument?) had set things in motion, how, just very occasionally these days, babies could live at six months, how there were various factors in her case which militated against a successful delivery, the fact that she was a long way from the kind of equipment needed to preserve life at that stage, the fact that very few hospitals apart from the teaching institutions in central London were equipped with really satisfactory intensive baby care units (that was a political point of course, she noted with sour passion), the fact also that it was not a particularly strong baby or, at any rate, didn't *appear* to be strong because it (he) had been, as she may have noticed, dead on arrival, not breathing, that is to say, possibly because it (he) had never wanted to or never planned to or had come to life too surprised and ill-prepared or (who knew really, they were only doctors) had just died the way we all do, at a bloody inconvenient moment.

They explained it. And the more they explained it the less she understood. They did not understand themselves. Their awkward, failed doctors' eyes told her that. She understood it even less than when she lay in that corridor, looking up at Jack and Spielman, waiting for a cry that never came.

They both stayed with her and she did not cry. It was right that they should both stay with her because either one of them could have been the father, always assuming there was a baby to be a father to, which in this case there was not. Both Jack and Spielman, however, were in some measure responsible for or involved with the tiny corpse that was taken away somewhere by people as uncaring and puzzled as those around her, and set out among flowers or placed in a silk lined coffin or burned in a furnace or freeze dried for scientific purposes or used as a football by grisly mortuary attendants with hollow sunken eyes and clammy hands, was somehow or other (she did not want to know how or where) disposed of, so that, for then and after, it was as if it had never been there. Him. Not it. Him.

In a room somewhere, away from the others, awaiting sedation, it seemed to Annie that all her hopes had died out there in the corridor – what was that line of Auden's?

As the clever hopes expire
Of a low, dishonest decade.

He was a lot of use, wasn't he, when it came to the crunch? Mr W. H. Auden. And she was the same. A few decades later, she was no better. Washed-up lady from the sixties. For Left Book Club read Flower Power or Student Revolution and she could be the same disease. What was it Jack had said? Something about them once imagining that they could change the world. Regret. Annie's creed did not allow her regret, because it had foretold these things, had predicted that she would feel like this and suffer like this and yes, if anyone wanted to know, at that moment it was a creed, a permanence to which she clung, although it offered her no comfort, and it said – "Did you imagine, my *dear*, my bright little bourgeois intellectual, my dear *butterfly*, that anything you did or thought had any effect on the grinding inexorable struggle of the oppressed classes? Did you really imagine that you were exempt? Safe? Your life is lived out in a charmed circle of sterility, one that bears little or no relation to anything or anybody – surely you didn't presume that you, *you* were capable of bearing children? All the children of your class, even the children who romped through higher education in the 1960's with flowers and bells in their hair, noses, ears, eyes and toes are sentenced by history to jostle in the darkness with the bankers, the judges, the doctors and the priests."

She did not speak. Had not spoken since the birth in the corridor. Since the death in the corridor. It had not spoken. It had not cried. There was nothing to say about it. Him. Not it. Him.

She was listening to her voice as they brought in the syringe. She was listening to them, registering the fact that Jack's face was broken up with horror and that Spielman was very still, his big brown eyes steady on her face. "And now," they said, "get the message. Give up. You were always so afraid for others, weren't you? And you should have

151

been afraid for yourself. Worry about Jack and his baby? Worry about your own. Don't try and tell them how to run their lives. Worry about your own. They're taking it away in a black van, its tiny hands clenched, its stone face cold against the world. Worry about yourself, Miss Clever Clever Middle Class Communist. Eh?"

Jack did not speak. Could not. It was Spielman who, she remembered, before the injection sent her under, lifted his huge, helpless hands to her face — something about the tenderness in his face reminded her of the sweet smile Hovis had given her back in the van, a look in the eyes that gave a hint, only a hint, that there were still people in the world who managed to care for others as well as themselves, who had moved from public to private concern, or from public anger to private compassion, people who were brave enough, yes, political enough, to take the responsiblity for others' pain without shrugging off into weakness or neutrality.

"Annie love," said Spielman, with unselfconscious gentleness, "We'll start again. *Again.*"

His serious, troubled face before her, something of the peasant about its overly marked features, reminded her of an extra in a passion play, or a solemn, purposeful worker.

The spark of hope suggested by his eyes shook in the air before her, then, under the spell of hospital valium, guttered into black, unknowing sleep.

PART THREE

I t was a notably awful summer this year – rain, green leaves and chilly evenings had provoked a spasmodic confusion as to the real season, so that sometimes things seemed to be just beginning, sometimes drawing to a close, and only rarely did you stop and decide that this was the height of everything – full bloom. Two years to the day, almost precisely, thought Jack, when the people who were now his extended family had met for the first time. Not counting Hovis. Hovis was the valet rather than one of the family.

Hovis was still peering at Nelly's list. Nelly did not write shopping lists as such. She wrote recipes for walks, rather in the manner of Baedeker or Fodor. "Walk past the tomatoes and do not go off down the side into the freezer place but go straight to the pasta department and get two long packets of the spaghetti that is in the blue paper, I think." Her clear, childish writing was marked by endless crossings out and alterations in spelling, and Hovis, blindly obedient to her command, traced and re-traced his steps like a man following a private system in a maze. Either, however, Nelly's recollection of the place was inaccurate, or else she was remembering a completely different supermarket. The tinned vegetables were not where she had said they would be. The meat had completely disappeared, while the flour, sugar and biscuits had been split up by some officious gremlin and placed at different ends of the store. Jack could hear Nelly's voice as Hovis read aloud the instructions for locating and purchasing something called Nice Bits of Foreign Salami . . . "eet eez just by the breakfast cereals, I theenk!" . . .

"We are not fulfilling our norm, comrade!" said Hovis, grimacing satirically.

Hovis, thought Jack, had been to the top of the mountain, or the bottom of the hole (depending on your political position), and was, perhaps, genuinely destroyed by the experience, whereas Jack, in order to try and keep himself together, had, so far at any rate, managed to

155

avoid going up the mountain or down the hole or indeed anywhere. But he was no longer a jelly. No one in their right mind could accuse him of being a jelly. He resembled, perhaps, an acrobat or high speed chameleon, no longer lumbered with Danby, Simmons or Jarlsberg, but equipped with a whole new range of methods of coping with the world.

"Sean, hi!" said a voice at his elbow.

"Hi!" said Jack.

Sean was popular around Shepherds Bush, or "the Bush" as he tended to call it. One of his plays had been staged in the tiny theatre above the pub – a comedy about a pack of dogs devouring a nun, who, it was subtly hinted, might have been, at one stage of her life, an official of the Women's Gestapo.

"Wargrave-Smith!"

Wargrave-Smith was a man of about thirty-five, dressed in a tattered leather jacket, muddy jeans and huge black flying boots. Westminster, thought Jack idly, or Winchester – anyway, for sure a slightly more impressive public school than the one Jack had attended.

"O'Connor!" said Wargrave-Smith.

Hovis was looking suspiciously at his companion. Did he know about Sean O'Connor? Surely he did. Jack no longer made a strenuous effort to conceal his *noms de plume*. Perhaps he had simply forgotten to tell Hovis.

Sean looked Wargrave-Smith up and down. Slowly. This was the kind of thing Sean often did. Being nobody's fool and a bit of Young Radical Playwright to boot, he looked everyone – theatre managers, agents, visiting royalty, even friends – up and down. Slowly. Wargrave-Smith, used to this kind of treatment from hundreds of Young Radical Playwrights, who cluttered up his theatre with tales of incest, sodomy, arson, multiple rape and other subjects beloved of the advanced bourgeoisie, sneered impassively. He was holding a huge tube of toothpaste.

"Derek Schooner," said Wargrave Smith, "was very excited about *Sodding Off*."

"Where – " said Jack, "was he thinking of sodding off to?"

Both Sean and Wargrave-Smith found this remark confusing. *Sodding Off* was the title of Sean's nun play. Wargrave-Smith, unaware that Sean was in fact a puppet being manipulated for his benefit by a master of disguise, attempted to twist Jack's comment into something comprehensible.

156

"To the *Play for Now* slot," he said, "but I suppose your agent deals with all that."

"Indeed!" said Sean. "Do you know Hovis?"

"Hi Hovis!" said Wargrave-Smith.

"Low Hovis!" said Jacк.

Hovis and Jack sniggered. Jack re-composed his face into Sean O'Connor, and Wargrave-Smith, deciding that Sean was probably on the verge of a nervous breakdown, backed away towards the breakfast foods.

"*Ciao*, Sean!"

"*Ciao* Ciao!" said Sean, mutating just at the end of the salutation into a kind of parody of Spielman. Hovis, when Wargrave-Smith had gone, looked at his friend, puckering up his face, thereby increasing his resemblance to a mummified Buddhist monk.

"Jack," he said, in his serious voice, "you're going to have to make up your mind who you are."

"Sez who?" said Jack.

A t the check-out counter Hovis continued to cluck, in motherly fashion, over the unhealthy way in which Jack was "spreading himself".

"You mustn't spread yourself so thin!" he kept saying, as the two of them crammed their purchases into a huge leather suitcase belonging to Snaps, "you'll spread yourself too thin."

Jack thought this made him sound like a processed cheese and said so.

Actually he enjoyed talking to Hovis about his identity crisis. Or rather, his lack of identity crisis, as he now liked to call it. Most people in Jack's current situation would probably suffer from an identity crisis. If any normal person were addressed as Sean, or for that matter Steve, Ron and Paul (all aliases currently in use) in the course of a week, they might well end up with what Nelly called "the screaming had-dabs".

But not Jack.

"Annie says," said Hovis, "that if you didn't use all these silly names you could be making quite a name for yourself."

"I am," said Jack, "making a name for myself. I am making five or six separate names for myself."

"Snaps," said Hovis, wheezing as they moved towards the escalator that leads from the north side of Shepherds Bush Green to the shopping precinct on the south side, "Snaps is falling behind in his quotas."

"Snaps," said Jack, "is fucking living off us. All of us."

Whichever way you sliced Snaps (and slicing him might not be a bad idea), he was a problem. Hovis, who was walking backwards at the front end of the suitcase, accelerated down the escalator in reverse phase, his legs whirring. Only his small, calico-coloured face was visible above the case, the rimless glasses glinting with panic.

"So-called bourgeois gravity," said Hovis, "is proving a problem for me, comrade."

Jack too discovered that his feet were moving faster and faster – unable to stop himself, he was having to run to keep up with the progress of the miniature lapsed Maoist. Hovis' head bobbed above and below the level of the suitcase as, at a truly shocking speed, they neared the bottom of the escalator.

"Newton," said Hovis, "the bourgeois empiricist charlatan, will not deflect me from my allotted function, which is to deliver this suitcase to the Workers' Commune of Sinclair Gardens. I maintain – "

But his legs, pedalling faster and faster, encountered a gap in the pavement and Hovis, giggling with hysterical nervousness, fell, pushing the case up and away from his glasses as he did so. The catch slipped and a rain of groceries, a technicolor yawn of packets, tins, fruit, meat and veg, reared up over the concrete, stalled and fell to earth.

"The work of saboteurs and wreckers!" said Jack.

"The Household will not be pleased!" said Hovis.

T he Household.
Jack shuddered at the word. At last, by a series of accidents and misadventures, they had arrived at that mystic state canvassed by Lucy

in the drab flat in Finchley two years ago. Was it only two years? It felt like twenty. The Household.

"Oh Lukey!' she had whined on countless occasions, "oh Lukey. Wouldn't it be marvellous? All of us living together and raising everyone's children together and the men sharing in it and everyone you love there, just *there*, sort of equal and participating."

Hovis and he began to pick up the week's food. The truth about Lucy was that she was becoming rather threatening. She had done her hair differently, she was able to speak, almost all the time, in a normal voice, she had a job, quite well paid, in a publisher's office and she had actually succeeded in getting her manuscript published. She had even been seen on television talking about Mothers' Rights and feminist journalists kept ringing her up for her views on clitoral orgasm or the Equal Opportunities Act.

They were, however, sleeping together on a regular basis. This was not good. This was committing. Also, however, extremely pleasurable. There was something liberating about going to bed with someone who could be quite as embarrassing as Lucy, and for Jack, who found sex an embarrassing business at the best of times, her cries of "Oh deeper deeper with your cock!" and "You love me so well with your huge self!" raised the act of copulation to so frenetic a pitch of embarrassment that it was very near wantonness.

"How are things," said Hovis, divining his thoughts, "in Studio One?"

"Studio One" was Hovis' name for the room in which Lucy and Jack slept. Studios Two and Three contained Annie and Spielman and Snaps and Nelly, respectively. Hovis slept in what he called his "hutch" – a cupboard between the bathroom and the lavatory.

"I feel pressured," said Jack.

"The Household feels, comrade, that, ideologically speaking, it would be satisfactory if you could lose your paranoid fear of the opposite sex and – "

"I know what the fucking Household thinks!" said Jack.

"Sorry, sorry!" said Hovis, meekly, packing toilet rolls into the suitcase.

Of course the Household felt that Jack should do the decent thing to Lucy. It was what they meant by this that was the problem. They couldn't mean marry her. Annie and he were still married, for a kick-off. The only reason they hadn't applied for a divorce was because everyone in the Household thought marriage was completely irrelevant and degraded women. That was their story anyway, and, for the moment, for their different reasons, they were sticking to it. Perhaps they would ask him to link hands in some grisly, impromptu ceremony at the dead of night – "With this hand I vow to maintain a permanent relationship with thee and thy meaningful son, Egbert of this parish!" The whole thing to be rounded off by some wanker reading from the work of Dylan Thomas or Adrian Mitchell or somebody equally awful.

He would call in at the Post Office at the bottom of Richmond Way to see if there was any post for Loesli. Saturdays were a good day for Loesli letters. He would have to work out an excuse to Hovis.

They had finished re-packing the suitcase.

"Well – " said Hovis, as they started off through the shopping precinct, "at least you're getting it."

Jack looked at Hovis, his small pointed head, his skin, his turkey neck, his birdlike nose, his wire glasses, his emphatic ears, his hair, resembling an inefficiently reaped cornfield, and his worried little eyes. Hovis had presumably never had a sex life. He was owed one.

"It's all this pressure that I can't take anyway," replied Jack, as they tottered into Richmond Way. The Post Office was in sight. He would have to dump Hovis. "Oh, by the way, I've just got to pick up something from the Post Office, OK?"

"Fine!" said Hovis glumly.

Unlike Jack, Loesli was a great letter writer. Not to friends (Loesli had no friends) but to the newspapers, public figures, industrial concerns, mortgage companies and car hire firms. As a reward for his industry, Loesli received long, oily letters, full of personal concern for his welfare. The letters were usually stencilled and Loesli's name (often mis-spelt) was typed into a space left vacant for it.

Today there was one from the bank, informing S. Loesli, Esq, that his deposit account was £8,000 in credit and that his current account was overdrawn by £356. Loesli, being a businessman, wasn't unduly disturbed by this. He knew that, in setting up any paying concern, a little credit is essential. There was also a letter from a firm called Buschenschaft, which read –

Dear Mr Loesli,
    We are delighted to be able to send you full colour reproductions of the Buschenschaft range of kitchen equipment, designed by our

160

kitchen specialists and in a variety of materials, woods, laminates and plastics.

We also enclose a descriptive brochure for our new kitchen range complex, *Terracotta*.

Yours sincerely,
Brian Laing.

Enclosed were pictures of kitchens – peasant-style interiors, warmly lit, Teutonic halls of gleaming efficiency, all giving promise of perfect homes in which clean careers and cleaner relationships could be acted out. The other letter was thick. Loesli, being a shrewd man of business, knew what was in it. He folded it into a tight wad and put it in his back pocket, making a mental note to conceal it as soon as he got back to the house. No one, but no one, must find this letter. Not yet, anyway.

C ooking for six people was actually blooming hard work, when you came to think about it, even though she liked doing it because Nelly's speciality was cooking, for Christ's sake, but cooking for Hovis (which made seven) was a different kettle of beans. Hovis was a vegetarian and, in Nelly's opinion, the best thing to do with vegetarians was to throw them to the tigers at Whipsnade Zoo. If a vegetarian showed his face in Auntie Gizzy's farm or Cousin Stanco's small-holding they would be run off the bloody property and no mistake. My God! Anyone living without veal cutlets and belly of pork and paprika sausage and bacon in the morning, not to mention goulash. One of these days she would sneak up on Hovis and force goulash down his funny little face, which might make him peek up a bit. God, he looked like a stick insect with VD.

There was a lot to be said for Communism, thought Nelly. Not that it seemed to do much good in the big wide world (My God, Communism was nothing but trouble in the big wide world with those filthy

161

Russians raping everyone) but at 23 Sinclair Gardens it seemed like a very good idea. With Communism, everybody had to be in for meals. It was a House Rule, which certainly made a change from the bad old days when Mikey would be down the pub pissed as a fart with some secretary. People obeyed House Rules. Apart, of course, from bloody Jack. Jack Jack Jack. Funnily enough, it was Jack, much more than Mikey, who was causing the real problem.

Having put the Hovis funny food on one side, Nelly started to carve the smoked ham with a serrated knife that did the job lovely. Part One of the Keep Mikey in Studio Three For Ever Plan was to go into action at lunchtime today, with Annie and everyone joining in, so she wanted to make it nice. Smoked ham and potato salad would do to start and then they could fill up on the mackerel fillets, pork with sauerkraut, the apple flan and the big chunk of Jarlsberg she had bought yesterday. Buying the Jarlsberg had been a clever joke because it was a way of getting at the names and although the names weren't the half of it they were a start.

It was Mikey's baby. It had to be. It couldn't be Jack's. Last year she had only ever twiddled with Jack, not so much twiddling as bloody rape in her minds, and it would be very unfair if something so stupid and unpleasant could lead to her having a baby. Blimey. If only she and the girls hadn't been so funny and secretive with each other last year when the men were up the road at Elgin Crescent, but of course that was inevitable when you had people coming and going with no one to keep an eye on them.

She began to lay the table in the front room, humming to herself, as, outside, the unpredictable June day went bright, faded to dullness and back once more into brilliant sunshine. The wind tugged at the locks of the trees outside. Somewhere on the other side of the road, someone was playing that pop song about crying in Argentina. Two plates on top of each other, a napkin between, small glasses for the Slivovic, wine glasses for the home-made plonk Mikey and she had brought back from Yugoslavia after they had all made it all up after the march.

Jack was the heart of the trouble. Because with a man like Mikey he might grumble and loaf all the time, but you knew where you were, whereas with Jack it was like living with eight different people. One day he was one thing, the next another and, even when you were having the simplest bloody pow wow with him about beans or sprouts or something, his eyes had that cloudy, faraway look, as if he was listening to some jolly interesting radio programme in his right ear hole that you didn't know about it. He was, as Annie kept saying, fucking slippery, and, in a well organised, well run household, that stuck out like a sore arm. Also, of all of them now, he was the only one who kept treating his woman like she was a cross between a doormat and a ground-to-air missile.

As she finished laying the table she saw Jack and Hovis staggering up the front garden with the suitcase full of shopping. For a moment she felt sorry for them – she couldn't have said why. There was a groan from the hall and she heard Jack thud up the stairs two at a time, while Hovis made a scrabbling sound with the suitcase like he was a weasel and trying to gnaw through the locks or something. Something about the way Jack was singing, loudly, to himself as he came in made Nelly suspicious.

He was up to something. She would have to go through his trousers pockets if bloody Lucy wouldn't. She stood back from the table, folded her hands over her huge, projected stomach and beamed maternally at crockery, cutlery, glass and linen. Lunch soon. Thank God for that.

H ousehold lunches, on Saturdays anyway, followed a strict pattern.

First they had bits of sausage and Slivovic and walked around discussing things, usually politics because that was the most important thing, apparently. Annie was running something called a Cuts Campaign, which Spielman wrote about in his new magazine (he seemed to start one almost every week) and this morning there was a lot of toing and froing about Cuts. Somebody or other had found a secret document about Cuts which said that the bloody Government was going to chop all the doctors and the nurses and the hospitals up into little pieces and unless you went with the bloody Arabs to Harley Street you were going to have to wait ten years to have your head examined if you fell off a ladder by which time – it occurred to Nelly – you would probably be as dead as a door handle anyway. Nelly did not join in this conversation but it was the usual thing about how, pretty soon, it was going to be necessary to give all the workers a Sten gun, and everybody, apart from Jack, agreeing that eventually the gutters would have to run with blood. This time, it was Annie who started in on him. Suddenly, without warning, she turned from a completely different conversation and said –

"Of course, Jack doesn't really think Cuts are the Issue. The real issue for Jack is *saying* publicly burning, passionate things and *doing* fuck all."

"That's it, love," said Jack, "that's me. And you do things all the time now, don't you? I mean you're always working at it and I think that's great."

He said this in quite a sincere way, but there was something so quirky about his expression that it only made it look even more like he was taking out the piss in a particularly subtle and underplayed way.

"Despite his flippant and counter-revolutionary attitude to questions of the day," said Hovis, "comrade Warliss provides a more than adequate contribution to the domestic economy of the glorious Workers' Commune of 23 Sinclair Gardens. In other words – he pays his way."

Nelly stationed herself next to Lucy, wondering whether she would get a go on Egbert before she moved into her Plan of Attack for Keeping Mikey in Studio Three. Egbert himself was running a red plastic lorry up Mikey's leg and looked more like the sort of person who had goes on you, rather than the other way around. Nelly wandered over to the table, super-duper casual and said –

"Vot about the agenda for the house meeting?"

"I would like to put a proposal," said Mikey, as they drifted towards their places, "that the house acquire Draught Guinness on a regular basis."

"Once a day sort of thing!" said Jack.

"Indeed, squire!" said Mikey.

"Seconded!" said Jack.

This was a good example of the sort of behaviour Jack brought out in Mikey, and Nelly found it more than usually irritating. Always egging him on like a bloody schoolboy when really Mikey was as responsible as the next persons. Hovis perched on the edge of the rickety chair that Nelly had given him. His lips were pursed and his forehead wrinkled. At first Nelly thought he had caught sight of the nut cutlets, then she realised that Egbert was banging his head against Hovis' bollocks.

"Draught Guiness – " said Hovis, "is an emetic!"

"It might not be a bad idea," said Spielman ponderously, "for us all to sort of, you know, state our *earnings* before we get into consumerism on that one, eh? Consumerism being a little bit . . . well . . . shall we say . . . Hopeless."

He said this like he was a nice Scoutmaster and Nelly, as often with Spielman, felt frightened of him. In fact, the more he looked gentle and nice, the more Nelly felt he was a great big bear and going to eat her for dinner. He was, anyway, on Nelly's side in this, because he found Jack's antics with Mikey quite as irritating as did Nelly, although for some blooming complicated reason, most likely.

"Ham and potato salad, you people," said Nelly. "I think we should deescuss Jack on the agenda!"

"Why – " said Jack, in his don't-ask-me-to-be-reasonable voice, "do you think it so important *I* should be discussed?"

"For a start," said Nelly, "you always are grumbling!"

"I'm a dissident!" said Jack, trying to laugh it off.

"I move – " said Mikey, coming to Jack's rescue, "that Hovis be on the agenda."

There was a bored kind of pause. No one wanted to discuss Hovis. Not even Hovis. There was nothing to say about Hovis except that he was a horrid little sarcastic vegetarian with a face like a dried up prune.

"I second the motion about Jack!" said Annie.

Jack looked at her. This wasn't like a normal house meeting. Usually people got terribly steamed up about things like the lavatory – just now they were all looking, or trying to look, jolly bored about something that ought to have been discussed when the cows came home.

"Eeet eez the names," said Nelly. "You have started weeth the names again. I theenk we should deescuss the names!"

Jack opened his eyes very wide and gave the kind of unconvincing laugh Mikey used when you asked him whether he had been trying to get up other women's drawers. Lucy cupped her chin in her hands and, shaking back her curls, she leaned forward on to the table. Really she had spruced herself up even more lately, thought Nelly; in that white petticoat thing she looked quite a saucy handful, when you came to think about it.

Egbert started to do a convincing impression of somebody arguing.

Walking round in a tiny circle on the far side of the table he nagged at himself, madly. "No!" he kept saying, shaking his index finger. "No! No!"

"What names, anyway?" said Jack.

"Sean O'Connor," said Annie.

"Steve Greatorex," said Spielman, "who writes rather bad pieces for the *Morning Star*."

"And Ron thingy – " said Annie, "who was writing for some Trot paper the other day. I mean Christ – have you got some jerk called Simon Carrington Jones up your sleeve who enables you to write for the Tory house magazine?"

"There's Paul Tennent!" said Mikey.

"How the fuck did you hear about him?" said Jack, rattled.

"Who is he?" said Annie.

"He was an actor," said Jack, "he's dead now. He fell under a bus. Under two buses. Driven by Sean O'Connor."

Nelly started to clear away the first course.

"Paul Tennent," Jack was saying wearily as she came back into the room, "was an actor with the BBC drama repertory company, if you want to know, and I faithfully promise you he jumped out of a window, depressed at the standard of his own acting. He is no more. He was only alive for two days, poor sod, I mean the average mayfly did better than Paul Tennent. Give the guy a break."

Spielman was shifting about in his chair doing the puzzled look he often used in house meetings – he might look as though he was one step behind, thought Nelly, but this only it made more certain that he was in fact two steps in front.

"Issue *is*, Jacko," he said, "issue *is*. I think. I don't know but I think that all of us are a Unit. Right. I mean there are differences in our area of interest but we are sort of working towards a common aim. Broadly speaking. Right?"

166

"The complete elimination of class enemies of both left and right and the annihilation of big landlords and robber gentry?" said Hovis, following this up with a muffled sort of laughter.

Annie and Spielman, and, to be creepy, Mikey, gave Hovis a look. From the smirk on Jack's face, Nelly realised that this was supposed to be funny. She didn't understand Hovis. He took the michael so much you thought he was serious. He was another one led astray by Jack. As she served the mackerel, Lucy spoke, twisting her heavy rings round her fingers as she spoke. Egbert watched her with awe as she said –

"We pick on Jack because he can't make up his mind."

A silence. It was funny. Whenever Lucy said something there was always a silence. It was as if she was, like Spielman, two steps ahead of everyone, and, at the same time, like Jack, several steps behind, or, to put it more fairly, it was like she was a million billion miles ahead and behind of absolutely the lot of them.

"Choice – " she went on, "choice is his right, his spirit."

There was another silence. Spielman slurped loudly. You could tell he didn't like her really but was too clever to say so on account of she was mixed up with all this women's liberation rubbish. She was talking still, and it was as if it hurt her to talk, as if somebody invisible was criticising everything she said.

"You can't chain a spirit to a historical process, can you? Even one it believes in. What none of you understand is that the historical process is of itself spiritual."

Jack did not seem to enjoy this any more than anyone else. Yawning, he pushed back his chair from the table.

"OK," he said. "Put me on the agenda!"

"Eet eez the first time we have had anyone actually on the agenda," said Nelly, wondering why he looked so sly.

They were not eating. Stupid of her to have brought it up at the meal really, thought Nelly, and, to get them all worked up, she went to the kitchen door so you could smell the loin of pork wafting out, rich, fatty, sumptuous, cut through with the sharp vinegar of the sauerkraut and grilled so the crackling was hard to the teeth, but you could nibble through until the white meat melted in your mouth. Oh my blooming God. Roast loin of pork. That was on the agenda all right.

It was then that Jack got up from the table.

"You finish?" said Nelly sharply.

"Er . . . thanks . . . but . . . er . . . yes thanks!" he said.

167

"That's OK," she said, really sweet as sugar although inside she was boiling at him turning up his nose at her food just because she put him on the agenda. Then, as Jack went out into the hall, she dashed to his plate, picked up the half-eaten pork and followed him up the stairs. He was going towards Studio One, and, still carrying the lovely loin and juicy sauerkraut, Nelly followed him in.

The room stank of sex. Blimey. What with that and the mascara on the sheets, the piles of crumpled paper that were Lucy's book, and the numerous tattered files that contained Jack's correspondence, it was a cross between a brothel and an office. Nelly waved the plate at Jack.

"Thees ees pork loin!" she said.

"I know it's fucking pork loin," said Jack.

"Eet eez done een eets own gravy!" said Nelly, feeling that she should not have to recommend food in this way to a normally healthy man. "Eet eez also – "

Then she stopped. On the carpet, beneath her feet, was a thick blue file, much smarter than any of the others. Instead of Jack's sprawling, disorganised handwriting in which no two letters seemed to be transcribed the same way twice, there was a neat, typewritten message on the front. That was interesting enough in itself. What was a bloody sight more interesting was that, when he realised she had seen it, Jack made a grab for the file, but little Nelly was too clever for him by half as much again mate. She put her shoe on it and peered down so that she could get a good look at whatever was written on it that he did not wish her to see.

She was quite calm now, although Jack was not, and when she had read it, twice over to make sure she had understood, she put the pork and the sauerkraut on the duvet to her left and smiled her sweetest, sugariest, most deadly Hungarian, butter-wouldn't-melt-in-my-mouth mate smile and said in perrrfect English.

"The Loesli correspondence!"

Jack kept his hand on the file. Nelly raised her eyebrows.

"Who is Loesli, Jack?"

He still did not move.

"Is he by any chance a relation to Mr Jarlsberg?" Jack looked up and straight into her eyes. Then he said, without blushing, softly,

"No, Nelly. No – he isn't."

Nelly knew when people were lying and she was as certain as she could be of anything that, for once, Jack was telling the truth. She

168

released the file to him and sat on the bed, next to the pork.

She felt tired and old. Nobody liked her. She was a funny foreigner and she cooked. That was all. She didn't want to go downstairs with the others. She wanted to stay here with Jack, for his eyes were as unhappy as she was.

"Loesli," said Jack patiently and slowly, as if he were telling someone all their relatives had just died in a multiple car crash, "is the name of a well known brand of yoghurt."

"I know thees!" said Nelly.

"And that," Jack continued, "is the only connection that Mr Loesli has with the mythical Mr Jarlsberg."

He was giving her about seven hundred volts of sincerity, which involved turning the mouth down and trying to make the eyes water by remote control. It seemed to be having some effect. As well it might. Loesli, for Christ's sake, did actually exist, didn't he? That was what was so frightening about him. If he needed further confirmation, he had about two hundred of the little sod's letters in the blue file.

"Why did you start in on me?" he said gently.

"Mikey . . ." said Nelly, "and I . . . are not . . . right . . ."

"Ah."

Of course. She was terrified it was his baby. Just as he was. And, in her housewifely way, she was trying to tidy him up, to arrange him on a shelf with Lucy, admittedly for more practical reasons than the gremlins down there. He patted the Loesli letters and put his arm round Nelly.

"I know – " he said, "that the kid isn't mine!"

"How?" said Nelly.

"Because – " said Jack gently, "I had a sperm test!"

"A *vot*?"

What an extraordinary thing to say! Jack had never had a sperm test – the mere idea of masturbating into a glass tube and allowing your semen to be passed around, prodded, boiled, whipped up and probably even drunk by a horde of medical students had always struck him as the lowest depths to which Science had persuaded Man to sink. But there it was. He had said it and it seemed to be bringing some comfort to Nelly, so it would not be wise to retract the statement.

"Yes," he said, "years ago."

"But why?"

"To see if I could have children."

"Weeth Annie?"

No. Not weeth Annie. Nelly would be sure to mention it to Annie. And Annie would wrinkle her brow and mutter, "Sperm Test? Sperm Test?" and then add, "He's lying again." Which he was. But he was lying for a purpose now. For some ridiculous reason he wanted to reassure this woman, even to make her happy.

"No," he said, "I had it on spec. She doesn't know . . . I'm . . . sterile . . . "

"Egbart," said Nelly in a puzzled voice, "is not your son?"

For one wild, lunatic moment Jack contemplated suggesting that he had had a sort of sperm remission in the case of Egbert, then decided that, even in her present amiable and credulous mood, Nelly might find that a little difficult to believe.

"No," said Jack solemnly, "but you must never mention that to anyone. Especially not to Lucy."

"Vy not?"

"She doesn't know I'm sterile. Has no idea."

"Then she has twiddled with another man?"

"Er . . . yes . . . I suppose she has . . . it's difficult to tell . . . "

"Christ, surely she knows when she has twiddled with another man? Or does she do it in her sleep or something?"

Jack's brain raced. Or, to put it more accurately, throbbed and writhed within his cranium at the strain this conversation was putting on his powers of fantasy.

"She doesn't know about the sperm test. I never told her. She mustn't know. No one must know."

NOT EVEN YOU! he thought of adding. He should never have got involved with the sperm test. It was proving pretty difficult to dismantle. Human beings, Jack reflected, are capable of believing anything, however harmful or absurd, to be true, and, if they wish something to be true, as Nelly evidently did this latest story, something as minor as implausibility will not stop them. If only he wanted to believe something. But no. He saw the process at work in himself and in others too closely. "You're a conjuror," Annie had told him once, years ago, "to you everything is magic. But you don't believe in it."

Nelly was still catching up on the sperm test saga.

"Who is Egbart's father?"

"A man called Hillmore," said Jack soberly.

He could see Hillmore clearly. Well, fairly clearly. He was bearded. He wrote poetry.

"My Christ!" said Nelly.

Then –

"When did you have thees sperm test?" she asked.

"When I was sixteen."

Surely she would not believe *that*.

"So eet weel not look like you," said Nelly eventually.

"No," said Jack.

The much vaunted resemblance of parents to children was another confidence trick, of course; the merest hint of biological flattery, a suggestion that hair matched hair or eyes, eyes and the proud parent discovered his or her identity in the stranger they had brought into the world with so much love and difficulty. Identity – that word again – the word at the heart of his problem, a circle around the unfaceable complexity of birth, that mystery he seemed, so far at any rate, fated to avoid or to be betrayed by.

That road to identity was barred to Jack, was it not? Although there had been times, especially recently, when he had felt able to cast himself as Egbert's father, the necessary star in his life, he could not, in the end, allow himself that luxury. There seemed no faith and no role to act as a barrier between him and what the philosophers called "world stuff", raw, existential static, pain and pleasure that could not be explained away.

"You just be nice to Lucy," said Nelly, catching at the direction of his thoughts.

"Lucy thinks she loves me," said Jack, "but I can't . . . I don't know . . . I can't believe anyone could love me, you see. I don't think I amount to that much. I think anyone who loved me would be an idiot."

"But you want to be able to love her, Jack, don't you?" said Nelly.

"Oh I *want* to, Nels. But it's hard, you see. It's so fucking awkward."

171

There was a pause. Jack looked at the carpet. Then at Nelly. She had a shrewd, tolerant face, he decided. Like most other things in his life, he had misjudged her.

"You see," he said, "if I could accept myself, I could accept her. But I don't see what I add up to. I can't make sense. I don't know. I need a Road to Damascus. Something. To let me see myself. And I've waited. I've waited so fucking long for it, Nels. I just sit here turning to stone. Like Uncle Spielman says, hopeless. Just hopeless."

D own below Jack could hear Egbert and Little Luke. They were rolling things down the stairs. He could catch the odd, distorted word from his son. Egbert now used a weird dialect, refining and elaborating the simplest words – "lorry" became "loreleiala" and "fork-lift truck" "fucka leefa ticka rack" (both these words loomed large in Egbert's current vocabulary).

Egbert. Egbert and Lucy.

He thought about Lucy sitting there on the bed with Nelly as outside the wind rose, batted through the shabby gardens and then subsided, making way for more fitful sunlight. New, successful, feminist Lucy. He felt Nelly's hand on his arm.

"Now," she said gently, "tell me about Mr Loesli."

"Loesli," said Jack, "is a guy I met this spring." He wondered whether to tell her. Finally he did.

"He would not be liked in the Household," he said. "He's . . . well . . . not to put too fine a point on it . . . he's a capitalist."

"Yes?"

"I don't think even your husband or Hovis would get along with him."

"Mikey is not a reactionary!" said Nelly, in the tones of one who might say, "Mikey pays his bills!" or "Mikey does not rape little girls!" Nelly, like most conventional people, had absorbed the habits of

172

thought of her environment and accepted them without question. If she had been living in a semi-detached house in Harrow she might well have developed a different but similarly coherent set of convictions about the best way to hang net curtains or the necessity of neat gardens.

"Loesli," said Jack, "sets up deals. He buys cheap and sells dear."

She was puzzled that Jack could even know such a person.

"But you like heem!"

"I keep his letters for him."

"Why?"

"He's on a few fiddles. He uses the Post Office up the road as a forwarding address. It suits him to have someone around to pick things up for him."

Nelly couldn't understand how Jack could have a close friend outside the charmed circle of the house. It was true that, since moving in there, the outside world had become even more remote than it had been. No one seemed to see their parents. Even when, like Annie or Spielman, they went out into the world with apparent gusto, they seemed to need the security of this communal womb.

"How can you like a capitalist?" said Nelly.

"I can't dislike them all," said Jack, "I even find myself acting with one."

"Then you don't have any principles. Poleetical principles."

"None that I'm not capable of breaking."

"You are like that weeth love I think, Jack!" said Nelly.

"Yes," said Jack, "I think I am."

He would do something for Nelly anyway. Set her right with that hopeless ex-crony of his, who was even now downstairs well into his fourth glass of rosé, his thin, dark face flushing cruelly with the alcohol.

"I'll sort Loesli out," he said, "and as for you and Mike, he'll be fine when the baby comes."

Always assuming biology does not reassert itself in too tactless a fashion. Always assuming it wasn't ready-equipped with glasses and red hair and a big nose and always assuming it was *there*, unlike Annie's –

He wasn't going to think about Annie's baby.

"Can I give you some advice, Nels?" he said.

"Vot about?"

"Mike."

"Certainly!"

Nelly looked very cunning at this remark.

"What you need to do with Mike is to take him in hand."

"I try to take heem een hand for bloody years and – "

"Mike essentially wants to be ordered around."

"Hein?"

This theory of Snaps' personality had obviously never occurred to Nelly. She seemed to suspect some kind of trap, possibly that Jack was a double agent sent by Snaps to confuse and torment her for, cocking her head to one side, she said –

"Who tell you thees?"

"It is obvious."

As indeed it was. As clearly truthful as the story about the sperm test had been clearly false. But it did not fit in to Nelly's picture of the world. The idea of Mikey as someone who might require ordering around evidently involved the rearrangement of a whole range of other preconceptions, in order to make way for this one. Nelly squinted at Jack, cautiously, through one eye, as if he was a potential bargain.

"Ordair heem around, eh?"

"Sure," said Jack.

"Put heem on the agenda!"

"Why not?" said Jack.

Nelly looked Jack up and down. Then she sniffed in the back of her throat and slapped her thigh. She looked, briefly, like a schoolgirl actress attempting the role of a bluff nobleman. After another shrewd shift of the tongue round the mouth she got to her feet, smiling broadly now, and, from deep within her, shaking her sturdy frame, making the black hair bounce on the tanned forehead, a guttural laugh spread in shock waves the length and breadth of her body.

"Put heem on the bloody agenda," she said through her laughter, "all the bloody men on the agenda, hein? On the bloody agenda, squire, and no mistake. Move ovair, brothers!"

T here was a lot of stuff then about how they should talk more often and how she had always felt recently that Jack was not on her side and other people in the Household had felt thees and they fancied each other a bit, didn't they? But not enough now to do anything about it and it had never worked out but that was to the good, wasn't it, with all of them living on top of each other you couldn't have everybody climbing into bed together and that they all respected each other's "space" (this was a word she had picked up from Lucy) and surely that was better, wasn't it? Jack listened, feeling only that Nelly was slipping away from him, as Annie had done last year.

The real question was – what was he going to do about Loesli's letter? The one in his back pocket, the one he hadn't brought out to open yet because he knew what it contained. He listened to Nelly's flood of talk.

Nelly's real wish, of course, had been for him to cut the slender, almost invisible threads of lust and curiosity that still bound them –

" . . . that first evening in the flat at Paddington I thought my God well here is a man who is interested in me as a person, you know? Who is also a responsible person not a bloody neurotic . . . "

Jarlsberg, of course, was in a way an early draft of Loesli, but he had none of Loesli's terrifying concreteness, his unpleasant clarity. Jarlsberg would have made a "good provider", wasn't that the phrase? Perhaps he had been shaped out of Nelly's unstated desires and dreams, but, of course, Jarlsberg wasn't up to satisfying them. Jarlsberg, unlike Loesli, was easily disposed of, a breath, a dream.

" . . . so all of last year when eet was all girls together and Lucy and Annie I didn't understand a word of it, mate, Household this and Household that eet was like a bargain basement I tell you and then you went barmy een the fog but you are not actually the rapeest type so I nevair told anyone don't worry . . . "

Getting old. That was at the bottom of it. Getting so that even his unpredictability was familiar. The other night, for instance, he had lost his keys and made an entrance, drunk, through the bedroom window. Once that would have been madcap, lovable Jack, the one you couldn't count on. Now it was about as unusual as rain in August or delays on the Southern Region.

" . . . eet ees weeth me and weeth you I have learned so much, you know? From you all, I mean baseecally thees women's lib and burn your bras eet ees quite a good idea and I have not been confronting the realities of my poleeteecal position vis-à-vis Mikey's sexism . . . "

The ease with which Nelly slipped into jargon to express her relief interested Jack – unlike Hovis' automatic self-parody, the familiar

175

ideological banners rolled pleasantly past.

" . . . sayeeng no more about it and it is a load off my mind and you are so right I have to go in there and sort my reelationsheep out because I too have not been facing up to the basic realiteez of the situation which eez basically the dilemma of all pair-bonded relationsheeps een capitalist society my God I weel sort heem out I should have done thees years ago but now eet eez a show-up and Gunfight at All Right Corral Christ Mikey you weel get a big boot up the bum and no mistake . . . "

Nelly's words were assuming the exquisite meaninglessness of crystalline structures or contour maps. Her face shining, she was picking up the remains of Jack's lunch and waddling towards the door. He was saying . . . "Yes, yes, of course. It's OK now. Don't worry. Don't worry. We've sorted *that* one anyway. Sure. Sure. Don't worry . . . "

Then she was gone and he was sitting alone on the bed with the Loesli letter in his back pocket, the Loesli file at his feet and the cracked mirror, daubed with Lucy's face powder, and scribbled on (by Egbert) with Lucy's subtle lipstick.

Dear Mr Loesli,

This is to confirm that the completion date for your purchase of 12 The Avenue, Banbury, is, as stated in our earlier letter, July 4th.

I appreciate that your business commitments will make it difficult for you to be present at our meeting with John Davis but have no doubt that he will be agreeable to your proposal.

Best regards
Alan Sammonds.

A decision would have to be made today. Banbury. Cool, anonymous, regular Banbury. A town which had never heard of communism, homosexuality, urban blight, fascism, or any of the other things that tormented Jack. Heard of them, perhaps, but pretended not to hear. And, acting dumb, had become dumb. The butcher, the baker, the major, the banker, part of the long swelling tide of money that was, for some, the logical process of our history.

Were they going to acquire a new neighbour? A sharp business man with a funny foreign name? A man in the catering trade? Or rather, a man who said he was in the catering trade? Were they?

176

T hey had left the table and looked a bit depressed, all of them, which was surprising because they had guzzled about half a side of pork and two tins of sauerkraut, not to mention the potatoes. They looked sort of glazed and Mikey was rubbing his tummy as if it hurt. What they needed was the apple flan with cream and she might add a few pancakes left over from Thursday night to perk them up a bit.

"Pudding!" she called gaily and they twitched back into life.

"I'm OK, actually," said Annie, being polite as usual.

"There's plenty!" said Nelly.

Mikey groaned and fell off his chair on to the floor, acting the bloody goat as he always did. Nelly gave him a friendly kick in the ribs.

"Mikey will help!" she said, starting the ordering-about policy.

One by one they came back to the table. Help is all, thought Nelly, if you did not force these people to the bloody trough they would die of starvation, like turkeys too stupid to see the grub you put out for them. When she had set the table, with Mikey's help, she went straight into the attack.

"I theenk," she said, "that Mikey also should be on the agenda tonight!"

"Comrade Chef," said Hovis, "this is going to be an immensely long meeting!"

Hovis laughed through his nose like he had got something wrong with his brain.

They were really tucking into the flan and cream. A bit slowly, so they could relish the brandy and the sponge topping bits she had put on the plates, as well not to mention the odd pancake piece. Mikey was pretending to look green as usual.

"Have you," said Mikey, "any specific proposals to put to the meeting. Vis-à-vis me?"

"You always make fun of me!" she said, after a lame pause.

"True," said Mikey.

"You are rude about me in public!"

"True," said Mikey.

"You are always saying you do not love me!" she said.

"True," said Mikey.

There was another, even lamer, pause. Really it was impossible to argue with someone as rude as Mikey.

"You carry on as if you cannot stand the sight of me," said Nelly, "when it is obvious that you really care very deeply about me."

"Is it?" said Mikey.

"Yes," said Nelly, losing her accent, "it is!"

"News to me!" said Mikey.

The other members of the house, probably to show how much they disapproved of Mikey's rude behaviour, were munching and slobbering like anything. Nelly decided to let him show up his own stupidity by giving him enough rope with which to strangle himself. Very, very cool, like that woman on the ITV who was a millionaire and bossed all the men around like crazy, she said –

"So. Mikey does not love little Nelly at all! Mikey cannot stand the sight of her!"

But she said it so satirically that everyone round could see she had Mikey's details all right. Just to cap it off, she added, very amused and up to the point.

"Mikey does not love little Nelly. Eh?"

"That," said Mikey, "is about the size of it."

The atmosphere round the lunch table was now getting pretty blooming unpleasant, considering, and, although Nelly did not mind Mikey's jokes, today they seemed especially rude. To make it blooming crystal clear how stupid he was being she pursed her lips, rattled her cutlery and said –

"Oh ho! Next thing we will be hearing that Mikey does not like my cooking or something!"

There was another silence. This time a bloody peculiar silence like when the mad scientist gets the answer to how to destroy the monster that is gobbling up the whole of Sussex on the television – as if she had said something that was super-duper important. Mikey's head did not move. He stopped with a forkful of cream, pancake, sponge and apple flan. It was quite a long time before he said, in a comparatively sensible voice –

"No!"

Nelly, too, found her fork was suspended between plate and mouth in a position not dissimilar to Mikey's. The house watched them like they were gunfighters or something.

"Actually," said Mikey, "I can't stand it."

At first Nelly assumed this must be an even more unpleasant practical joke on Mikey's part. But something about the quality of his reply made her lean her elbows on the table and ask, in quite a kind and jolly sort of way –

"Oh Mikey, now. Come along. You eat it, don't you?"

"I eat it," said Mikey, "but I can't stand it."

Both of them lowered their forks to their plates. Nelly's heart was going pit-a-pat-a-pit-a-pat like a metronome. Somehow this was the one area in the whole of the region of Mikey problems (which, when you thought about it, was not so much a region, more a bloody country or continent) that she had not considered. She had been prepared to think that he didn't, on occasions, eat her food, in order to spite her or to get back at her for something. She had been prepared to think that in many ways he thought her a bit of an old football boot, but, after all, that was the normal state of affairs between husband and wife, was it not?

But the idea that he actually did not *like* what she cooked, was, well, ludicrous. It was mind bending. It was a bit of turn up for the book, squire. After all, when you came to think about it, what was she doing all this cooking for?

"I know you like to joke about my food, Mikey," she said, eventually, "and to wriggle out of eating it to spite me from time to time. Thees eez men all over. But for God's sake, Mikey, I am a bloody good cook. In fact I am fantastic when you come to think about it."

There was silence in the room. Then she said –

"OK Mikey, what do you like to eat?"

Mikey looked her straight in the eye. In a low, choking voice, full of emotion, he said –

"Beans. Baked Beans."

Baked Beans.
    Weren't they little round slimey things in tomato sauce? Little white horrible globs of horrid muck in red, oily gravy. In tins.

"How," said Nelly, trying to salvage something from this reply, "do you cook baked beans?"

"You don't cook them," said Hovis, "you open them, comrade."

Nelly turned on him.

"Listen, you horrid little vegetable, Mikey and I are having an important discussion so you keep your horrid little trap shut, eh?"

"Yup," said Mikey.

They had never talked as intimately as this before. God it was amazing really that they were saying all these things in front of other people. But worse was to come.

"Vot else you like, Mikey?" she said, quietly.

"I like sweetcorn. I like frankfurters. I like tomatoes. I like nuts. I like everything you can get in tins," he replied, equally quietly.

"Mikey!" she said sweetly, "What please is little Nelly to do when she has opened these tins in two minutes flat and bunged them on your plate as if they were blooming dog-food or something, eh?"

Mikey sucked his fingers thoughtfully.

"She is to concentrate," he said, "on being less obvious. Sexually."

Hovis got up from the table and tried to head for the door but Nelly stopped him with her foot. If Mikey wanted to make a fool of himself then that was his affair, wasn't it? She put her head to one side and asked, as nice as pie:

"*Vot* do you mean? Sexually obvious?"

"I mean," said Mikey, "that going to bed with you is, on the whole, more predictable, less hair-raising and altogether less spectacular than eating one of your fucking nine-course meals. And I should like to see a little less emphasis on stomachs and a little more emphasis on – "

"Cocks," said Annie, dryly.

"Please, Annie," said Nelly, "I weel feeneesh thees een my own way."

Was she sexually obvious? Maybe she was. What did that mean anyway?

"Vot you want," she said, "I should wear lacy nighties and so on?"

Spielman and Annie had their faces well down over their plates, clearly as embarrassed as everyone else by this ridiculous request of Mikey's for saucy underthings. Nevertheless, aware that something important was happening, Nelly continued with the discussion before anyone had the time to make an excuse and leave. Lucy and Little Luke were having a hug and ignoring everyone else.

180

"Vot else must leetle Nelly do?" she asked.

"She must," said Mikey, "display a working knowledge of the English language."

She wished in a way that they had had this conversation before. In any marriage, as the Doctor had said in last week's *Family Circle*, there were bound to be ups and downs and it was important to take the smooth bits in connection with the rough ones. After all, if all she had to do was to stop cooking for a few weeks (Mikey would come back to *cevabcici* and courgettes and goulash and the things that really mattered), God that was nothing, squire.

As far as sex was concerned, well, she had never had any complaints before but they were nearing a crisis in their married life as everything did every seven years, and, as Lucy said, this was the whole problem with capitalism, was it not? But anyway it was easy to solve the sex problem, she would buy some of those red underthings from that rude shop in Tottenham Court Road and wave her bottom around before, after and during and maybe say a few naughty words as well. Gasping. That was it. They liked you to gasp to show you were coming and even though these days she would rather have a nice piece of veal for preference it was important not to make the man feel he was doing it to a sedan chair or something. Mentally ticking off underwear, gasping, tempting tins and telling herself for the thirtieth time that her English was first hole anyway, and she'd like to see fucking Mikey get his tongue round the simplest Hungarian verb or noun, she gracefully accepted his awful rudeness –

"Okay," she said, 'I weel do what you want. But you must do what I want, eh?"

Mikey looked haggard.

Nelly started to eat again, feeling the worst was over, remembering a conversation she had had with him ages past, oh, before she had met any of them, when it was only him against her and her against him. It was about the only other time Mikey had talked crazy like this and it had gone on and on and on but in the end he had said to her something like he would never leave her because however awful he was she could take it on the bloody chin. Oh yes, thought Nelly, looking at Mikey's handsome, haggard face, the shiny black hair and the lively, malevolent eyes, oh yes, little Nelly will stand on her head in a bucket of dog's doings if Mikey wants her to – she will wave her hands around her head and wear leather bras and green suspender belts, feed him off lizard's eyes and chopped up toads if Mikey requests. But after all that is over and when she has hung upside down by her toes from the roof for a few years and been walked on, used up, spat on, ignored and generally buggered about then she too will make a few requests and they won't just be for the salt and pepper. Squire.

"What do you want?" said Mikey.

"I want – " said Nelly, and realised that, this time, she was being asked to decide exactly how much she required of him, that this time she would have to know and yet that she had no way of knowing, so grown over with stupidness and bloody lies were things between them, "I . . . can't . . . "

Annie and Spielman made a move to go.

"I don't want anything, Mikey," she said, finally, surprising herself by the courage of her answer, "not from you."

P eople were getting up from the table and Nelly, for once in her life, was making no attempt to stop them. People were scraping bits of apple and sponge on to floating masses of pork and cabbage, cigarettes were being lit and the smoke was billowing out in clouds in the tall rays of early afternoon sun, but Nelly could not focus on what to do next or what to rustle up for them if they wanted it. She could not now conceive of poaching or frying or grilling or roasting or baking or stewing. Moving her mouth very slowly, as if her tongue were lassooed to her lips, she said –

"I don't think that we love each other, Mikey."

Mikey looked back at her.

They had never, in all the time they had known each other, used such language, and Nelly had never before felt this almost physical pain, the weird sensation that every phrase meant something awful and tremendous.

"I . . . don't . . . know . . . " said Mikey, looking embarrassed.

182

Lucy was showing Little Luke some pictures in a book. Annie and Spielman had drifted away towards the kitchen. Hovis was twisting his mouth around as if his bum was landed on something sharp.

"Look, Mikey," went on Nelly, "it's a bit stupid, isn't it?"

"Is it?" said Mikey.

"Well — " said Nelly, "I cook these horrid meals and you hate them and — "

As she started to speak, Mikey grabbed a plate from Spielman, who was shuffling after Annie like he was a Bavarian waiter or something and held it right up high. His face was even darker red than usual and he seemed to be hating this even more than Nelly. The funny thing about Mikey was that he would never say anything like that. It occurred to Nelly, as she goggled at him and his plate, that she had not in fact got a blooming clue about Mikey's thoughts and if conversations like this were anything to go by the less she knew about them the better. She should have let sleeping dogs lie down in front of the fire.

"Look — " said Mikey, "forget the beans. Huh?"

"Mikey, we are now realiseeng that our relationsheep eez een a very bad way and — "

"Forget the beans," said Mikey again, urgently, "for Christ's sake forget everything I ever said but for Christ's sake especially forget the fucking beans."

"Maybe we have not been honest weeth each othair and — "

"Pork, veal, lamb, goulash. I love them, especially goulash. Goulash, goulash, goulash, goulash. The Goulash Archipelago!"

And "archipelago" (a word with which Nelly was not familiar — was it a kind of stork?) was the last word he addressed to her on the subject of their relationship for, lifting up the plate that now contained bits of potato salad, smoked ham, mackerel fillets, pork, sauerkraut, cream, apple, fag ends, bits of paper, other people's spit, grease, dust, roast potatoes, etcetera etcetera, watched by an amazed Household he began to tip them down his throat, his face blazing with embarrassment.

Nelly stopped in mid-sentence.

"Mikey," she said nervously, "what does this mean, please?"

"It means he's eating," said Spielman irritably, "OK?"

"Mikey," she went on, her voice near breaking, "I didn't mean to — "

But Mikey paid no attention. All eyes upon him, he poured the last fragments from plate to mouth and then, like a dog snuffling round after a feast, picked his way through the plates and dishes that were scattered across the table. He licked out the dish of cream, he gnawed the remains of a French loaf, and he swallowed the last drops remaining in every sticky glass. He sipped, nibbled, chewed and gulped up the rubbish, the leftovers, the junk from the floor, the stuff at home that you'd feed to the pigs, he ate it, acting it up, flagrant, paralysed with embarrassment.

Nelly discovered herself to be crying.

"Mikey," she sobbed, "please, Mikey. Please!"

But he was not to be stopped. She wrestled with him over the saucer containing the last pieces of the Hovis nut cutlet but he forced her away, sending her spinning back into Annie's arms. She pulled at his arm and begged that he might stop but he continued like a gannet or a wolf or a man starved for years, suddenly let loose in a millionaire's pantry.

"Mikey," she wept, "I did not mean it I get ideas about how we should carry on I don't know look Mikey thees eez stupid I don't know about loving each other or any of that eet's all too complicated for me eet eez the sort of crapola that everybody talks een thees house I don't geeve a sheet about any of that Household thees and Household that I tell you all I want is a few good meals and to see you reasonably happy oh for God's sake Mikey not the blooming vinaigrette you weel be seek for God's fuckeeng sake eet has got black peppair een eet – "

But on he went. And, as he ate, she found herself saying worse things still. Things that everyone in the house would hate but she could not find herself able to stop saying them and the words tumbled out as the tears smudged her face –

"Oh Christ Jesus all bloody mighty Mikey eet eez so up an' down I can't tell you I don't understand any of thees poleeteecs eet makes me seek I don't care about spiritual values neither if you want to know Lucy I could not geeve a monkey's fuck about spiritual values nor about Marx or Lenin or any of the beeg turds far as I'm concerned you do as you bloody like Mikey twiddle weeth as many women as you like oh Jesus Christ I love you Mikey honest I do I love you."

She had firm hold of him now as he finished the last drop of sauce Hollandaise (what had she been making sauce Hollandaise for? – she must be going barmy) and, to her intense relief, felt his arm go round her shoulder and felt him pat her, lightly, on the cheek, a sign that he was, if not actually pacified, not actually going to chop her up with awful substances, or, worse still, to leave her in the cupboard.

It was, she thought, the nearest Mikey had ever got since they'd married to being nice to her, but she was buggered if she cared about that. Oh God, all of it – self-respect, politics, relationships, Jack, Hovis, Spielman, Annie, Lucy, they could all go and jump in a lake so long as she had Mikey and Mikey had her. She looked up at him through her tears, knowing that he felt the same, which was not surprising because where else was he going to find a bleeding doormat as high quality finish as her and said, in a voice full of concern, because from now on they were going to get on so well –

"What did you mean, sexually obvious?"

Mikey continued to pat her, but slowed the patting to a regular movement so it was like he was testing her for springiness.

"It doesn't matter," he said, "let's not discuss it, shall we?"

But it does matter, thought Nelly. Next week I shall buy the lacy undies. Then I shall buy a corset with a red ribbon on it. Then I shall buy a record for pronunciation and after that as many bloody beans as he can stuff down his belly. After that – sport, sex, pronunciation will all go hand in hand in hand.

This is the way in which it will become better. Better and better and better and better. You cannot imagine how better it will get in course of time.

T he grey, full-bellied clouds were strung out like barges on a river, and, from the breaks and gaps, light slanted prodigally to earth, yellow against grey, promise of the genuinely celestial. It was six o'clock.

Annie was sitting with Spielman, arm in arm on one of the benches in the shopping precinct at Shepherds Bush, looking at a shop that sold freezers, and reflecting on the irony that had brought luxury goods so close to the homes of those unable to afford them. For, above their heads, ranks of vacant windows, piled up towards the clouds, winked the dumb signal of the badly off — those for whom Annie felt herself to be fighting. Things hadn't got much better for them over the last two or three years, she reminded herself.

Spielman chewed a match ponderously and said, in his best cracker barrel philosopher manner —

"The only thing on the agenda tonight is Warliss."

Annie started. In the window opposite she saw a hard-faced woman in a headscarf. Her.

"Sorry, love?"

Spielman chewed his beard and made little stamping movements with his large, ill-clad feet. Did the beard suit him, Annie wondered, and then rejected the notion of anything "suiting" Spielman. Nothing, be it beard, nostril or item of clothing, would dare do such a thing.

"I mean," he went on, "I mean . . . when you think that here we all are. A kind of unit of vaguely progressive people, right? Or at any rate a unit of people potentially influenced by what we might describe as a hard core of progressive people, that is to say me and you, dear, and what are we discussing? Rhodesia? Unemployment? The Official Secrets Act? The National Front? No. We are not. We are discussing one Jack Warliss. Why is this? I ask you. Why? Jack is a perfectly decent guy. A man I've tried to talk some sense into on several occasions. But he is, basically — "

"Hopeless!" said Annie.

"Hopeless!" said Spielman.

The relaxing thing about being with Jake was that there was no fear, at least on the surface anyway, that he was being sent up or got at. His manner took care of that. He was, there was no denying it, a powerful personality.

"People always discuss families," said Annie, "especially the family black sheep!"

"I didn't realise we were a family," said Spielman, pulling a face of theatrical gloom, "I thought the family was the basic unit of capitalism."

"OK," said Annie rather sharply, "collectives always discuss the collective black sheep."

"In collectives," said Spielman wryly, "colour is a concept that no longer applies."

186

Annie did not want to go on with this conversation.

Her child was still with her, carving lines of worry in her face, turning her into the harder, more aggressive woman she seemed to have become. He played a cruel trick on her, punishing her by his absence, so that when polite people at parties, or old acquaintances, or, worse still, people who had known her when she was pregnant, asked her about "the family" she pretended to understand, by that, the ill-assorted band of men and women at Sinclair Gardens. Where lay an even crueller irony. For they – the Household she had resisted so strongly last year – had now become her family, her only family, and her concern for them was a mother's concern.

The doctors had told her that it would be impossible for her to have another child. She had told no one else. One day she would have to tell Jake, which would make their precarious relationship even more fragile. If only she could believe that she, all or any of them, could love and care for others' babies as if they were their own. If only her political creed would crack and sweeten and let out the bitter note that was leading her away from the Party and towards some ghastly no-man's land where hatred for the exploiters was the only thing illuminating the scene. There was a technical term for what had happened to her, a term Hovis would have seized on with whoops of sarcastic joy – she had developed "ultra-leftist" tendencies, while Spielman, perhaps encouraged by the success of his latest venture (a magazine that combined in-depth sports coverage and classy political theorising), seemed to have drifted to the right. They had met in one of the burnt, scarred, deserted patches of ground that separate the ideologies of the left, and co-existed there in a comfort that was too uneasy to have become anything else.

Getting back to Jack – there was this question of money.

When the house had been set up, in the wake of the disastrous march, Jack had declared his income at £6,000 a year and his contribution to domestic funds had remained at a rate related to that figure. But it had been after the invasion of Sinclair Gardens that the latest in his long line of lucky breaks had begun, and he had managed the lucrative metamorphosis, to use his own self-deprecating words, "from Hack Jelly to Trendy Radical Playwright and Columnist".

Where was the money going to?

"Lucy," continued Spielman, "is of the opinion that Jack's problem is that he did not attend the birth of his son Little Egbert, or Eggie as we call him, believing as she does that the human spirit in the raw,

187

etcetera etcetera. *Who* knows? She may have a point."

"This is the mission of man, is it," said Annie, more harshly than she intended, "to spend years of your life preparing yourself to face the birth of a fellow creature. Christ all bloody mighty, does that woman think that fucking and dreaming are all anyone needs, I mean – "

She stopped herself. She had not intended to call Lucy "that woman". That was the sort of phrase Annie's mother might have used.

"We'll sort out Jack tonight," she finished.

"Look, Annie – "

Spielman started to say something that looked as if it was going to be hostile. Then decided not to. He, presumably, had his doubts and fears about her, just as she did about him. She didn't want to know his doubts and fears. Probably the affair was hopeless. Soon it would be over, like all her past attempts at satisfactory love.

T he house meeting was at eight.
　　　Accordingly, Annie and Spielman made their way out through the north side of the precinct and up the steep slope that shoulders the Green above the blind end of Richmond Way.

The sun drifted further to the west and the clouds had dissolved into a splendid wreck. It would be fine tomorrow, thought Annie, as she and Spielman leant on the wall, not speaking. They did not need to say much, since they disagreed about so little, and yet the silence was not entirely companionable; there was a nervous, unappeased quality to it, as if, soon, some unspoken quarrel would have to be resolved.

It was because of their silence that Lucy and Jack did not hear them. They were standing facing the pub, backs to Annie and Spielman, and, from the way they were both looking down at the pavement, it was clear that they were in the middle of yet another of the what-do-we-mean-to-each-other conversations that disfigured life at Sinclair Gardens. The angle of Jack's head suggested that he had been struck with a dreadful form of nominal aphasia, and would never frame a coherent English sentence again. Beyond them, Egbert was playing a complicated game, involving the transportation of bits of road grit from A to B and back to A once more. Occasionally he would break off to go into what looked like an impression of an aeroplane, or to point at his parents, as if his gesture would turn them to stone. He talked constantly, his words, when audible, appearing to refer to lorries and the necessity of mending a car.

Spielman made no attempt to disturb them. He seemed to be making no attempt to listen either, and anyway would be unwilling to reveal the fact that he was eavesdropping, even to Annie. That was part of the coolness and constraint of their affair, she mused, wondering again whether over-cautiousness would kill it before too long. To all intents and purposes, the two of them were admiring the beginnings of the sunset over beyond Earls Court, where the steady line of planes trundled towards Heathrow through the almost golden clouds.

"It isn't just Eggie," said Jack after a while, "it isn't just him. I mean I like him now."

"Because you avoid responsibility for him!" said Lucy.

Annie leaned forward over the wall, daring either of them to turn round. They would soon. Or surely Egbert would see them? Before this had time to happen, Jack said –

"You and bloody Annie. One moaning because she's got a baby and the other maimed for life because she lost one. Christ. And now I have to be sort of publicly reprimanded at some fucking meeting!"

"You think you can dodge anything, don't you?" said Lucy. "You think you're above everyone and one of these days you're going to climb back into your spaceship and – "

"I think, actually," said Jack, "that I'm reasonably objective and – "

Lucy, wicked in this kind of dispute, would not let him go.

"You think that you're an artist or something. Or rather you're somebody who wants the privilege of being an artist without the responsibility, or no, actually I'll tell you what you are, you're basically a fast moving layabout, a sort of bloody *child*!"

She had succeeded, as Lucy usually did, in getting a response out of Jack that bore little or no relation to his idea of how the scene should go. Watching them, still wrapped in an intense, private circle of misery, Annie recalled similar disputes with Jack in which she had been able to arouse nothing stronger than violent self-deprecation or what Spielman

189

had described as "terminal silliness". Jack, so often embarrassed by Lucy in public – admittedly less so these days – seemed quite undisturbed by the intensity of the dialogue. Perhaps that was a measure of how much he had changed since living with her. He turned and his chubby, haggard face was hot with anger, the bookish glasses slipping forwards precariously along his nose, and his curved, angular shoulders craning over as he said, jabbing his finger at Lucy's chest –

"Listen. As far as I'm concerned the *lot* of you can fuck off. The *lot* of you. Because I am going. I am going somewhere where none of you can get at me or bother me or tell me what my responsibilities are. And this time, lady, I mean it. I am going somewhere where nobody, but nobody, will know me. You won't know me. None of you. You won't know me."

Lucy suddenly became calm. She put her hands on her hips and looked up into Jack's face.

"Oh Jack," she said, "I don't know what your latest scheme is. I'm not *interested*. But remember, when you think you've got us sewn up, you haven't, why, Jack, you don't know Eggie and me, if I told you that Eggie – "

She stopped, in either assumed or genuine panic at what she had just said. In private, Annie thought, Lucy was an actress of some distinction – for now, theatrically tossing back her curls, she backed towards her son, who had removed his sphere of operations to a nearby gutter and was scattering small stones and rubbish as if conducting a small, enthusiastic orchestra. Jack, acting up to her mood in a manner that suggested he was enjoying the prospect of revelations about Egbert (provided they were not, in the final analysis, to be taken seriously), marched after her, threequarters on to her retreating figure –

"What," he said like a Victorian hero, "what about Eggie?"

Lucy, moving from melodrama to grand opera, threw back her head and gave a stagey laugh. Annie was quite surprised that a knot of spectators had not gathered, or that Egbert was not about to pass round a tiny hat to collect some reward for his parents' efforts.

"What about us?" she repeated. "What *about* us?"

She tossed her curls once more, stamped her foot, and, picking up Egbert, stormed off down Richmond Way, closely followed by Jack, who was looking right and left to an imaginary batch of spectators, appealing for their sympathy at the depressing way in which the conversation was being handled by his partner.

190

"Annie love," said Spielman as they left, "I don't care about your not being able to have kids. I mean, I know you can't. Things get back in a set-up like ours. OK? Actually I don't mind. Actually. But you do. And until you can sort that one out. Until you can stop . . . I dunno . . . *hating* things . . . well you and me . . . it's . . . "

"Hopeless," said Annie bleakly.

"Hopeless," said Jake, quite definitely and utterly Jake rather than anyone else, a kind, tough, serious person, who was being lost to her by the grief that would not let her be.

There was a slow tone of wonder in his voice, thought Annie, as if he had been considering the statement for months before delivering it, and, when he turned from the street to look at her, she felt him to be still preoccupied with the import of what he had said. So much so that he did not seem to want her to look at him or follow him, which she did not, staying at the wall above the road, watching Jake follow Lucy and Jack and Egbert, watching all four until they were out of sight and she was alone with the quiet summer street and the sunset, grand as a state funeral over to the west.

L ucy and Egbert crossed into the drab streets that lead from Richmond Way down to West Kensington and the Hammersmith Road. She did not look behind her. Seemed unaware that she was being followed.

The fact of the matter, Jack thought, was that Loesli was of a different order from any other of Jack's *noms de plume*, for, unlike Simmons, Danby, O'Connor, Jarlsberg or the rest of them, Loesli had a genuinely independent existence, i.e. the people who believed him to be real (two estate agents, a bank manager and a business consultant Jack had met in a pub) did not know of the existence of those who would, if informed of his identity, expose him as a fake, a fraud and a betrayer of everything that they held most dear. Financed out of the sudden flowering of

O'Connor and his ilk, Loesli was a creature designed only for getting and spending. He knew only getters and spenders, people from the world of work, uncontaminated by ideas.

No. Loesli in his way was quite as big a responsibility as Warliss. He was a whole, alternative person, and being Loesli, assuming he went ahead with the crazy scheme, would be a twenty-four-hour-a-day, fifty-two-weeks-a-year occupation. And, unlike Warliss, Loesli was not buried under a whole heap of false names. He was clearer about his political intentions than his *alter ego*. Unbothered by schisms, he went about his business in the comforting knowledge that, in order to be a good capitalist, he *didn't have to worry about politics*. While Warliss was such a depressing specimen that the woman who lived with him did not even care enough about who he was to check up on whether he was building up a false identity and planning a clearly loony moonlight flit to Banbury in order to open a restaurant. Just now she hadn't seemed to want to know, even when he had been about to confess.

Was he going bananas? This had to be considered. Ahead of him, Lucy had put Egbert on the pavement. Egbert took small and important steps as his mother, moving more slowly now, turned into Hammersmith Road and right down towards the Broadway. Jack matched his pace to theirs.

Loesli versus Warliss.

Loesli, although he was made up of limitations and negatives, knew himself very thoroughly. Apart from his slightly worrying tendency to write off for kitchen units, he could be relied on by whoever it might be he intended should rely on him. He got things done. It could be argued, by Loesli anyway, that what Britain needed was not more theorising and attitudinising, whether of left or right, but men who added to the wealth of the country.

Wealth versus gaiety. Was that the problem?

Lucy was carrying Egbert across the Hammersmith Road by the fire station and setting a course for Hammersmith Bridge and the A4 out of London.

He was ill in the head. No doubt of that. Psychiatry needed here. But, of course, he would have a way of coping with psychiatrists as well, wouldn't he?

They were under the Hammersmith flyover now, facing the bridge, and Lucy and Egbert were some sixty or seventy yards in front of him. Over the bridge − its funfair gothic arch suggesting that, on the other side of the river, the traveller would encounter some kind of commercially sponsored fairyland – the traffic seemed to be restricted to one lane and there were an unusually large number of policemen lining the road before them.

Unlike the policemen encountered and miraculously dodged at Alie Street last year, however, these constables seemed keen to impress on passers-by that they meant no harm. "We are wearing uniform," their fresh, young faces seemed to suggest, "purely as a means of self-identification. We are, in fact, Having Fun!" To prove this, one of them was wearing a bracelet of bells, while another, a man of about forty with a large, badly shaped behind, was doing what looked like a bump and grind with his hips. He was wearing (there could be no doubt whatsoever about this) a flower in his hair. From over the water came the sound of a steel band, as, into Jack's vision, prancing (insofar as it is possible to prance from the confines of a wheelchair), chanting and rolling eyes and elbows, came Derek Schooner, closely followed by Hovis, who carried none other than Gobbo on his back.

Behind them came a ragged line of elderly youths with shaggy hair and glamorous, yet dated clothes. They carried a poster that read –
WEST LONDON COMMUNITY FESTIVAL
HI THERE!
"Hi there!" muttered Jack sourly, and followed Lucy and Egbert into the advancing crowd.

"Crowd" was an optimistic way of describing the hundred odd revellers, some black, but mostly white, who were rumba-ing their way across Hammersmith Bridge, bearing placards, balloons and banners of a strictly non-controversial nature. Indeed, the vast majority of them, men and women of about Jack's age, seemed vaguely depressed – apart from two or three West Indians up on a float marked *Kensington Law Centre*, who were getting into quite a respectable go-go routine, the most abandoned members of the crowd seemed to be policemen.

"Yeah!" shouted the constable with the large behind. "Hit it! Yeah!"

"Right on!" carolled another helmeted figure, who could not have been, according to Jack's reckoning, more than about twenty years of age.

Eight o'clock. The house meeting, he thought, as Lucy with Egbert turned back with the crowd. He was not going to be there on time. Already they would be discussing him, going through his things; they had probably already discovered the Loesli file, already decided, by unanimous vote, to throw him out of the house and out of their lives, before he had the chance to make up his own mind about whether to go or stay. Jack pushed his way through the revellers to Lucy, who had been avoiding his eyes, and, whenever he appeared to be close enough to talk to her, dancing off to another part of the celebration. Finally, however, as they turned up towards Shepherds Bush, he reached her side.

"What," said Jack, "about Eggie? And what about the house meeting, eh?"

"The house meeting," said Lucy, in a passable imitation of Nelly, "we are deescussing Jack."

"We are," said Jack grimly.

"You like that, don't you?" said Lucy, tucking her bum forward, and grinding her pelvis down at the ground.

Things, as so often with Lucy, were not going in quite the way Jack had intended that they should. Putting his hand on her arm, he said –

"Look, about Eggie – "

"Not till you dance," said Lucy, "everybody must dance. Didn't you know?"

"I mean it," said Jack, "I am going to leave. Leave you all. I swear it. I am going to walk out."

"Where to?" asked Lucy.

"Banbury," said Jack, without meaning to, and Lucy threw back her head and laughed, hips now vamping to the right, feet kicking wildly to the choppy-water rhythm of the steel band: "Banbury? Hey? Banbury!"

"Jack – " Lucy was saying (the rhythm of this music was, it had to be admitted, infectious – it was hard to stop oneself from being a nigger's whiteman, and physically exhausting to avoid converting the hop and shuffle into a bump/grind/bump/grind), "Jack – all this stuff

194

about getting away from it all and not knowing yourself and Christ, Jack, all this identity crisis shit is just that. Honestly. I mean just that. You haven't got an identity crisis, Jack. You're only trying to make yourself interesting."

"And aren't I interesting?" said Jack, rather feebly.

"*I* think you're interesting, love," said Lucy, "even if no one else does."

"No one else does, eh?"

"Not really," said Lucy, "not deep down. I mean it's very hard to find *one* person to really love you. You seem to want everyone to really love you. Can't you be satisfied with me?"

The rhythm of the band had changed. In a brighter key they tapped staccato now, no longer *dam* be dam de be dam dam dam, but ah didedadadadida de be damdamdam day di da da dam di damdam di −

Jack's feet were sketching out the beginnings of steps. Out of his control they had started to weave the same up, back, down as Lucy, the policemen and the numbers of other Irishmen, girls, boys, jokers and pedestrian punters who had swelled the body of the carnival or festival or whatever it called itself. Not *interesting*? What did she mean, not *interesting*?

"In that case, dear," he said, "why is it that the whole of fucking Sinclair Gardens is having a house meeting about me? Eh?"

"Chance," said Lucy, bounding Egbert up and down under Jack's nose, "and if you go they'll find someone else to talk about."

"Essa talkaboulla!" said Egbert.

"Oh, I only really exist when I'm with you, do I?" said Jack bitterly. "All you want to do is to tie me down to being another fucking husband and father, even if those aren't the words you use, that's what you *mean*. Your crap about communes and Households is the same old dangerous female rubbish that has loused up men through the ages. And you want me to be as ordinary as you are. There is no arrangement, domestic or otherwise, that will allow men and women to shed what you call their stereotypes and I call their fucking destiny. I won't, I won't, I won't be tied to you and Egbert."

Against his will he was now actually dancing, and the amusement in Lucy's eyes continued as, be-bopping, shaking, hula-ing, twisting and rocking, they followed the stream off the Hammersmith Road and down one of the drab roads that lead (oh *no*!) towards Sinclair Gardens. She met his eyes, pursed her lips, and said −

"Husband and father nothing, Jack. You may not *be* Egbert's father."

"Nota Egberta fallerather!" said Egbert.

And grinned, in a friendly fashion, at Jack.

L ucy had had a lover. Lucy had been with another man. She had sighed, screamed, been embarrassing, been Lucy, been the Lucy he had always assumed that only he knew completely, perhaps because no one else would *want* to know her completely, oh God if she had betrayed him then . . . then what?

He had betrayed her. He had betrayed her from the beginning. But not seriously. No. That was wrong. Seriously then. Not seriously then. He hadn't told her his name. *He* hadn't done anything. He didn't love her then, of course. What? He loved her now, did he? Whatever he had come to feel, he knew that the thought of her with anyone else was unbearable to him. And the thought that Egbert might actually be somebody else's was . . .

What was it? Egbert always had been somebody else's, hadn't he. What was with this? Was Jack casting himself as a family man then. Someone who wanted to own and control a woman and her children. Oh Jesus Christ, Jack thought, why is it that I have been carefully inventing problems for myself, the spectres of commitment, identity and all the rest of the claptrap, when all the time, here in front of me, has been the real and serious problem.

The band was now playing a much simpler song with a fast, four-inthe-beat bar, that was working up some genuine gaiety among the participants. There was an incomprehensible verse and a chorus that went –

Oh-h-h
We're keeping moving
Oh-h-h
We're gettin' on.

Some of the company were joining in this ditty, clapping their hands and glaring out at the uninvolved evening, as if daring it to join in –

Oh-h-h
We're keeping moving
Oh-h-h
We're gettin' on.

Mouthing the words made it easier. From mouthing it was a short step to singing and from singing the road to dancing was an easy one as, hands clapping, eyes on the slide and head held high, Jack found himself with only the merest of British blushes, the slightest trace of diffidence or irony or whatever it was that had stopped him from living all these years, singing and dancing to –

Oh-h-h
We're keeping moving
Oh-h-h
We're gettin' on.

He jerked an almost happy glance to Lucy and shouted –
"OK. Who's the other father?"
Lucy did not answer.
"If I," said Jack, "am not Egbert's father, then who is?"
Lucy smiled a faraway smile.
"Snaps," she called back, "Mike Snaps."

I n the darkened front room at Sinclair Gardens, Annie sat looking out at the empty street.
"My God!" said Nelly, "thees baby of mine eez bloody quiet tonight.

I theenk he eez planning something!" No one responded to this remark.

We ought, thought Annie, to be having a house meeting about me, except that I don't have the knack of making my sorrows public property. Public property is, in a sense, all my sorrow is and even those close to me here would not admit to the existence of Annie the Crossed in Love.

"Say something!" she wanted to scream, "say, 'Annie's really difficult these days.' Say, 'Annie's a problem!' Say, 'Can we talk about Annie and what happened to Annie's baby?' Say – 'Annie's on the agenda.' Eh?"

As usual, of course, she was chairperson.

"Look," she said eventually, in her briskest voice, "even in Jack's absence there is a question I wanted to raise."

"Which is?" said Spielman.

"I have reason to believe that he's . . . contracted out in more than a purely social sense."

"Uh?" said Snaps.

"That Jack," said Annie, clearly and slowly, "has not been honest with us about the amount of money he is earning."

"Serious one," said Snaps.

She looked across at Spielman.

"What," Spielman said slowly, ruminatively, "do we do with People Who Don't Come Clean?"

"Shoot them!" said Snaps and giggled nervously.

Annie stretched, feeling more depended on her answer than the question of what to do about Jack. Spielman was biting his nails in a worried fashion.

"I don't think," said Annie, "that we can accept people who don't accept our rules."

"No-o," said Spielman, even more slowly.

"I think that involvement in any community, however small, involves participation in the responsibility deemed to be communal by that society."

"Look," said Snaps, "if he wants to go – let him go. Eh?"

Spielman paused and addressed his next remark to the carpet.

"The question is," he said, "not whether he wants to go but whether we want him to. The question is – how far should any group go to retain the loyalty of an individual, without compromising its principles or forcing the individual to do the same."

198

As usual at house meetings, the discussion had developed into a dialogue between Annie and Spielman, with Annie feeding him questions and Spielman, with peasant thoughtfulness, steering the group towards an acceptable decision.

"Vot do we do?" asked Nelly.

"As far as I'm concerned," said Spielman, "young Warliss represents a fairly typical example of a radical member of the middle classes unable to make a final commitment to what I would regard as a party committed to the . . . er . . . victory of the working class and so on."

"As far as I am concerned, mate," said Nelly, "eef he has been cheating us on the money he can bloody well cough up."

"The two things, surprising as it may seem," said Spielman, "are interrelated."

He lowered his huge, gargoyle-like head into his hands and was silent for some moments. The others watched him with reverence. Annie wondered why she felt this conversation to be so intensely personal.

"You see," he said finally, raising his bleary eyes to the rest of the group, "I'm against any form of censure if there is a chance that the individual will make his contract with the group of his own accord. In other words, as far as I'm concerned, where there's a chance that an individual will obey a rule out of choice then we ought . . . well . . . to leave him alone. The only thing to do with people like Jack is to wait. They'll come to you in time."

"The Lord," said Annie sourly, "rejoiceth more over the sheep that was lost and found than over twenty obedient citizens or else – "

"Annie," said Spielman, "you're chasing something other than the issue in hand. A communist society ought to be preoccupied with the exercise of charity, both of individual members to the group and of the group to individual members. Kollontai – "

Annie knew all about Alexandra Kollontai. With an unpleasant sense of having been manipulated into saying this by Spielman, she cried –

"Don't give me Kollontai. Russian revolutionary lady, daughter of a fucking *general*, yet she could be me all over, Jake. Revolution will end the family and all that there'll be will be soup kitchens and men and women prancing around in blue overalls. I've never heard such crap. Revolution has nothing to do with the family – all it will change is corporations and industries. You can't do away with the fucking family, Jake. Fathers and bloody mothers and bloody babies, as soon as they get the babies they piss off somewhere and start the perfect Fascist unit, don't talk to me about babies, Jake. I haven't *got* a baby I haven't *got* one I haven't *got* one and I want one and I – "

She stopped in horror at the sound of her own voice. It seemed to be doing everything she most despised, breaking with self-pity; it belonged to a woman she did not know – a woman who had been cheated of her conventional role, who had been there always, presumably, at war with her better self. "This is what you and Jack have done to me!" she wanted to scream at Spielman. "Even those men who pretend to understand the condition of women are doing no more than acting."

Then, Nelly rose to her feet and said, quite calmly –

"I don't know about cleengeeng to babies but I think I am blooming well about to have one."

N elly's baby had been something of a political issue from the very first.

For a start there had been the question of the father. Nelly had not exactly implied that it could be anyone else but Snaps, but from chance remarks Annie had overheard (the best way of finding out anything about other Household members) there had seemed to be the faintest of doubts. Snaps, at any rate, whether from knowledge or natural coarseness, was constantly making "jokes" on the subject.

She had refused to attend any form of clinic, Natural Childbirth class or other form of aid to pregnant women devised by the twentieth century. She was not even registered with a local GP and, whenever asked anything about her condition, would reply – "Eef peegs can do it so can I."

It was as if she had no desire to acknowledge the reality of the foetus growing inside her. Annie, who had pored over maps and diagrams, felt that there was something both arrogant and foolish about Nelly's attitude, but, over the months, had almost forgotten the baby was due to be born. Perhaps Nelly had forgotten as well. She looked puzzled. Annie hurried to the phone.

"Hold eet!" said Nelly.

Annie stopped.

"Do not please phone a bloody ambulance. I am haveeng a baby and not a heart attack eef you please!"

"Look, love," said Snaps in a tone of terrified concern, "don't panic. I'll phone for an ambulance."

"Christ all bloody mighty!" Nelly snorted. "Eet eez not necessary. I weel lie on the sofa."

And, hitching up her skirts, she proceeded to do just this. For one terrible moment Annie thought she was going to remove tights and knickers and have it on the spot, but Nelly, perfectly composed, folded her arms and stared at the ceiling. Perhaps she was so frightened by the realisation that she was about to give birth that it would be necessary to introduce her slowly to the concept of midwives and delivery rooms, breech and Caesarian births, gas and air versus epidurals, over the period of her labour. Prepared to start this crash course in Birth, Annie said, with a casualness she did not feel –

"Have the waters broken?"

"Wheech watairs?" said Nelly.

Totally baffled by this reply, Annie wondered whether there was a Hungarian/English dictionary in the house, and, if so, whether it would contain at least some of the more important technical terms used in obstetrics. Snaps was hovering by Nelly's side, the picture of fatherly concern and anguish, while Spielman still seemed preoccupied with the conversation of a few minutes ago.

"Look," said Annie, "er . . . are you having the baby at home?"

This was yet another important issue that had remained undiscussed.

"Looks like it!" said Nelly, and, covering her face with her hands, she giggled shrilly. She was nervous, there was no doubt about that. Not so much nervous as stark bleeding terrified.

Snaps was certainly going to be no help whatever. He was at the window, tweaking the curtain back like an agent in some spy film – perhaps he was hoping for a passing ambulance to catch sight of him so that he could signal to it, undetected by his wife, and resume the role of father in some hospital waiting room, littered with cigarettes and battered plastic chairs.

"Look, Nelly," said Annie, "after what I went through – "

She broke off. Spielman was watching her closely.

"It doesn't matter . . . "

For some reason she regarded Nelly as her problem. The thing was, presumably, to get her into an ambulance, or to persuade her to see a doctor, without frightening her. In her present state she seemed capable of doing any number of dangerous things. Sitting next to her on the sofa, and taking her hand, Annie whispered –

"When did the contractions begin?"

"Vot contractions?"

"Well, presumably you're having contractions?" said Annie, throttling a desire to giggle.

"*I* don't know," said Nelly, suddenly full of the Slav gloom that occasionally struck her, "I am so blooming fat."

"You're not fat!" said Snaps, in his new role as responsible lover, husband and father-to-be. "You're great. Great."

This, Annie decided, was getting them nowhere. She went back to her first line of approach and said –

"Look. After what I went through . . . "

There was a hushed silence in the room. She had not spoken of this to anybody. Still Spielman (Jake?) was looking at her.

"After what I went through . . . I mean it's scary. It's very scary. The whole thing is scary. But you mustn't think about the scary part. Because however bad it seems, I mean it isn't actually as bad as it seems I mean even with me Nels, look at me look what happened to me but if I'm honest it isn't bad it isn't the end of the bloody world because I can still feel and I can still feel for your baby and there's still *life*, it is happening and we ought to glory in that oh Christ I don't know what I'm saying but really that is all we ought or need to know I mean it's beautiful Nels really it's beautiful isn't it?"

She was crying and giggling at the same time now, as was Nelly, though Nelly was doing rather more crying than giggling – her huge breasts rising and falling like a restless sea, she held out her arms to Annie and said –

"Thees ees vot eet eez all about Annie oh my God."

And the two of them collapsed, sobbing, on to the sofa.

Curiously enough Annie found that her tears did not feel real (and she had not cried or laughed since the death of her baby) until she felt Jake's (not Spielman's but Jake's) arm round her shoulder, dry, reassuring, steering her back to sanity as life shook back into her in great gusts of tears and laughter. Jake, she thought, it should have been bloody Jake all along and I was too stupid to see it.

"Come along," said Nelly, "we weel go into the hospitals!"

How they would to into the hospitals, or, indeed, which hospitals they proposed to go to and whether they would accept them were not stated, but it seemed churlish to argue as the three of them, Annie, Jake and Nelly, made their way into the hall, crying, giggling and chattering excitedly. Snaps followed a yard or two behind, anxious father to them all, as if unsure who was to be born via whom. Annie felt as unsure as Snaps looked. It was, after all, Nelly's baby that was making her shake and flutter and see Jake's face as more than that of a friend and counsellor. It was Nelly's baby but hers too, she supposed, since she was holding her friend and guiding her, and since she felt that there could be no question of ownership in the matter of birth. Such an assumption would make nonsense of the passion she felt, would it not? What she felt could only be meanly discriminated from what Nelly felt. She was not prepared to allow the other woman to embark on her adventure alone, and since she, Annie, the once blighted, was so evidently needed to support her friend, how could she be arrogant enough to suppose she was not necessary?

She shambled her way through the hall, dimly aware that Snaps was now ahead of them, opening the door on to the June night, now no longer breeze-ridden but close and tacky. Perhaps, she mused, there really is an ambulance out there. Nelly stopped abruptly.

"Blimey!" she whispered, stone-cold sober and big-eyed with wonder, "eet eez on eets bloody way out!"

F rom then on Spielman took charge.

Nelly lay on the dirty red carpet, and Snaps, without being asked, retired to the kitchen to boil water. No one, as it turned out, knew what to do with boiling water, but boiling it seemed to make Snaps feel better and anything, Annie felt, that lowered the available

203

amount of hysteria was to be commended in the circumstances.

Nelly seemed to have passed the point of no return – in a sudden access of frenzy, she was howling in a mixture of Serbian and Hungarian and occasionally making a noise that sounded like "ouf pouf" as Spielman (it was curious how, in a group of people, Jake edged back into being Spielman, but even more curious how that no longer made Annie feel distant from him) bent a practical eye on her organs of reproduction.

"Practically five fingers dilated," he said, "presumably the weight's concealed the contractions."

Feeling like Tinker to his Sexton Blake, Annie said –

"Right. We'll deliver here."

"Yup," said Spielman, "waiting is – "

"Hopeless," said Annie.

"Hopeless," said Spielman.

For a second it was conceivable that the two of them would dissolve into helpless laughter (again, for the first time in their relationship) but a reversion to the clichés of the quarter deck helped Annie through –

"I'll get some water and we'll scrub up," she said.

At this point Snaps re-emerged from the kitchen and started babbling about the boiling water. Annie asked him what he proposed to do with the boiling water.

"Sterilise things," said Snaps weakly.

"It's a bit fucking late for that, comrade," said Annie, feeling two stone heavier and twice as cheerful as she had done for months. Snaps disappeared, gibbering, into the kitchen to boil yet more unnecessary kettles.

Spielman was bent over Nelly calmly and solicitously. He looked more like a doctor than most doctors – his ability to rationalise and stay aloof from the social connotations of such a tremendous event had lent a spuriously professional calm to the scene in the hall. Annie brought in a bowl of warm water and the two of them scrubbed their hands vigorously.

Nelly was being extremely unprofessional. Blitzkrieged by contractions, she was yelling, swearing and screaming in three or four languages (Annie could have sworn she heard her say "*Donner und Blitzen!*") while her stubby fingers banged on the floor in imprecation. There was something heartening about her refusal to be "dignified", a sense that, whatever else you could call Nelly, there was no way in

204

which she could be described as ill or at risk. If anyone was at risk it was Annie or Spielman as they ducked between her thighs and shouted encouragement up at her, like removal men at the end of a gigantic wardrobe.

"Push now!" Spielman was shouting.

The other amazing thing, Annie reflected, was that the baby, as befitted a baby of Nelly's, was anxious to be out and dining off something more substantial than intravenous sludge from the umbilical cord. A tiny pink square could be seen thudding against the walls of Nelly's labia – terrible, beautiful and strangely full of threat.

"Busy little bugger, isn't he?" said Spielman.

"Soddeeng hell!" Nelly shouted back, "Vot you theenk I am fuckeeng doeeng?"

At this point Snaps stuck his head round the kitchen door.

"Did you say it was a boy?" he asked.

"You can't tell from the head," replied Spielman.

"Can you see its head?" whispered Snaps, white with dread.

"Sure," said Spielman, "come and have a look!"

"Fine!" said Snaps, and fainted clean away.

Nelly was oblivious to her man's failure to comfort her in the traditional manner, by sponging her forehead or holding her hand. Indeed, you would have had to have been a qualified rodeo rider to hold Nelly's hand for longer than two or three seconds at a stretch, as it flayed the air wildly in all directions.

"Push!" shouted Spielman again, "Push!"

Annie understood most of it now.

How in the future she must balance her private and public concerns more carefully; how, in the future, without regretting her time spent with Jack, she must understand how much she needed Jake and how much he needed her; how much her mission to arrange and order the lives of others must be exercised with charity ("Annie's like me, *dear*," she heard her mother saying, "a terrible *bosser*!"); how much this child did indeed belong to her as well as to Nelly and its father (if indeed he was the father), who was now groaning feebly from a supine position some two or three yards behind its mother's head.

Best of all, though, she started to understand the necessity of optimism again. As that pink square widened, as Nelly swore, and another life edged forwards to the midsummer night she saw, or thought she saw, how love as well as force was to be the midwife of the new society.

That was Marx, wasn't it? Force, the midwife. Presumably he had not thought it necessary to mention love, since the word is understood in so many Jewish households, but for those like her, who had come to their social faith from the stony wilderness of the British middle classes, the discovery of that word was like the unambiguous revelation offered by dreams. And she saw dreams too, as Nelly (improbably) started to sing in a deep bass voice (had she been sneaking a look at Annie's Natural Childbirth literature?).

Doo wa diddy diddy
Dum diddy day
Doo wa diddy diddy
Dum diddy day!

She looks good
She looks fine
I am hers
She eez mine!

Dreams about how their household would be organised in future and how its members would act in the world outside. They hadn't got *started* on that yet. Dreams about the humbling of the rich and the liberation of decent instincts. Dreams about class forces, noble workers, wicked landlords, clever leaders, more work, higher wages, beautiful people – a whole host of new possibilities.

Ve vorked on
To my door
Zen ve keess
A leetle more

Woa yeah
I knew ve vere falleeng een ler-erve and
AAARGH!

Snaps, bravely, sang on with his wife, even through her lapses into hysteria, as Spielman moved from mother to baby, baby to mother and back again, shouting, cajoling and arranging limbs or hands. If only Jack were here. Would he always be too late to understand things?

206

Annie wanted to be able to tell him that it was all right. That she had let go of him and that that, in its turn, had enabled her to want him again. She wanted to be able to see that he knew what to do about himself, for it was, of course, in the end, his affair and no one else's. He must come. He could see for himself. She wouldn't try and put herself between him and the world any more. He would, must, grasp the bravery of so many new beginnings – Nelly and Snaps, she and Jake and now whoever it was pushing their way stubbornly forward to the light as his or her mother wailed and shouted and swore.

"Push!" shouted Spielman.

Jack, thought Annie, *you must not miss this.*

But you probably will.

"Snaps," said Jack, as the carnival drew nearer and nearer to the house wherein dwelt the offender, "why Snaps?"

"It was only once," said Lucy. "Annie set him to spy on you, you know."

"I know."

"The joke is that when we did it I didn't know. I mean I didn't know he was Snaps. I didn't know his name. So it didn't really count, you see."

They had both modified their dancing to a kind of loose body shuffle that made serious interchange of views easier. Hovis, once again drunk, had appeared and he and Egbert had broken away from the main body of the dancers and were jiving along the pavement together. Egbert (who got on well with Hovis) was joining in a song called *Brown Girl in the Ring* in a rubbery series of labial vowels that approximated to most of the sounds around him. Jack looked at Egbert, wondering how Lucy's revelations affected his view of the child. It didn't, somehow. Had he been unequivocally Snaps' child, matters would have been different, but things at Sinclair Gardens were already so confused, in the area of paternity, that it seemed logical rather than otherwise that Snaps or he might be Egbert's father. After all, Little Luke called Annie, Lucy and Nelly "mother" quite indiscriminately. He, Snaps or any number of unknown foreigners might or might not be the father of Nelly's unborn baby, while he and Spielman had shared the brief life of Annie's unfortunate child together. It wouldn't, given the state of affairs at Sinclair Gardens, have surprised him to learn that he was really Nelly's mother or Snaps' aunt, or that Lucy had been left in a handbag on Croydon Station at the age of six months and was, in fact, his very own sister. Lucy was talking about Snaps.

"I knew there was someone following you that summer. There was always this yellow car parked up the road and once or twice I saw this guy sitting in it, drumming his fingers on the roof. I don't know what I thought about it. I was afraid of him. I was afraid of everybody then. He's difficult to make out, is Mike."

"Oh sure."

"Then, one afternoon, I was sitting by myself and I saw him on the pavement outside. I called to him. It was really strange. We hardly talked at all. I said, 'What's *your* name then?' and he said, 'Oh – names aren't important. It's what you do.' I don't think that's quite true, actually. I think you do something and then you name it and the name becomes part of it. But you mustn't let names rule you."

"So what happened then?"

"He came in. Like I said, we hardly talked. Most of it was really edgy. Like, 'So who *are* you?' you know? But it was mysterious. It's always been my dream, you know, to go to bed with someone and not see them again, not name them or talk about them and then . . . it's like it's never happened . . . "

"But it fucking *has* happened."

"Has it?" said Lucy. "I might just be teasing you."

"For Christ's *sake* – "

"It certainly *could* have happened. You could ask everybody concerned. Not that you'd be any more certain then. You don't really know anything about other people, Jack, except what they choose to tell you. But that's what I choose to tell you. Wasn't it funny? After you'd talked to me about Snaps. Out of the blue. Do you think you wished him to appear? Out of the sky, a sort of nameless event, a thunderbolt."

Anyone less like a thunderbolt than Snaps it would be hard to imagine, but Jack did not find it easy, as he once would have done, to become amused at Lucy's biblical style. He could not be sure whether she was sending him up or not. It was true that Snaps always seemed to bring news of change in his life, like some malevolent herald, he was always the signal, if not the instigator, of great events. Jack tried again to feel jealousy, but the simple emotion would not come. Of course he had never wanted to be the sole male responsible for his child. He didn't want to be the father (fathers were tyrannical, ludicrous figures), he wanted to be the father *from time to time*. Well, not from time to time, more always but not quite always, a sort of part-time father, a half father . . .

That wish seemed to have come true with a bang.

"You wouldn't come and see Eggie being born," said Lucy.

"No," said Jack, "I'm sorry."

"That's OK. You see, you can choose. Being a father to someone isn't conceiving them. Any idiot can do that. Like having a baby. It's what you do to the child that counts – all of this crap about 'real' fathers and 'real' mothers that poor kids get lumbered with is just so much crap. It's just another set of useless names. You can be a Father to Eggie *if you want to*."

"I do want to."

"Good. Before you start to live, Jack. Before you can even think of beginning to do all those things that you want to do – politics, writing, *business* if you must, I don't care, you have to be able to live. Do you see what I mean? Because at the moment you *do* these things but you don't live them. That's the problem with all you people."

"All what people?"

"Well. You and Annie, I suppose. Clever people. Not Nels. I used to think I could never have anything to give you in the way Annie could, but I don't think so any more. You see, you're like all these terribly clever English people. You find it difficult to live. And what's the point in setting out to do all these good, brave and wonderful things when doing them only seems to make your hard heart worse? OK, you'll have won parity for building workers or written a masterpiece. But look what you'll have done to yourself."

"I don't think," said Jack, "that you necessarily destroy yourself in achieving things."

"Not *necessarily*. But it can happen. Admit it to yourself, Jack – you're so fucking preoccupied with what you look like, and the effect you may or may not be making on others, that you're not, come on, you're bloody well not *living*!"

"So what have you got to do to live?" said Jack.

"Oh Jesus. Care for things. Love. Love me for a start."

"And Egbert," said Jack dolefully, reducing his own attempts at car-nival dancing to an arthritic hop, "and Spielman and Hovis and Annie, Snaps I suppose, and Luke and Nelly."

"Start with me," said Lucy, winking rather saucily.

"And the men in the Underground and on the Clapham omnibus and the white Rhodesians and the black Rhodesians and the Communists and the Fascists and the rich and the poor and the – "

Lucy interrupted.

"I'm not saying you have to love everyone all the time. But I am say-ing that you must be able to find it in your heart to do so."

A s they came to the traffic island at the junction of Sinclair Gardens and Richmond Way, windows in the houses opposite opened, and streamers, toilet rolls and fruit rained down on to the crowd.

"You're saying," said Jack, limping after Lucy as doors of houses in Sinclair Gardens opened and a bizarre stream of flat-dwellers, single girls, married women, off-duty traffic wardens, Greeks, West Indians, Cypriots, Germans, in short, fairly typical Londoners, poured out on to the pavement, bringing beer and wine and spirits with them, "you're saying it's not what I *call* myself, it's what I am. Right?"

"Right," said Lucy.

"I was going bananas, Lucy. I was going to call myself Loesli and go and live in – "

Lucy was not interested in Loesli. It was interesting that, now he had told someone about him, Jack was not particularly interested in Loesli either. Loesli was floating away like a balloon, and, to Jack's surprise, he found he didn't miss him. Loesli wasn't all the story of course. There was Steve and Paul and –

"Darling," said Lucy, "I don't care about Loesli and Jarlsberg and Danby and Simmons and Bin-End and O'Connor and Toastswitch and Marbellana and Hindendorf – "

Hindendorf? thought Jack. Who is Hindendorf?

"As far as I'm concerned, the whole lot of them can go and jump in a lake. But you see, if they don't want to jump in a lake they needn't. I mean I love you, Jack. I love *you*, even if you don't know who you are. I love you."

"Do you love Jarlsberg too?" said Jack, "and Toastswitch and Bin-End and Loesli?"

"I love all of them," said Lucy, "especially Bin-End."

"I'm glad," said Jack, "Bin-End needs a lot of love and affection. He has a terrible disease of the skin that makes him smell. In *fact*," (he was enjoying this conversation) "in *fact*, he caught it off Jarlsberg. At a swimming pool near Cracow."

"I love all of them, Jack," said Lucy, "absolutely all of them."

"Well," said Jack, "what's good enough for Bin-End is good enough for me. I mean any woman who could love Bin-End seems to me to be a saint. Because he's incredibly difficult to live with. Apart from the smell, he has a sort of awful thing he likes to do with rats."

"Jack," said Lucy, rather too seriously for Jack's taste, "if you can love one person with your whole heart then you can love everyone. It's difficult. But you can. Everyone, and every part of the one person you love. I swear it."

For Jack, things were not quite so easy. Some tiny part of himself still resisted the thought that his problem had been that, like the boy next door, he needed the love of the girl next door (in this case Lucy) before making a start on the world.

Then, as Lucy and he drew level with their house, they saw, in the light of the hall, Nelly, flat on her back before the waiting crowd, delivering her baby to the crouched figures of Annie and Spielman.

Lightning, he told himself for long afterwards. It was lightning, and then some.

H e and Lucy, now hand in hand, goggled their way up the path to number twenty-three, watched fearfully by the now stilled crowd – for, among them, the rumour of the extraordinary scene taking place in one of the houses in the street caused an almost physically

211

noticeable change of tempo and the citizenry turned one to the other, like extras in a Shakespeare play, and began muttering (or bawling) about this thing that was come to pass at number twenty-three. What the thing was was not always clear to the participants in the now temporarily stationary West London Community Festival. Though it began as a birth, by the time it had made the rounds of several hundred inebriated people it was an explosion, a drugs raid, a fire, an orgy and even, some said, a member of the Royal Family.

For Jack and Lucy it was a birth – there could be no question of that. Nelly, her legs high in the air, was grunting rhythmically – Annie was holding her right leg and Spielman, his usually white face red with strain and heat, coaxing the child out of her, as, behind, Snaps, looking pale green and shocked, peered forward timorously. Little Luke was somewhere up there in the shadows as Lucy and Jack, followed by three black ladies and Egbert, approached the circle surrounding Nelly. Somehow or other, Egbert was handed back to his mother. Showing no interest in the events before him, he was waving wildly back at the black ladies shouting, "Yeti ah! Yeti ah hah!"

Jack had not imagined it would happen so quickly.

He knew about labour and contractions and how babies work their way forward and down and out, but he had not imagined that the child would come, when it came, with such a rush. For a second there was no child. There was a woman groaning and struggling and there was a seething mass of flesh between her thighs, a marbled civil war taking place in one, apparently, individual body. But then, at the next moment, the logic and training that would have led him to describe Nelly Hortobagyi/Snaps as one person, as a bundle of doubts, fears, mannerisms and appetites, was confounded, routed and dissolved because, as the child's head nodded out, it dawned on Jack that he was, in fact, looking at two people, at the supreme paradox for one who had always suspected identity to be a matter of sleight of hand, and reproduction to be a mechanical affair. It was, indeed, reminiscent of a large, gleaming machine sloughing off yet another perfect product, but even to use the word "reminiscent" was dangerously like pretending that it was in some way "like" anything else Jack had ever seen or ever would see. For, while the words that came to him – minting, casting, modelling – had mechanical connotations, the event itself was cheekily spiritual.

Then again, to call it an "event" was to underestimate and over-describe it, because the child's body followed the head in a slither and a rush, the arms and legs twisting like an Indian dancer's, the surface of the body, blue and crisscrossed miraculously all over its surface, like that of a unique stone cut sectionally, wired with patterns like a – . Still, as attempts to describe it foundered on each other's heels, the child offered yet another excuse for bestowing it with intellectual faculties, explaining its foreignness by an imagined similarity to oneself, for Spielman (who didn't look like Spielman at all, but some elder from a South American tribe) held the creature up tenderly, and, hesitantly, like a motor car engine on a cold morning, or a bird too timid to sing, a miniscule, hacking cry began – irritation at having been wakened too soon, Jack thought, or tears at something suffered that he would never guess at.

Spielman laid the baby on Nelly's stomach and said –

"We have a girl, everybody. We have another girl."

Snaps' face curved upwards into a huge smile, and, still grinning benignly, he fell back into the darkness of the hall, his last gesture being a sketch of a comradely wave at Jack, Lucy and Egbert. Annie was at Nelly's side, her face full of smiles and quite as soft as if she herself were the mother, while Spielman monitored the glorious progress of blood and guts from Nelly's womb that seemed to be causing no one, including Nelly, any bother at all.

In a sense it was nothing to do with Jack, since he might not have been the father. In another sense it was everything to him, because he might be. In the best sense of all, no such consideration applied, for, for the first time in his life, Jack could not have cared how he ought to be labelled or what role was expected of him. Indeed, he found positive pleasure in the circle of faces, the confusions of parenthood and pairing that made the six, no, the nine of them, indistinguishable from a family, but not a family wished on him, instead an elected group, sustained by the delicate balance of affections. He stood, he and Lucy now part of the group around the mother and child, with his face aching from the strain and the laughter, and he said –

"Lucy – "

But that was all he said to her, for this time he did not need to add, to justify or to explain, and so he simply turned to Lucy, looked downward slightly and let the glance tell her everything that she wanted to know.